GENTLE BEAST

By

Margaret Afseth

ISBN:978-0-9921638-2-2

This book is dedicated to all the babies who never got to grow up: those miscarried, aborted, or selfishly murdered in our world.

TABLE OF CONTENTS

A Guide to the creatures of this tale:

NOOR: a humanoid being with exceptional psychic abilities, the degree varying with each individual. Some also have the capability to separate its mental essence from the physical body.

-In a conjunctive male: the two halves exhibit themselves as two separate physical entities.

example: Liam/Loki

-In an introvert female: the two display as different personalities; only one dominates at a time.

example: Tilk/Susa.

FELINE: man-size intelligent cat beings.

example: Dia, Kimon, Uel

BEAR: a giant bear being-intelligent, protective, used as body guards

ROOT: tree-like beings. Said to have little empathy, a trickster and devious.

example: Theee, More and Zaba

ROOG: large dog-like beings. Not necessarily highly intelligent; very aggressive and predatory.

SLITHER: snake-like creature with chameleon abilities. Also able to remain invisible for long periods of time. Usually a light blue-green, but color darkens when they are about to attack. Only emotions it is capable of are protective instinct and anger-attack. When a Slither emotionally attaches to a being not of their kind, it will protect for life.

BOM: a cross-breed Roog/Feline

LIAM/LOKI: a cross-breed Noor/Feline

Other NOOR/FELINE are: Twila and Jabek; Shiveron and Reon

TUSHA: a HUMAN/NOOR

Other HUMAN/NOOR: Nyle and Kaudy, Moriah and Iora.

SLITHER/HUMAN: Sith and mate Serene

BEAR/HUMAN: Wadi and mate Rimu

Enjoy the story.

PROLOGUE:

Shiveron could hear the growling and hissing from where he stood guard at the double doors of the medical centre entrance. He took off running, knowing any disagreement was detrimental to the recovery of the patients. As he loped through the occupied beds, he pulled at the laser weapon on his belt.

It has to be that half-dog in the bay again, picking a fight!

The ship was Feline built, owned and operated by Dia and head physician Kimon. True, the two were a soft touch when it came to mixed species beings, and tended to adopt them, when no one else would give them a place in society, but though their crew included a sprinkling of many universal and mixed races, such as half Slither, half Bear, half Human, half Noor, half Feline, half Roog, and any other unfortunate combination, it mainly was staffed by Felines.

Because med bay physicians were mostly related or fosters, the entire craft was family orientated, and a hospital Zone. None were ever turned away, whether of mixed or pure persuasion. This was a ship devoted to healing.

Only one could boast the mixture Roog/Feline, and however obnoxious he might be, he was part of the cat race. Felines tolerated him, but many of most species disliked him exceedingly. This merely amused the Roog half, and he lived to antagonize, often taking advantage of the benevolent nature of this ship and its proprietors.

Why doesn't that creature stay on the prison facility he is supposed to be governing? In that establishment, he can fight when he pleases, taunt, mock; tease and torment his inmates to his heart's content, without fear of reprisal; there he has a captive audience. But no, he chooses instead to make life miserable for those who serve here.

Arriving on scene, Shiveron pulled up short, shocked as he realized the one who had risen to the challenge was none other than his half-Noor, foster brother; the respected and caring instant healer.

What can have caused such a lapse from the norm? Loki seldom argues, let alone fights!

The tormentor towered over him. Droopy ears, snarling face and the slathering, barred teeth of a bulldog; head dark black with tan muzzle, indeed that of a dog, but on the body of a cat.

His appearance was more the mangy feline than canine/Roog: long shaggy black coat, matted bushy tail, tan feet and paws, the claws fully viciously extended. Standing eight feet tall, and smelling like the sewer he frequented: unwashed, unsanitary, fowl; a travesty in a vessel dedicated to sterilized curing. This was Bom, the bane of all Feline!

Appearing the smaller of the two, because of his usual humble attitude and stance, Loki was actually a bit taller, at eight foot three. He had been raised in the cat world, but normally, there seemed little evidence of feline in this male.

Face mostly man-like, except for the blue feline eyes with their elliptical-pupils; his humanoid features were topped with a thatch of ginger curls, hiding his tiny cat ears. The back of his neck and shoulders showed a light short fuzz of fur, but otherwise, he appeared of human origin, though in fact that was deceptive, merely an indication of his mixed Noor blood, instead.

As the typically tender, careful hands ministered to the sick and injured, his weapons were usually pulled in, concealed from view; these claws were now extended. The seven-foot, shorthaired tail, always kept invisible, was presently in frantic motion, out in plain sight, both these unusual occurrences indicative of his extreme agitated state.

Loki hissed, returning Bom's challenge. He hadn't yet used his Noor talents, but Shiveron had never seen his foster brother this provoked; he might still put them into play.

The door guardian, stood there clutching his weapon, holding his breath, uncertain what to do.

****

Kimon heard the commotion, the god-awful yowling, as he worked on a small Root female. He knew immediately the culprit was Bom. Hissing his disapproval, he handed his patient over to another, and moved purposely to the area of the ruckus.

Why is it, when that male has off time, he insists on provoking the staff in my med bay?

Kimon determined, before this day had ended, he would put a stop to this once and for all. He didn't dare attack the prison warden himself, but the other contender would be discouraged from participating in such behaviour again. If this weren't dealt with swiftly, Bom would stop at nothing, not until death was visited upon his adversary.

This is a place of healing, not a brawling tavern!

But Kimon had hardly expected to find the culprit to be one of his own Noor fosters.

Loki and Bom locked into a body clutch just as he came upon the scene.

And even more infuriating, Shiveron, who was suppose to police such an incident, stood frozen in indecision, his weapon in his hand.

Such a useless enforcer!

Fury in every movement, Kimon charged forward, and grabbed the guard's ray-wand as he past him.

To his credit, the physician could not be blamed for what he did not know. It had not occurred to him, that the weapon would not be set to stun. It was in sleep mode; the setting still at negative, to ensure it was non-effective for anything save a Noor.

His half Noor children were seldom a problem; that setting only used to drain their energy, if they were injured, became disoriented, and lost control of their powers. The wand had a two-fold purpose: for those of Noor blood, one of restraint for the safety of others, and when set to positive, an active weapon against aggression in another species.

To make matters worse, Shiveron's last encounter in battle had required the second setting to be at Kill. Negative/Kill was only used as a last resort. To execute a Noor!

When Kimon raised the weapon and fired, his foster son folded abruptly, hitting the metal floor with a jarring thud.

Loki was the strongest half-Noor male in history; generally even a deathblow could not fell him, unless he was in a weakened state, or in heal-back. And through this day, this Instant healer had cured many, by taking in their injuries into his own body. He had been at his lowest energy, not quite healed back from his last repair of a patient.

Perhaps, that is why he so easily lost his temper?

The huge male went down hard. His image shimmered, like a neon sign losing power, but it did not blink out.

Not dead, at least!

Those around stood in horrified shock, Kimon not the least of those. His jaw dropped open in disbelief. Only, when his foster daughter, Twila, wailed plaintively behind him, did he clamped his teeth shut with a snap, and moan disconcertedly.

What have I done?

Bom laughed, as he stood over the victim, finding the situation playing out to his extreme satisfaction. When Kimon glared at him, he shrugged, then growled deep in his throat.

"He attacked me!" he thundered defensively.

Kimon rather doubted that.

Aware of the obvious scepticism, Bom still pressed his point. "He challenged me! I am his elder, and a superior besides! This requires punishment for aggressive behaviour. You are pledged to treat all with dignity, are you not?"

Kimon ignore the question, going right to the core of the matter. "If he was misbehaving, I will deal with him…"

"I want him punished, not by you, by legal means." He snarled derisively. "He is Noor," he stated with contempt, as if that alone were a crime. "A Noor is not permitted rights! They are non-creatures, beneath us!"

Kimon knew he'd best hold his temper, or this would end with him in a prison facility, as well. "He has a right to a hearing, as any other. The facts are needed here…"

"I have judged him! I will sentence him! It is my right as the affronted!"

"You are not my superior, Bom! We will take it before the council. They will determine if a crime has been committed."

Encouraged by her Foster's bravado, Twila spoke timidly from the sidelines. "Loki was defending me, Papa. Bom wanted...but I was unwilling to accept his advances. He wouldn't leave me be. Loki stepped in, telling him to leave. Then Bom...said...put down of momma Dia, dishonored her with...many explicit derogatory names. He kept at it until it drove Loki to anger...and then to fight."

"As is Bom's usual tactic," Shiveron agreed in a low tone, at his side.

Kimon grunted. The beast was trying to staff his prison med-bay again.

"You take the witness of a female over me? And another Noor mixed one at that," Bom challenged. "I sentence him! To my prison! He defied me!"

"First off," Kimon declared hotly. "On this ship, as in other Feline establishments, a female's word is law! Whether of mixed breed or pure, the females rule our society, and while you are in our company you follow our rules. You are not on a dog compound! We will take this to the Universal council, if you persist!"

"So," growled Bom. "You wish to challenge me too? Have you forgotten my father stands as head of that council?"

Kimon sighed. He knew what was coming, and how such a procedure would end.

Into the dead silence that followed, Bom snarled. "Put this Noor scum in a drain belt!"

Kimon nodded to an orderly. "Set it on low."

"No!" thundered Bom. "It goes on high!"

Kimon shook his head in surrender. Bom was the son of the highest Universal command, and if they disobeyed him, this ship would be closed down, not permitted to treat casualties, maybe even, all present would find themselves in the prison under Bom's devious whim. Everyone knew the surety, that's why it always ended the same. Bom got his medical staff in the end. But until this moment, he had never taken their Instant healer.

What is the half-dog up to this time?

As the unconscious giant was contained, Kimon asked meekly. "How long is his sentence to be?"

"I will have him for a year."

"No," Kimon moaned. "He will never survive so long in the drain belt. Think, Bom," he appealed. "Who will you have to torture, should he die?"

Bom laughed, conceding. "Six months, then. And I will quickly extend that should he offend me again."

Kimon's shoulders sagged. Out of the corner of his eye, he saw Liam rush into the bay, assess the situation, and narrow his eyes as if for retaliation. There was no need to explain what had gone before to Loki's telepathic conjunctive twin; he was their mental half; the holder of their powers. Loki was merely their physical strength.

Do nothing.

Kimon knew Liam would read the thoughts he projected, because they had communicated in such a way before.

If you remain separate, Bom can do less harm.

Obediently, Liam backed away into obscurity, so he would not be noticed.

CHAPTER 1

Althea was the first to acknowledge, the average person had it hard. But as far as she was concerned, right now, her life sucked big time! More than usual!

It wasn't because she was sick. She had the usual handicaps of those her age: false teeth, nearsightedness, which required trifocals, and a prolapsed bladder, also taken care of with an inner pessary that had set her back nearly a hundred bucks. But otherwise, for sixty, she was exceptionally healthy.

Nor was her problem her income. She had managed to qualify for the meagre government early retirement pension. And recently, she had also started a sideline in-home business. Though not exactly in demand, she made enough from writing instructional copy to supplement that income. She would never be rich, but she had enough to pay the bills, and still eat adequately.

The building in which she lived on the fifth floor was not overly plush, but it did sport a mini common area at the elevator doors on each floor. This twenty-foot square visiting space contained two nondescript compact loveseats, one on the outside wall, another across from the two elevators, with a sturdy block coffee table between. Usually, the area was seldom if ever used, and those that did linger, came and went quickly.

The problem was Althea's living room was situated directly behind the elevator. It seemed when they had constructed the complex, the designers were under the impression the steel frame of the elevator shaft would cushion sound; if they had insulated at all, it had been sparingly. They had also failed to sound proof the hallway. As a result, the tenant behind the public lift heard not only every conversation from the corridor outside, but also any dialogue carried on in the visitor corner.

Althea had lived here for over six years. The floor was usually quiet, both at night and during the day, a perfect place to work silently at your computer undisturbed. That was until recently.

Two month before, an older couple had moved into the two-bedroom suite across from the comfy elevator sitting area. It appeared they thought the common space was an extension of their own personal living quarters for, as often as not, the husband could be found lounging out there with a book.

When he vacated the space, his wife took up waiting out there, clearly intent on enticing a visit from anyone riding up from below.

When guests would come, instead of retiring to their rented rooms, these were entertained in the common visitor area. For the life of her, Althea could not understand why their own suite was unsuitable for entertaining, but this seemed to have become a condition she must live with.

At one point, before she realized they were responsible for the constant disturbances, Althea had confidentially shared with the couple the fact that her walls were paper thin, and she could hear every word spoken, but it had not made the slightest difference in their behaviour.

She had also spoken to the caretaker, who had informed her it was a public area, and as it was the middle of the day, there wasn't much he could do. If she had a complaint, she needed to take it to the building's owners. Althea feared that would cause her own eviction in the end, so she was loath to put action behind her annoyance.

And so the situation had continued to go on unchecked. It seemed the favourite time for entertaining was mid afternoon, just as Althea got down to the nitty-gritty of editing her work, in preparation for sending it out at the four o'clock deadline.

The couple was usually soft-spoken in there dealings with Althea, but their guests were inclined to be of a much more raucous breed. Today they were exceptionally loud, and she was finding it impossible to concentrate. Unbearable!

The group sounded like a pack of dogs howling and challenging each other. The hissed whispers, grating gravelly lower tones, and barking strident laughter, was driving her to distraction. Althea toyed with the thought of going out there and confronting them, but she was a timid person, conflict terrified her, so she clenched her teeth and tried to finish her work.

And got nowhere. In her frustration, she almost accidentally deleted all her hard won copy.

A burst of hard laughter, and a new voice joined in the fray. Althea couldn't identify the newcomer, but she seemed extra vociferous.

Who the devil is that?

The newest arrival seemed to monopolize the conversation. In a voice high enough to aggravate, yet too unclear to distinguish words clearly, she went on and on recounting some supposedly humorous yarn. After ten minutes, Althea could take no more.

Against her inner warning, she pushed out her chair, stood and made for the door to the hall. She would just peek around the corner to see whom the voice belonged to, explain they were disturbing her.

But when she saw who it was, her temper got the better of her.

"Man! Are you guys ever loud!" came out of her mouth, without conscious thought.

The fat mannish woman was from down at the end of the hall. She had a nickname, a man's name, Althea couldn't presently recall. Her tone held scorn and was dripping with sarcasm as she replied.

"Well sor…ry! Are we bothering you?"

"I can hear every word you say out here! My living room is right behind the elevators and the walls are not sound proof."

The woman leaned into a elderly woman on her left, whispered something indistinguishable and both chuckled. Ignoring Althea, she raised her obese form with effort and started for the elevator, pressed the button, waiting for the doors to open.

And Althea just had to say something else. "You know, this space isn't where you're suppose to be visiting, that's what the large common room downstairs is for."

As the doors opened and she stepped though, the plump woman gave Althea the finger. The portals slid shut, and the coward escaped downstairs.

Althea went around the corner to whispers from the two remaining women. That angered her farther. Though she was visibly shaking, she unwisely turned back to go another round.

Rounding the corner a second time, Althea lit into her neighbour. "You know, I could report you. This isn't an extension of your own private quarters; that's what the coffee room downstairs is for."

"I don't like it down there. I won't go there."

The woman's elder companion rose, choosing to escape rather than take part. Althea waited the few minutes it took her to get out of earshot.

"If you continue, I will report you. What you've been doing is disturbing to your neighbours and I'm pretty sure it's not allowed. I've already talked to the caretaker. He says I can complain. Just keep this up. I will report you! Do you hear?"

Althea trembled inwardly; her neighbour said nothing, sat there with a peaceful, condescending smirk on her face. Althea turned and went home.

Later, when she had stopped shaking enough she could breathe properly, she grabbed her keys, and made for downstairs to get the mail.

The woman also had gone to her suite, but in the downstairs coffee room the fat lady sat gossiping, leaned over and whispered into the ear of her companion, when Althea showed up on the ground floor.

Althea started shaking again. All she wanted to do now was hide in her rooms and never come out.

What have I done? It will be all over the building by morning that I've thrown a temper tantrum, and been unreasonable. No one will even ask my reasons, nor will they defend me.

She'd run a fowl of these gossips before.

****

Pan turned on her companion, as he sat complacently with his book in the armchair.

"I earned my freedom!" she growled. "I'm not going to let that pissy woman wreck what we deserve!"

She paced the floor, agitated, as she raged. "I gave them over thirty fetuses for their delight! And you fathered hundreds…to score this surface retirement! I won't let her ruin it!"

She strode the opposite direction, then back once again. "If we offered them a fresh edible heifer, they should jump at the opportunity."

Her male live-in looked up from his book, but said nothing.

"I want you to set it up. They prefer to deal with a male. If you don't, you can kiss your cushy retirement goodbye. Do you want to go back to the dungeons?"

He finally put his book down. "I'll see what I can do."

CHAPTER 2

Althea was beat.

She had started her morning slinking down to the ground floor, hoping she would not encounter anyone who knew about her blunder.

A few people were in the common room. Though they saw her through the glass wall, they paid her less attention than usual, even turning away, as if ignoring her. Her neighbour, Pan, was there big as life, having coffee with a group of other women, when she had blatantly stated she would never come down.

Althea cringed, knowing she was the subject of animated conversation.

Anyway, something was accomplished. She is now visiting down here, rather than in that small elevator lounge.

That was a point in Althea's favour.

She slipped out into the street pulling behind her the handcart she always packed full to the limit with store produce. When empty it wasn't that difficult to drag along, and she walked the many streets of the half-mile to the store in quick time.

After, unsuccessfully browsing the clothing stores at the mall, stopping for a burger at the fast food counter around lunch time, and spending an hour and a half picking out her groceries, Althea felt she'd had enough down time to settle for working without complaint on the morrow.

Another half hour awaiting the bus, then lifting her cumbersome cart-bag, which seemed to weigh more than she did, up the steps of the public transport. A fifteen-minute ride, and repeating the process in reverse, made her wonder:

Do they deliberately put the buses with steps on this route to frustrate us less fortunate people, who have no vehicle and must lug their groceries home?

Once off the bus, half a block, and across the busy roadway, another half block to home, tugging the uncooperative loaded cart, wore her to uttermost frazzle. But the icing on the cake was, though she gestured frantically at those on the other side of the glass entrance door, none would buzz it open for her. She had to unpack her purse, fish for the keys, before she could swipe her own fob across the sensor.

Mercifully by then, everyone who had been sitting in the foyer had disappeared to parts unknown, or they might just have been exposed to a second tirade of tenant rage.

Man! Am I fed up with this!

Finally in her suite, exhausted but unwilling to sit down before all was in order, Althea went about her kitchen hiding her purchases: emptying cereal into her containers, slicing vegetables to store with less bulk, and packaging meat into one-person meals, placing the last in the freezer of her storage room.

At long last, finished with all, save to discard the smelly meat wrappings, she escaped to the hall, heading to the garbage disposal chute, leaving her suite door unlocked.

As exceedingly weary as she was, her vision was narrowly focused and her hearing on mute. Her back turned toward her apartment, Althea failed to hear the door to her neighbour's unit stealthily open. A shadowy figure loped to her unlocked portal; pulled it open, and furtively slipped inside, unnoticed.

Dumping her garbage, the fatigued woman turned back, just after her door quietly closed, and retraced her steps.

With a sigh, Althea shut her outside door, and turned the deadbolt, effectively shutting the world out for the night, or so she thought. As she past the storage room folding door, she realized it stood slightly ajar, and pushed it firmly in place.

Thought I closed that?

So tired; so tired. I just want to go to bed. But it's still a little early. Only four o'clock.

Althea ran a hot bath, got her pyjamas, undressed and stepped in.

Awww! So wonderful! Relaxing.

She wasn't one to soak in the suds, and tonight was no exception. Her whole cleansing took a mere twenty minutes.

When dried off, Althea took care of her medicinal needs, applying the hormone cream as per doctor's prescription, then dressed in her loose-fitting pyjamas and cleaned the tub.

Exiting the bathroom, Althea closed all the blinds, and stepped into the kitchen to make herself a sandwich.

Slamming the fridge door, she dumped the makings on the counter top: sliced ham; mustard and mayo; an English cucumber; lettuce and tomato, and of course, the bag of whole wheat bread.

She thought she heard the storage room door slide open with a thump. Althea listened. Silence.

Must be mistaken.

When the sandwich was completed, she opened the fridge, put back the fixings, held it open with her foot, as she grabbed a glass from the cupboard, filled it with milk, and let the fridge door slide shut again.

She turned toward the living room, and let out an involuntary gasp.

Between her and that sitting area stood the biggest dog she had ever seen. Resembling a Rottweiler dressed in shorts, it towered six feet at least, standing upright on hind legs, its teeth bared, salivating.

The full glass of milk hit the floor, shattered, the contents splattering across wall, fridge front, and bare feet. Althea hardly noticed; her last and only thoughts:

How did it get in? I never leave the door open. Where did it come from?

And then the formidable creature sprang toward her.

She didn't even think to scream, nor did she have time.

CHAPTER 3

Nyle entered the office shortly after ten pm. He had been told to report to the supervisor after shift, but when he arrived, he was surprised to see a stranger behind the desk.

"Come in; shut the door."

As Nyle settled into the chair across from the man, all he wanted was to go to bed. He'd just finished a twelve-hour shift, and didn't need this hassle, whatever the problem was.

As far as he was concerned, if these people wanted to pour out money like water to keep the men working around the clock to build this place, it was no skin off his back. The reason he was here was because of the exceptional pay. A hundred dollars an hour for overtime would pay for his new condo much faster than any other job. He just hoped this wasn't another lay off he'd not planned for. They were often shut down because the government regulators insisted the workers must have their time off. At least, that was what he'd been told.

Never mind, when they open up the shifts again, if this is another layoff, I'll just turn around and apply for the next three-week stint. I'll be back in a week or two, just like I've done in the past. The heck with government bureaucracy!

The eighth Irish in him sometimes raised its ugly head, especially when Nyle was tired. Tonight was no exception. The reputation associated with the reddish cast of his blond hair had been well earned.

Right now, I just want this over with, so I can head to the showers and catch a bit of shuteye, whether I'm to carry on my workload tomorrow or fly back home.

His name in the Irish tongue meant 'Island', and true to it, Nyle was a loner. In his thirty-four years he'd been provoked by many, especially, incessantly by his ex-wife, and the only one to ever irrevocably steal his heart was his young daughter, Kaudy.

Not that my antagonistic ex-partner will often let me see my jovial youngster.

Last time he had talked to Seline, she had said she was moving, and needed to leave Kaudy with him for a time. It was unusual that she would let the girl loose like that, and as he was at the whim of the woman because the courts had favoured the mother, he had been quick to agree.

I'll be free as soon as this work period ends.

Nyle wished fervently Kaudy could live with him always, but Seline considered the teen to be her meal ticket, and would never part the ways.

I sure hope she doesn't change her mind.

She was notorious for doing it in the past.

Nyle scowled at the bent his thoughts had taken.

Is this guy ever going to get to it?

"I was expecting the super," Nyle challenged, to break the unnatural silence.

The man behind the desk ignored the implied question, shuffled the papers in front of him one last time.

"You've been working for us more than a year, I see," he stated, finally looking up. "Do you like this kind of work?"

He was a hawkish looking man, with a thatch of black hair that fell to his chin hiding his ears, and a beak-like nose. Beady black eyes probed at Nyle, like the beacon on a lighthouse lamp at the edge of an ocean cliff.

"The pay's good…"

The other nodded, didn't seem to notice he'd evaded most of the query. "Your supervisor says you do excellent work."

"I try to do my best. You have to, so it passes inspection, needs to be up to codes."

The man cleared his throat in preparation to state his demand. "If you had a chance to advance in your trade, would you consider it?"

Nyle frowned.

I already have the highest of training; the only thing I have to do is take a test to go into business for myself.

"You mean as an electrician?" he clarified. "Wasn't aware you could go higher. I'm industrial grade."

"Yes…yes." The man seemed somewhat preoccupied.

What is this? Are they kicking me off?

But the man went another direction. "Do you realize what is being built here?"

"Not really, just follow blue prints, and obey Super's direction."

"Never questioned what is forming under your hands?"

Nyle shook his head. He had noticed the weird shape of the building: domed, as if it was some sort of spaceport, but he knew nobody on Earth would build a space centre up in the far north of Canada.

Or would they?

"What are you building?"

"What does it look like to you?"

Nyle chuckled good-naturedly. "Like some sort of futuristic movie set, a space station actually. I couldn't begin to imagine what you are really constructing."

"It is a transport portal."

Nyle was suddenly very much awake; his eyes went wide in surprise. "A what?"

Again the man sidestepped the question. "We are near finished on this side. As I asked before, would you consider advancing your learning? You are such an exemplary worker, we wondered if we might persuade you to come help complete the receiver on the opposite side."

From dealing with his ex, Nyle had learned to be a suspicious man.

There is something fishy here.

"Where is this other side?"

The man cleared his throat again, as if the response required some thought.

"First allow me to explain…as you have noted, I am not of this work detail. I am from off world…"

Nyle almost laughed.

Is this guy some escapee from a mental institution? Surely, he can't be serious?

"You mean, like…off the planet?"

"Yes."

"Seriously?"

"Most serious…"

This time Nyle did laugh.

"You look…human to me."

"I am of human mix. That is why I was selected to approach you."

Now that Nyle looked closely, the man had a humanoid face, but the hair of his head, and facial beard shadow had a bluish tint. He had thought it a mere trick of light and shadow.

"You mean, there really are intelligent beings in outer space?"

"Contrary to human belief, those on other planets have a higher aptitude than many among you. And we are not all malevolent, nor do we wish to exploit you."

"Been watching our television a lot, have you?"

"Were we to judge you with the same measure as you do us, I would never have approached you. No, we observe, and make our own conclusions."

"This is not some prank? You're for real?"

Never once had the man laughed. It was as if he had no sense of humour.

"Shall we get to the matter at hand?"

Nyle shrugged, nodded.

"In the outer worlds, your planet is called the 'Forbidden world', so named because it is a prison facility, and in the sector appointed to the Roog. They resemble the dogs you have domesticated, but in reality are quite hostile and much larger."

"Giant dogs? Here? Haven't seen any."

Once more, the sense of amusement was lacking. "Humans see very little of what actually takes place around them. But…that is beside the point."

For something to do with his hands, the man shuffled around in the paper of the desktop, then when he thought the pause was sufficient, looked up again.

"Some time ago, it came to the attention of the universal council, that the surface of this planet Earth was peopled by intellectual beings other than the Roog, but as the territory was a substation under the devilish dog breed, we could only covertly approach you. After much secret deliberation, it was agreed, if we could build a transporter site, limited immigration of the surface kind would be permitted."

"You're saying you want me to emigrate to another planet?"

"Because of Roog patrols we operate in secret; they claim you as chattel. In their thought, you belong to them."

"Oh, like hell we do!"

A small smile escaped the stoic countenance. "Our thoughts precisely! Now, back to my proposition. Would you be willing to come to the outer worlds, be trained higher in your field of expertise?"

The idea sent shivers through Nyle.

What an opportunity!

"Would the pay rate be the same?"

For the first time the being looked pained, as if to say:

'Why is it humans always are so money oriented?'

He sighed. "Our immediate responsibility will be to train you, to bring you up to our standards. Then your labour will go first toward the repayment of the cost for your transfer…"

"How am I supposed to eat, to pay for a place to live?"

"In many off worlds, at the completion of a four day five hour work week, these necessities are free."

Whoa! Is he kidding? The basic necessities are free?

Nyle didn't have to think twice about accepting this.

"Would I have to go alone? Is this just for a limited stay?"

"Actually, no to the latter. Once intergraded into universal life one cannot return… unless we develop a later treaty with your peoples."

"So, I have to leave my family behind? I have a fourteen year old daughter."

"The daughter may join you. What of her mother?"

"She's not in the picture," Nyle quickly asserted.

"You must understand, secrecy is of the utmost necessity. No one may be told of your going, or of your whereabouts."

"Okay. How do we go about this?"

"It will be a few days, until we have junction with another port. You would be one of the first to use this portal."

"Okay. Can you give me a time frame here?"

"Shall we say, three weeks hence? You and your daughter are to be here at a given date and time; I will see you are notified as to the moment. Your larger property will be traded for lodging at the arrival site. Small property is to be sent through the portal at our convenience. You need do nothing; we will see to the dispersal and movement of all possessions."

"Okay then. Do I need to sign anything?"

"A verbal agreement is binding. We have this conversation recorded."

"Okay, right then!"

Nyle stood to his feet, still in a daze, amazed that he'd made such a decisive decision.

This is one way I can free my girl from the clutches of that abusive bitch! She has always done her level best to keep Kaudy from me!

****

As soon as he arrived at his apartment two days later, Nyle called his ex-wife to set up the time to have his daughter.

Two can play at the game of moving beyond the reach of the other. And what Seline doesn't know, can't come back to bite me.

Or so he thought.

Hopefully, she'll agree to let me keep Kaudy during this time frame; otherwise I might have to steal my girl away, kidnap her. I hope it won't come to that.

But isn't that actually what I'm doing, anyway?

At least, if she does sic the police on me, they will never find us.

CHAPTER 4

Loki arrived chained hand and foot, like a defenceless human. He hadn't bothered to tell them the fetters were useless. Except for the drain-belt he now wore, he could get out of anything. He was half Noor, after all. But if it made those around him feel safer, he felt it best to be submissive; less trouble that way.

Because of his height, Loki had to duck when passing through the exit door of the craft. No one offered to support him as he descended, and with his ankles bound as they were, he could only take one step down at a time. The Slither guard was urging rapid decent, but Loki took his time, being careful. Because of him, the line moved at a snail pace.

"Move it, Noor!" hissed the Slither guard, impatient to be done with his cargo. "I ain't got all year!"

It was common knowledge, Slithers had no compassion, in fact they seldom showed any emotion at all; that's what made them such efficient warriors and protectors. It was rumoured, they were incapable of anything but fury, and were they to display that emotion, it was the prelude to a vicious attack.

Forewarned also by a change in the creature's hue, as its scales turned a darker green, Loki quickly stepped to the side, at the bottom of the flight of steps.

Gazing about him, Loki found his surroundings what he had expected. He stood on the metal receiving wharf of an underground sea. Knowing the installation was deep within the core of the planet, and each entry port securely guarded, he knew he'd not get far should he try to make a run for it. One or another of the sentries would have a ray-wand set on kill, and would use the belt he wore against him within seconds of his move.

As he waited, Loki realized Bom wasn't going to show. That male was evidently so confident he'd won the upper hand; he didn't even deem it important to meet his famous prisoner.

The other convicts were led away; the shuttle pulled back out and left. Still Loki stood alone, waiting, shackled hand and foot, appearing helpless to all around him. An example. A joke. Ignored. The mighty Instant healer brought down, put in his place.

Loki knew that was Bom's intention.

After a considerable time, the door at the end of the facility cracked open, spit out a small Feline male of about five foot four, and squealed shut again. The newcomer loped across the slick grey floor, and panting, came to a stop before Loki.

"Sorry. So sorry" he wheezed. "He didn't tell me I was to get you until now."

Loki said nothing.

What was there to say?

"I am Uel," the attendant admitted. "I am pure Feline." Without preamble, he asked pointedly: "Can you teleport?"

"Not while in a drain-belt. Sorry. That's why they have me in it, so I can't get away."

"Shoot! Shoot! Thought I could get around them, and not have to take the long way. We'll have to go through the cages."

"The cages? You mean the other prisoners?"

"No, no. We are never kept in cages. That's for the cattle. We must work off our sentence. We are given rooms. In med bay we even get cooking space. Very posh...for here."

"So what did you do to tick him off?"

Uel knew instinctively, Loki meant Bom. "I did not side with him," he admitted. "But if I do not offend him in the next four months, maybe he will let me go home again."

Loki uttered a short derisive laugh, which was ignored.

"Come," Uel ordered. " We had better get moving. I must take you to get the chains cut off, and only More can do that."

"More?"

"He runs the supply. He's Root."

Loki could have easily removed his own shackles, and saved time, but he'd learned a long time ago, the Felines were as intimidated by his size as any other species, so he always let them do what they felt most comfortable with.

As they shuffled forward, Uel continued to talk. "Bom has assigned you to the med bay facility. It's nothing like what you're used to, but...we do our best with what we get. Zaba is head physician; you will be under him, as we all are. He's another Root, and lacks empathy. We try to make up for that, but don't let him see you doing it. Tree people are unpredictable."

Uel opened the door to the inner world of the prison. When that access had squealed shut again, and their eyes had adjusted to the gloom, he continued his introduction to life in the compound.

"You might want to hold your breath as we go down through here," he suggested. "These are the meat stalls; the Roog like them live. They are processing a new shipment, so they need the room. They'll orgy every night until they've eaten all of these, and sleep half the day after. The stalls will be empty again by the end of the week."

"Lucky for us they don't like cat," he added. "They prefer us for entertainment; like to torture us to hear us howl. It arouses them."

Because it was mostly dark in the rows between the bared cages, Loki at first did not see the occupants. But moving slowly hobbled as he was, he finally caught sight of a small round face atop an obese body. In shock he realized, it was humanoid!

"They're surface humans?" he questioned disbelievingly.

"Yes, Bom keeps a breeder farm down here. He has both young females and male studs. The Roog troll the surface at night; even go directly into their nests to take them. Then they sort them into placement: breeder, stud, meat or worker, depending upon age or size. We get the pleasant duty of tending the pregnant cows."

"Have you become so callus you do not realize these are thinking beings?" Loki challenged angrily.

Uel sighed. "I know what they are, but I am prisoner too. There is no way out of here. Many have tried to escape, and lost their life in the attempt. We must accept what is done by the Roog; this is their holdings."

"But Bom is part Feline."

"Ha! Matters not. And sometimes I wonder if he is."

Silence reigned between them, and now Loki could hear the low moans of the said 'cattle', the quiet tears of despair.

"You can smell their fear and despondency," Uel quietly observed after a time.

Loki could smell more than that: urine, feces and vomit, among other things. "Why leave them so filthy? There must be innumerable diseases growing in these pens. You must be down here tending sickness continually."

"We are never called here. These are not treated. They pass through so quickly…then the new batch comes. It's the cages you smell; they are never cleaned."

Tears of abject misery flooded Loki's eyes. Sympathy formed deep for these unfortunates, and moisture spilled over, coursing down his cheek, dripping from his chin.

Uel looked up, saw. "You will harden, after a time," he encouraged.

No, I doubt I ever will.

****

It seemed like hours until they passed out of the meat pens. Just before they went through a connecting door, Uel pointed out a side passage.

"That's the kitchen down that way," he told Loki. "Those that are too skinny to eat or too old to breed are made to work there. They grind the meat, or cook the fetuses. The Roog like them five months or term; it's considered a delicacy cooked in mother's milk."

Loki gagged.

Mercifully they passed beyond the human hell into a less sickening atmosphere. Here were rooms of furniture, clothing, trinkets. Other spaces held packaged and canned foodstuffs.

"What is all this?" Loki asked.

"These are the confiscated goods from the surface. When they take the humans directly from their nests, the property is also removed to disguise what has taken place.

They then set a fire or cause an explosion to make it look like a disaster. Humans above never realize the true happening."

"Oh, God of the mighty universe!" Loki exclaimed horrified. "They get away with this? How come no one in the outer worlds is aware of this?"

"It is Roog territory. They are permitted to do what seems best in their worlds."

Before Loki could comment further, the two arrived at More's Supply and Stores. The gregarious Root was deformed and ancient, yet pleasant.

"Ahhh! It needs the chains broken!" he observed delighted. "I like to break things. Bring him over," More instructed.

****

Half an hour later Loki had arms and legs free, and they were on the way again.

This time their course took them through the breeder pens which were much cleaner, and on into comfort-care, where the females in advanced pregnancy were given better food and soft beds until they came full term or were aborted, which ever suited the masters.

"How are they bred?" Loki asked, curious.

"The female is given a drug to make her extremely needful, then when she is beyond herself, a male is put in with her. He too has been enhanced to utter sexual need. They go at it until she's found to carry."

"Just like animals," Loki decided in disgust. "When will we get to the med bay?"

"I just want to show you one more thing," Uel insisted.

He led his charge around the corner, to an area backing directly off the medical centre. As Loki entered, he felt the vacuum immediately. When he stepped around Uel, he stopped short. In the direct centre of the darken room stood a coffin-like glass container. Inside was a dim pulsing light.

"Do you know what it is?"

Loki didn't answer; he was too appalled to speak.

Uel went on to tell him anyway; totally oblivious to the knife he was twisting.

"This is the Essence of the most powerful Noor ever to exist, a Noor Queen!" Uel proclaimed proudly. "The Roog tortured and killed her physical, and managed to capture the Essence just before the other died. They have kept it here since before we were born. They keep her here in a vacuum space so she cannot escape. But I think she is dying now; the Essence is much dimmer than when I first came."

So this is what they do to the Noor. No wonder Dia and Kimon keep us isolated. This is why I can never choose a mate. This is what they would do to her.

"They say her name is Tilk; an Introvert mental," Uel added. "Good thing she can't get out. She could greatly harm us."

Loki knew it wasn't true that she could not escape. Because he had a mental himself, was a Conjunctive Noor male, he was familiar with the Essence make-up.

She is not a captive! She could easily escape through the vacuum, even if extremely weak.

An Introvert female was his counter part, the perfect mate of a Conjunctive male. Instead of being able to split into two physical appearances, as did the male, her two parts were a physical outward form, and an Essence, or spirit, which remained inside the other.

Liam/Loki, of which he was the physical, could separate, or junction together as the need arose. So could an Introvert, but did it rarely, as the Essence was said to be too unstable to remain apart. Without a physical, only a very strong Essence could have survived this long.

Loki knew this Essence did not escape because she was conserving that last bit of her energy. She had no power source, and no physical to join with. It was as if she were waiting for something…or someone.

Does it wait for me?

He would give anything to rescue her, yet while he remained in this drain-belt, he could not give her energy. He could do nothing; he was useless in this condition.

But he would wait; time could change circumstance.

As they entered the med-bay proper, Uel had one more thing to say.

"I am not one of those who agree with the annihilation of the Noor species," he declared vehemently. "Like my Feline queen, I do not think it is a plague to be eradicated. I am not your enemy Noor half, but many here are. Be careful. I will help if I can."

Loki sighed.

It is always so.

****

When at long last Loki was allowed a sleep time, a moment alone, he sat down and reviewed the day's events. It was then it hit him how grievous a situation existed here, not simply for himself, but for all in this hellish establishment. And he knew he was powerless to change their situations, though he longed with all his heart to do so. His only recourse was to help the injured and the sick, as he had always done.

His helplessness overwhelmed him; empathy charred his soul, and...Loki wept...

Violently, the shuddering sobs overcame. At last he feel asleep...lonely, heart sick, and defeated.

Bom had won! Again.

CHAPTER 5

Althea moaned as she awoke. Hurting in every muscle, as if she had been fighting, she stretched to alleviate the pain. Feeling the presence of someone near, she tried to open her eyes, to find only the left one would open fully, giving her a distorted blurred image.

Where are my glasses? And where am I? Not in bed.

She raised her hand to her eyes; the right was swollen shut.

I have a shiner? How did I come by that?

As it passed by her nose, her hand came away wet.

Blood?

The right side of her jaw was sore, as well.

She sniffed to rid the blockage in her nasal passages.

What a god-awful odour!

Where the devil am I?

A faraway gravelly voice came from above her. "Better put your prey with the others," it ordered. "The thing's awake."

"It's mine! My supper! I earned it!"

"You deserve one, yes, but not this one. Bom gets to choose first morsel. Always!"

"This one won't be to his liking. It's too small; not much meat on its bones."

"Never know," the first disagreed. "His tastes are sometimes strange."

Althea tried to inch away unnoticed.

"Better catch it, or it'll get away! Put it in the cage. Now!"

Her legs were caught in a giant hand-like paw; she flew through the air, and was slung roughly across a shoulder covered with coarse long hair. That's when recollection hit her.

This enormous, ferocious, demon dog was in my home! It attacked like something from the gates of Hades.

Am I dead? Have I gone to hell to be torment for my sins? Or is this a nightmare?

As the creature strode along the passageway, her nose was forced deep into the filthy fur of the giant canine; she had no choice but to endure the gagging body stench of the thing that held her.

Her surroundings rocked, like a boat on the high seas, making her nauseous, and she had to swallow back the gorge that rose in her throat.

Before she baptized her captor with the contents left in her stomach, Althea was unceremoniously dumped onto a straw-strewn floor, and the barred door slammed shut.

And now, she was no longer alone!

It seemed there must be over fifty people in that one eight by ten foot cell, all battered and bleeding as she was, some sitting, others pinned against the outer bars, the rest lying on top of one another. Most were women, some held children, and the few men present seemed stunned, and of no protection to their families.

Althea crawled to a corner, hoping to hide there.

****

Hours passed. The cage gate squealed across the metal floor, and Althea peered through the throng to see two dim shapes, dog-like again, standing blocking the way out.

"Come out!" the large dog bellowed. "One at a time. Move it! Move it!"

Those at the front scurried to obey. As the cage emptied, some held back, Althea one of them.

"Go in there, and push them out," the loud beast growled.

The second monster dog came toward Althea. She rose up quickly, and ran for the entrance.

"Get in line!" barked the first. "Move it! Move it!"

Althea scurried forward, joining a line of others, which lead off down the corridor. A young teenage boy came from behind her, pushed in ahead, apparently trying to get near a girl of about the same age standing just in front. Another older man also joined him, again forcing ahead of Althea. Two more women took up position at the rear of the line, behind.

The column abruptly stopped. Their guards seemed unconcerned, began growling to each other in low tones, as if conversing with each other. The prisoners relaxed somewhat; the humans inched forward in hesitant sprints and stops.

Finally, as she rounded a corner, Althea saw and heard what was going on. In panicked disregard of her own safety, a mother with a child was screaming and struggling with another dog sentry, as he attempted to wrestle the infant from her arms.

"Stupid thing!" growled the large creature. "You are breeder! This thing is meat! Let me have it!" He cuffed the woman soundly, tossed the howling child to a comrade, as its mother dropped to the floor. Two other canines then dragged the woman away in a semi-conscious state.

All Althea wanted to do was get out of there, but the way was blocked behind by the two who had forced them out of the cell, and the way ahead, though it lead away in three directions, each was equally fortified by giant Rottweilers. There was nowhere to go.

At the convergence of the four-way passage sat another small-breed dog. As each human passed, he sniffed the air and declared in a confident voice his verdict.

A skinny older woman came even with him.

"Worker," it decided, and the others pushed her toward the middle passage.

A plump short man with white hair came next. "Meat!" And he was pushed to the entrance through which the child had been taken.

Althea began to tremble visibly, as the meaning of the terms hit home.

The young girl just ahead of the boy and the man, who had forced their way ahead of Althea, came even with the bloodhound.

"Breeder." Wailing, she was shooed to the left, to stand in a row of girls already winding away out of sight.

The young boyfriend came abreast of the creature. "Stud!"

Althea shivered.

Are we like mere cattle to these things?

The older man was next. "Worker!"

It was Althea's turn. The bloodhound sniffed, sniffed again. She held her breath. She was older; by this time, Althea knew the pattern. She was either worker or meat.

"Breeder!"

A sentry nearby growled. "That's no breeder," it challenged. "It's too old."

"She smells fertile! Can you not whiff the hormone?"

The other stepped forward, sniffed at Althea, and stepped back puzzled. "Looks too old, but does seem breeder."

Althea stood stunned.

I've not had a period for ten years. What do they smell?

"Move it!" the guard from back by the cell growled. He'd come up behind, his bark causing Althea's heart to jump frantically in her chest. "Move along!"

Because they were nearing the end of those who had come from the cages, all had gathered round these last to be processed.

"It most likely does not understand," defended one of the other guards.

"Yes, it does!" declared the larger one. "It should! I have my throat translator on just like you. Move along, you stupid animal. That line!"

It pointed to the left passage, and finally Althea came to her senses. Fleeing to join the younger women, she was just relieved and thankful that she had not been declared 'meat'.

****

This new line moved quickly forward, and around another bend, finally spilling everyone into a large room.

Again a smaller dog manned this station. Obviously a female, she wore no shorts as had the males behind, and her gender was apparent.

She sounded like a barking excited Shihtzu when she shouted at them. "Strip! Strip! Only two garments to keep; the rest go in the chute!"

Althea only had two pieces. She was still wearing her pyjamas.

But like the rest, she shed her clothing, clutching them in front of her to hide her embarrassment.

"Put on the benches!" they were ordered next. "Leave! Leave! Into the next room, naked!"

Oh, golly. What next?

When all the women had descended into the lower chamber, the door slid shut with an ominous bang, sealing them in.

For a moment, nothing happened.

Then from every direction, boiling hot water came out of tiny jets, ceiling, walls and floor. There was no escaping them.

And it was not enough to simply scald them; the liquid also contained some sort of disinfectant that made the eyes sting and weep, and caused uncontrolled fits of coughing, if it was breathed in.

The screams and desperate dancing of naked bodies continued until the flow abruptly stopped again. It had only been ten minutes, but to each, it seemed an eternity.

And then, the blowing air came to dry them, frigidly cold.

The outer door finally slid open again. They did not need to be told to vacate the room. Shivering; with blistered skin and teeth chattering, they fled back to find their clothes.

And in the ordeal Althea realized: sometime during her capture, she had not merely lost her valued freedom, but she was missing an essential for survival: her false teeth. Without them food would be more curse than benefit.

****

From there they were placed in another holding cell, and yes, fed. The brown gruel was course, consisting of large, tough chunks of half-raw meat, and hard uncooked granules of some sort of grain. A milky substance held it together, and apparently they were expected to eat with their hands, or slurp it up with tongues. The moment Althea tasted it, she gagged, for it was exceedingly bitter, slimy, and rancid, as if it had been kept day after day until it should all be used. Even if she'd had her imitation teeth, she would not have been able to stomach the meal.

CHAPTER 6

"Oh, crap!" hissed an exceedingly pregnant middle-aged woman, as Althea and the young teen that had been taken with her were brought to the new cage. "Don't put them in with me."

"Move back, bitch!" growled the Dog that held Althea by the arm.

"Don't put her in here! There are other cages. Can't you wait until this one is empty? I'm the last one; I was next to go to comfort care. Now, I'll have to wait 'till these two are bred, before I'm taken. Double, double hell!"

"What's got this female in such a dither?" the second guard wondered. "You'd think we were threatening her."

"Beats me. Can't understand their yowling when they're not fitted with a translator," his companion answered.

"They should fit them with one as soon as they arrive instead of only when they reach comfort care."

"Back! Get back, or I'll hit you! Do you hear?"

"This one is called Lana," offered the other. "Maybe if you use her name, she'll be less aggressive? Try a little gentleness; they get miserable when they're near term."

"Nice Lana. Move back now; we don't want to hurt you."

"Like hell you don't," growled Lana, in a softer tone, sounding much like a dog herself, but she did move to let them in.

"See, it's all in the way you treat them."

The first barked a laugh, as he slid the gate closed.

Lana turned with a snarl toward Althea.

"They're going to fight," warned the second guard.

"Aock! Leave them be; they'll get used to each other. They do this all the time. We got better things to do than police them. Still got the others to deal with."

As their voices receded, the hostile Lana demanded: "Man! How old are you hag?"

"I'm not a hag…"

"They'll never breed you; even an old stud would find you ugly. What is your age, anyway?"

"I'm only sixty…"

Lana laughed, with long drawn out and raucous mirth. When she finally caught her breath again, she stated the obvious. "They'll never get nothing from you. And," she added. "Now I'm stuck here until the two of you are carrying. Which will be never…forever."

"Damn! Damn!" she mumbled, as she moved away to a corner by herself. "Got to do something about that."

****

"I need to go pee!" declared the young teen, dancing in place. "Where do we go?"

"Over in the corner." Lana pointed.

"In what?"

"You pull back the metal floor, and go through the bars."

"There are people down there," the girl objected, as she followed the instructions.

"So what. They're just meat."

As she did her business, the teen thanked Lana, then told her name. "I'm Beth."

"Don't care who you are. We're not friends."

Beth came back and sat with Althea near the barred cage door, as much for comfort as to get away from Lana.

"What do they mean by 'meat'?" hesitantly whispered Beth, after a time.

Lana heard her, but answered in a roundabout way.

"Guess what they do with the fetus?" She didn't wait for an answer, simply carried on. "We're just cattle to them. Like cows. This thing inside me will be eaten; it's a delicacy to the Roog. They'll cook it on a slow boil, simmer it in my own milk, then when they eat it, they'll break off an arm, and slurp off the meat…"

Althea's mind rebelled; Beth gagged and leaned forward.

"If you're going to puke, do it in the corner," Lana said coldly. "Don't need your stink to make me upchuck too."

Beth made for the corner, where she became violently ill. Althea found it hard to keep her own churning stomach at bay, but then there was nothing in it at the moment.

****

An hour later they came with food.

"Yummm! I'm starving!" Lana proclaimed, joining them at the bars.

"Move back, little humans. Back, back, or I can't get it through to you."

They moved back a few steps, as bowls of the brown gruel was past through a space near the floor on the sliding door. Lana grabbed at hers, and headed away with it to her space in the corner.

"Better give them fruit, too," ordered a second small female dog. "The one is pregnant, in final stage. She should have been in comfort care by now."

A small basket of apples, oranges and bananas was passed through along with the gruel, and their attendants moved off out of sight to the cages beyond.

"Leave me the apples," Lana snarled. "You can have the bananas, they make me sick; the oranges too. I hate citrus!"

Althea approached the large dish, took a banana and an orange. Beth took the gruel. Althea left her bowl by the bars.

"If you're not going to eat that," Lana said casually. "I'll have it."

"Be my guest," Althea agreed.

Peeling her orange first, Althea sucked at the juice. Even if she couldn't chew it, the moisture and vitamin D would fortify her. She swallowed most of the wedges whole; hoping her system would digest that bulk, giving her fibre. Then she started on the banana.

This was her first real food, and it tasted heavenly.

As they were eating, Lana chose to discourse. "You know what kind of meat is in the stew? It's the old ones; Roog don't like tough meat. They grind them up and feed it to us; sometimes the kitchen workers are too lazy, so they just chop them into pieces and put it to boil. The bottom burns, but the top never gets cooked. You're eating human…Beth."

Beth stopped with a fistful half to her mouth, the bowl went flying and the girl headed to the corner.

"Oh, gee. Look what you've done now. I could have had that bowl too."

Althea gagged on her banana.

"You going to bring up, too?" Lana challenged. "This place is going to reek!"

Althea wasn't about to give her that pleasure. She swallowed slowly, near choking on the slippery mash as it went down; she held her breath until the gag reflex stopped, breathed out a sigh, and took another bite.

Lana giggled, and went for the second bowl on the floor by the bars.

CHAPTER 7

Bom wanted a special one for next time. He was almost finished with the one he had now. He strode the corridors with his prison supervisor at his side.

As they past the tunnel that led to the breeding pens, he stopped. "Let's try down this way?"

"But sir, those are the holding pens for impregnation. Surely you don't want to take one of the valuable stock for mere consumption? Think of all the young you will forfeit."

"Is it not my installation, my livestock to do with as I please? I set this up! Haven't I kept my fellow canine well supplied with food?"

The other made no comment, knowing his chief held the lives of all in his hands. He dare not disagree, or he would end up in the entertainment cycle awaiting torture.

"We go this way!" Bom ordered forcefully, tolerating no argument.

Again they paced along cages filled with humans, but this time only females looked back at them.

The studs were kept apart, in another area of the compound, well fed so they would always be virile, their stamina kept at peak, until they were needed.

Perhaps I should choose a male? But no, too much lost if I pick one of those. One stud can produce thousands.

Surely, there is some delectable morsel among these breeders that can give me a challenge, before I gut and feast on her live struggling carcass.

His mouth began to salivate at the very thought.

"I like to play with my food," Bom stated. "It's the cat blood mix in me."

"Breeders aren't very quick," the other dared to offer.

"Yes. Some. But they taste better, and fight back. I like that."

He stopped at the bars of a cell; something had caught his eye as they were passing.

Did I see a flash of red?

This cell held a pregnant one. "Don't want one that's carrying," Bom said aloud.

His eyes roved over the other two cuddled together against the gate bars; the one was a mere adolescent, just into puberty. But the other...he could tell from her condition, she was a fighter!

****

Althea wanted to slide away and hide, under the scrutiny of the formidable beasts peering in at them. The larger one especially was an unusual anomaly.

As he knelt down to her level, he pressed a fingered paw to a small oval medallion on the band around his neck.

Is that the throat translator they talked about? They are each wearing one.

The male's face came into close proximity to the bars; his eyes level with hers, his breath rancid, smelling like bad meat. His head was that of a bulldog, droopy ears folded back against the black head, brown-tan muzzle, the thin dark lips pulled back to reveal viciously long canine teeth on either side; an attempt at a smile that had resulted in a fierce grimace instead.

Althea shuddered.

Next a hairy paw-like hand inched through the bars, catching one of her legs quickly. Althea tried to draw away with no success. Her foot was held firmly with incredible strength.

"Red toes," the creature stated in a soft whisper.

In shock, Althea's eyes tracked to her feet. She had forgotten; for the fun of it she had polished her toenails a brilliant red. Her coloured toes had always been hidden from the eyes of others, her one indulgence, but now because her feet were bare, they were exposed for all to see.

"I like red toes. Pretty red toes."

He released her foot, and quietly stood to his full height.

At least eight feet of muscled formidable giant, he had long shaggy black fur, and a matted bushy tail like a cat. He waved that appendage with a nervous twitch as if ready to pounce, stood there thinking.

Is this a canine or feline? He appears to be of both species. Is that even possible? If I hadn't seen it with my own eyes, I would have never believed it.

The reeking giant turned to his comrade. "I will have Red Toes! Keep her here until I come back. Do not breed her; I don't want the inside beast slowing her down, it'll make her too emotional and weak. This one is mine! Do you hear?"

Then he strode away purposefully. The other stood a second, then turned and went the opposite direction.

Silence reigned for a moment; then Lana spoke.

"You know who that was?" She chuckled. "You got the attention of the owner of this grand hotel. They call him

Bom. He's a crossbreed, between a dog and a cat, and oh... will he have fun with you!"

Althea shivered.

"But that still leaves you in here with me. Now I'll never get in comfort care," Lana added bitterly.

****

Loki was tending to a dog guard who had challenged another for his prize. The two had fought, inflicting deep slashes and gouging bites upon each other. Which one had won out the physician didn't know, but he would treat them both equally.

They just better not pick up the fight in this med bay!

Bom pushed open the double doors to the bay, striding in with a gait that told everyone, he was pleased about something. All heads turned his way expecting reprimand, then turned away relieved at his amendable manner.

"Your attention, please!" Bom bellowed. "I am making a new ruling." When all eyes had turned his way again, he dropped a most unexpected bombshell. "I have noted the inmates serving in this facility work harder than most, with little perks. Today, I feel benevolent. For your good behaviour, you may each pick a human pet for your pleasure. It may be chosen from the kitchen workers, and will live with you in your compartment. You will feed it from your rations, and may train it to help you. But...when you are discharged, it remains behind, and is to be returned from whence you took it."

Bom turned to Loki specifically. "That means you too, Noor."

Loki scowled.

Humans aren't pets! They are intelligent creatures!

"I mean it Noor! I'll be watching to see if you obey. I'll give you time to make your choice. I realize you are kept quite busy."

Then he turned once more to the group in general. "And make sure you tat them, so we can tell which belong to you, or they might just get eaten by mistake."

Chuckling hilariously at his own joke, Bom advanced with purposeful gait to the exit opposite that by which he had entered. The doors swung shut soundlessly behind him, whooshing at the air as if giving a fond wave in farewell.

CHAPTER 8

Beth was awakened by Lana's panting. When she muffled a scream in grunting discomfort, the young girl wondered why the woman hadn't moved to the corner latrine area to take her dump.

The young teen could just make out the older lady, Althea, still near the bars, as she lay dead to her surroundings, curled in on herself for warmth. Beth had gone to the bathroom in the night, but had been too sleepy to crawl back to the comfort of the elder, had fallen asleep closer to Lana.

The agonizing groans began again, and Beth turned to watch the pregnant woman. She was sitting with her back against the far wall, her knees pulled up, the skirt of her shift up around her waist.

What a strange way to go to the bathroom.

That was when Beth saw what was between her legs. At first, it looked like a small ball was stuck there. Then she realized it was the head of a baby.

In abject terror, she began to scream with all the energy left in her.

****

Althea woke with a start at the strident screams. She felt disoriented, and at first could not place where she was. When she realized it was the young girl Beth making such noise, she peered about the stall looking for the reason.

There were no guards inside with them, in fact Althea had realized after a few nights, the guards were never around during the sleep time; nor in the first few hours after lights came on. They seldom put in an appearance until feeding time, at what seemed to be the noon hour.

With her nearsighted vision, Althea could barely make out Lana against the far wall. The woman was sitting up, doubled over. By the sounds she was making, she sounded like she might be experiencing a contraction.

Beth was closest to her. And then it dawned on Althea.

Why, I bet the child has never seen someone in labor. That is why she is so upset.

Lana gave a long drawn out screeching groan, and Althea tensed.

Oh, my, gosh! She's pushing! She is giving birth!

She had a choice either to go to Beth and comfort her fear, or help their nemesis deliver her baby.

And that was a no-brainer.

"Beth!" Althea hissed. "Beth! Be quiet! You'll bring the guards down on us. She's only having a baby."

Whether the young girl understood or not, her screams softened to a muffled moaning in the background, as Althea crawled to the unfortunate Lana.

But Lana would have none of her assistance.

"Get away from me, bitch," Lana yelled with a vicious snarl. "I don't need no help. I've done this dozens of times. Ain't the first time in a dirty cell either."

But Althea was loath to leave her on her own.

"I can help when the baby comes out…"

"It's already here! Get back where you were, or I'll do something you'll wish…" The words ended in a scream, as Lana went into another pushing contraction. "Get away from me!" she growled when she could catch her breath. "I don't want you near me!"

Althea inched back, just out of reach.

"That's not far enough! Back by the door…where you were before. I'll kill you if you come near me! Do you hear?"

Althea knew it was better she obey. The woman was upset enough already. So, reluctantly she crawled away to Beth, and led her to the gate, where they had spent most nights together.

Five minutes later they could hear the liquid sucking sound as baby escaped its comfortable shelter; then the hard thump as it slid onto the metal flooring. A feeble indignant cry followed.

At least the child is alive.

"Let me help you clean it," Althea pleaded.

"With what? No rags or water," came from the far darkness. "Never mind! I've done this before…"

****

Morning came, and the lights came on.

Lana was bending over her infant, her back to them. It sounded like she was licking the baby clean.

Or is she?

The woman gagged.

"Lana? You okay?"

The woman growled low in her throat, like an animal, went back to what she was doing. Her back still hid her actions.

"Crap! Crap!" a voice behind at the bars exclaimed. "Par! Par!" the guard yelled. "I need you down here! This human is eating her young!"

Suddenly another joined him, and the gate was squealing open.

"Keep the others back!"

A third dog-guard burst into the stall, and Althea inched back, guiding Beth, holding her face to her breast so she wouldn't see what was happening. The girl, who had just begun to relax, began to whimper plaintively.

"Little bitch must have given birth in the night. Help me get it from her!"

Lana growled, like a beast fighting for her prey. The guard cuffed her soundly against the side of her head.

Lana dropped like a stone.

The guard tossed the bloody dead infant to one of the others. "Take that thing to the kitchens. Not good for anything but stew now." And the male disappeared from the cage with it.

Lana stirred. The first guard kicked her head, and she went out again.

"What's the matter with these things that they act like this?" asked Par of the other.

His companion shrugged. "They get violent and bestial when they are reaching the unbreedable status. Sometimes at that age, they even take their own lives…or they live on in a state of despondency working as kitchen staff."

"How long have we had this one?"

"Twenty, thirty years."

Par shook his head in disbelief. "That's longer than I am old. What now?"

"We put her back in to be bred. That'll appease her."

"No room in the breeder tank, at the moment."

"Then we leave her; watch her, 'til there's room. Let's get out of here before she wakes up again."

CHAPTER 9

Bom strode angrily into the med bay, a battered human slung over his shoulder. He dropped her with force upon the empty examination pad in front of Loki, just for emphasis.

"My meat's not responding."

Loki frowned. He looked to the young broken female laying on the cot.

"That's because it's near dead. What do you expect me to do?"

"Fix it! Heal her! You are half Noor!"

"I seldom can bring the dead to life at any time."

"It's not dead yet! Haven't you the kinetic healing touch? Heal it!"

"I cannot; not while I'm in this belt. That's why you keep me in it, so I can't use my powers…and so I can't teleport from your prison."

"You are lying to me! I've heard it said, the Noors are unable to tell an untruth."

Loki laughed bitterly. "Just as you, I am a half, part Feline. And Felines lie all the time."

Bom growled. Taking Loki's offensive remark personally, he defended: "I am more Canine Roog than Feline, you stupid cross-bred cat!"

Loki, rarely in a foul mood, was weary from lack of rest. So he chose to be unwise, but brave this day; to give back point for point. He had little more to lose; he was already in this bizarre prison.

"Well…" he challenged. "Is that why, for most of your younger years, you lived among your mother's cat people? I've heard your father didn't even acknowledge you were his, until you were full grown, and began to fight and dominate, causing trouble."

"True, I came before the council on a charge, but when I declared I was his son, he was quick to absolve me. He was proud of my nature! I was Roog, like him. But I am the only one of my kind. I'm special!"

"Yes, and so now your father boasts of the rape he committed. How come you don't live with him, if he is so proud of you? Not really accepted in their world either?"

"Watch your tongue, Noor! If I had a wand you'd be suffering."

"I'm sure there is one around here. Want me to get you one, coward!"

The dog male growled low in his throat.

Loki stood there, eye to eye, not flinching, nor backing down.

After a moment, Bom seemed to think better of fighting. He returned to his first demand.

"Fix it!" He pointed at the hapless creature on the cot.

"So you can hunt it, torture and finally eat her?"

"That's right! My prison; my stock pens; my rules! And you are my prisoner!" Bom snarled.

Loki shook his head in disapproval. "If we were at home, you would not behave like this," he rebuked.

"You think not? Remember who my father is? I am son of Clio; he heads the universal council! You've tried to buck him in the past. Remember? And you're the one in the belt now. Don't mess with me further. I'm warning you, half-breed."

Loki finally admitted to himself how hopeless this challenge was. If he provoked the male anymore, he'd be in here for life, if he weren't already.

"It's beyond help, Bom," he returned in a more conciliatory tone. "I can't help her."

"Fine. Leave her to die then. I have another in the cells to play with. Dispose of this one in the kitchens. Never liked carrion anyway," he grumbled, as he turned away.

Suddenly, he turned back for one last try. "You could heal it without powers," he declared. "I know this. You can infect her…however it is Noors do that."

"I would never do that to another. To be Noor is a curse!"

"Ha!" Bom laughed, pleased that he had finally cowed Loki. Then he turned and strode rapidly away. Just as he went through the swinging exit doors, he fired back. "Take it to the kitchen!"

Loki sighed, resigned, and gently picked up the battered human. While they had faced off, she had escaped this torturous establishment, breathing her last. He almost wished he could do the same.

CHAPTER 10

Althea felt the weight of the warm body as it crawled on top of her.

Beth must be really chilled to come to me so aggressively.

Without opening her eyes, she allowed the closeness. Then when a frigid fist slipped under her shirt, the smell assaulted her senses.

Whew! Man! We are beginning to reek like something from an outhouse.

Althea held her breath, so she wouldn't breath in the stench. She enclosed her in a comforting hug, still too relaxed by sleep to open her eyes and look at the girl.

The cold fist was joined by another, which moved down Althea's body, and into her pyjama bottoms.

Her eyes flew open in shock, and at her involuntary gasp, she took in a lungful of the fetid air around her, and coughed.

This isn't Beth! She wouldn't do this!

It's Lana!

With all her might, Althea began to struggle; fighting in a desperation akin to panic, but the other woman seemed to weigh a ton.

Then the lights came on, and the sudden glare direct into her eyes, blinded her.

Fingers from the hand in her pants forced deep inside Althea. As the fist opened up, the slippery goo in it slid in like backed-up sewer water. Althea squirmed, fought harder, but the woman was remarkably strong.

"See how it feels, old lady," Lana hissed in her ear. "You want to be treated like one of us; like you're young again? Need a man? I'll make sure none of the studs will ever go near you…"

Althea knew now what the overpowering odor was. Excrement. The other woman's hands were covered in her own bowel movement.

And now, the damage was done, with no way to reverse it.

Althea fought anyway, rocking from side to side, as the mad woman smeared the foul slime across her legs, moved up her side too the chest, and finally, to her breasts, where she rubbed vigorously to infuse the odour deep within the flesh.

"They'll love your perfume now, pretty Red Toes," growled Lana, like the beast she'd become. "Never know, maybe the brute dog will like the scent. Now, you smell exactly like he does."

Althea thrashed, bucked, rolled, but to no avail. Lana stayed with her at every turn, until she was ready to give quarter. Finally, willingly, Lana eased back.

She smeared one last streak of the brown mess from her hands across Althea's cheek, and abruptly stood up. Slowly, she walked across to her side of the cage, laughing hilariously at the disgusting deed she had just accomplished.

Behind her, left lying on her back, Althea went limp. She broke into uncontrolled sobs; the pent up agony to this point buried, finally coming to the surface. Tears flooded from her eyes, coursed down the sides of her cheeks, wetting the hairline, eventually absorbing into the grey curls.

Her misery continued for long minutes. When at last Althea quieted, the room around her was silent.

Althea pulled in a breath to steady herself.

Where is Beth?

She rolled to her side. And there sat Beth, not five feet from her, cowered against the bars next to the hall, hugging her knees and rocking in distress.

She had watched the whole thing…and done nothing; a victim of her own paralysing fear.

Althea crawled to her, but she pulled away.

And then, there was no further chance to give her the comfort Althea had planned.

The guards could be heard approaching.

****

"Oh! Yuk! Do you smell that?" growled Par to his partner, as they came around the corner. "Look at these two! They've been fighting. Open the darn cage! Gross! We'll have to hose them down before any male will approach them."

The barred gate slid back with a squeal, and the huge caretakers moved in upon the women.

"Take the young one to the breed tank; it appears not to have been involved. I'll deal with these two."

Beth whimpered pathetically as she was grabbed aggressively by her shirt and lifted off the floor.

"Sure you can handle the other two alone?" her captor asked from the entrance.

"I'll manage! Just get her out of here before she gets ideas."

The other disappeared, while the remaining watchdog studied the two women with disfavour.

By now, all the fight had gone out of Althea; she wasn't going to resist. But Lana had other thoughts. She made for the open doorway at a run.

The enormous canine took one large step, caught her in mid-stride, and holding Lana suspended by her hair like an errant pet, swung toward Althea.

Par gave a visible shudder. "You're more filthy than this one, but guess I'll have to touch you. You'll most likely make a run for it if I walk you…"

Althea hadn't even thought of that.

Where could I go? Perhaps I can hide from him, but for how long?

Before she could formulate a plan, the creature had her by the hair, and Althea swung through the air. She raised her hands in defence, clutching at his hairy arm. He shook her violently, until her head was swimming, and she dropped her arms to hang there limp.

"That's more like it," Par declared, but gave her one last malicious shake anyway.

Althea felt her neck crack. Sensation immediately numbed from the shoulders down, and she suddenly felt very old and tired.

She closed her eyes, surrendering; hung suspended without dispute, as they passed through the dark corridors.

I wish he would just kill me.

****

After the shower door had slammed shut, when she tried to rise, Althea could barely stand.

Lana was giggling gleefully, as she moved off to a safe distance. As the hot jets exploded from the walls and ceiling, she spread her arms out in obvious ecstasy, as if it had been a very long time since she had received a bath.

Althea also was grateful for this opportunity. She tore at her pyjamas, paying no mind to the heat of the scalding steam. She had to wash away what was on her skin. Yet more importantly, if she was to survive, the filth inside her must be eradicated.

Though the searing water blistered her flesh, she persisted, dancing naked, leaving behind her soiled garments to soak clean on their own. She spread her legs, and when the boiling liquid shot within that delicate private space, making it burningly raw, she clamped her jaws together, so the scream would not escape her lips. It became a moan instead.

She lowered into a crouch, her knees spread, until she was sitting right over the forceful scalding jet in the floor. But just then, the water abruptly shut off.

Althea knew it hadn't been enough to ward off contamination; the disinfectant in the water hadn't had time to go deeply enough to be effective. She would still pay the consequence for the feces that had been rammed up inside her.

The cold breeze didn't come to dry them. Instead the outer door banged open, and the guards were upon them again. The one that had taken Beth away was back again to help the other, and each male grabbed a human by the arm.

Her captor gave Althea no time to catch up her sodden garments, so she was led away naked. As Par left the room with Lana, he ordered:

"Put that one in a separate cage. She belongs to Bom."

"He picked this scrawny thing? There's hardly any meat on her."

"No reasoning for his choices. He's always been a bit weird."

"Better not let him hear you say that, or you'll be in the stocks for certain."

Par grunted in irritation, and disappeared with Lana.

Althea was jerked roughly forward, almost dragged down the corridor, and at last, pushed violently into a darkened cell. She hit the floor with a savage crack, and lay still, as once again, feeling deadened in her extremities.

She knew it was meant as punishment. The cell remained unlighted, and later when she heard the clatter of the meal cart, no sustenance was brought her way.

By then Althea didn't much care.

****

Quiet had descended; the sentries left for parts unknown.

Althea soon felt rawness in her throat, a burning cramping in her belly. She grew unbearably hot, then chilled to the bone.

Shivering, trembling, she at last fell into a fitful fevered sleep. Reliving her capture in vivid nightmare, she cried out hopelessly for someone to rescue her.

She was still in oblivion when the lights turned on. The food they placed just inside the bars went untouched. Darkness came again; night passed. Lights once more brightened the stall. Even as a third night brought the dimmed lights, Althea knew none of it.

Nor did anyone notice her delirious state. In her fevered dreams she fought with family, asking why she had been abandoned, crying out with a hoarse voice that no one but she could hear.

Why did you leave me? Why don't you look for me, son? Don't you love me? Don't you even miss me? How could you so easily forget me?

CHAPTER 11

Standing at a distance off to the side, as Nyle and Kaudy stepped off the transporter pads, a tree-like being waved them over. Leaving the upside-down horseshoe shaped entry gate behind, they approached cautiously.

"I am Theee," that individual declared, when they came abreast of it. "I am a Root."

Seeing as the creature seemed quite serious, Nyle tried not to grin. To him it was obviously a tree not a root, but...whatever.

It had the appearance of something that belonged in a park on Earth, with its gnarled rough brown bark, and rust and green leaf-like hair. It had eyes resembling knotholes, no nose, and a crack for a mouth. Tall and skinny, it stood approximately seven feet tall, and Nyle had to look up to it, as it continued its instructions.

Theee turned to a waist-high square post at its side, studying the data on a computer screen. As the symbols scrolled by, Nyle wondered what they said. The device spit out a small glass inch-square card, and Theee handed it to him.

"What is this?" Nyle asked.

"Please do not speak. You hear my words in your tongue; but to me, what you say is gibberish."

Wonderful!

As a second card shot from the console, and he was handed it, the Root continued.

"These are temporary identity cards. Until you are processed at Universal centre, keep them on your person at all times, or you will get lost in the system."

Nyle slipped both cards into his front jean pocket.

"Keep your female always within your sight."

Nyle didn't need to be told that twice. Now that Kaudy was with him, he didn't intend to part with her. He turned to leave, gazing about in perplexity.

How am I to ask where to go, if the thing can't understand? I have no idea what these signs say.

"Just one more moment of your time," Theee requested. "All beings must be fitted with a throat translator."

Nyle turned back. The Root held a small inch and a half wide circular band in its branch-like fingers. Where it had come from, he had no idea.

"First the little female. Will you allow touch? Just nod."

Kaudy nodded agreement, and as Nyle watched protectively, the Root bent forward, fastening the instrument around her throat like a choker neckband. The centre held a quarter-sized medallion, which he pressed inward before stepping back.

"I have activated your device. Please say something in your tongue."

"What should I say, dad?" Kaudy asked.

"That will suffice. I clearly understood." The Root turned to Nyle, and suddenly a second band was in its hand. "May I touch?"

Nyle nodded. The band was thin, light weight, comfortable, and hardly noticeable, when he too was fitted with the instrument. Pressing the centre, Theee stepped back.

"Speak, please."

Nyle cleared his throat, suddenly intimidated and tongue-tied. "Ah…thank you."

"Good. That will suffice. Now, you should both understand others, and they you. Please keep your translator on at all times while you are in Jump Centre. For a private conversation, one may deactivate by pressing the centre orb, but it is not recommended while in public. Now, please proceed to the tunnel at the far right. It will take you to your next destination."

Theee turned away, seeming to abruptly dismiss them with these words, moving to greet a group of many species just stepping off the transporter pads.

Thus released, Nyle took Kaudy's hand, and made for the exit to which he had been directed.

The tunnel was made from what appeared to be see-through Plexiglas, with a moving conveyor belt running down the centre of the floor, much like what could be found at any department store mall back on Earth. Kaudy, immediately finding it familiar, stepped confidently on it, and Nyle followed. With awe, they watched the night sky of space, as they were slowly carried forward.

"Oh, daddy. I can't wait to tell mommy all about the things we've seen. She won't believe we went to space for a holiday!"

"It's our secret. You can't tell anyone."

He hadn't told Kaudy this was permanent. He hadn't wanted to deal with all the fallout, and it had been the easiest way to get the girl away. Telling her they were going on an outing her mother would object to had kept the girl excited by the mystery, and silent so her mother wouldn't interfere, as Seline dropped their daughter off.

"Not anyone?" Kaudy clarified. "Didn't you even tell your mom…grandma?"

Oh, crap! I forgot to call mom! Didn't even get to say good-bye.

And I forgot to call my sister too!

I'll never see either of them again. Dumb! Dumb!

When he had failed to answer, Kaudy fell silent. A few minutes went by; then the panoramic spectacle outside the glass caught her eye, and sent previous questions to the background.

"Daddy, look!" Kaudy pointed to the left, and when Nyle followed her gesture, his jaw dropped in amazement.

Interspaced at various points out in the obsidian darkness were star-like clusters: a large centre star shape with ten smaller star structures circling around it. From the bottom end, similar to the one they rode, five tubes of varying length extended in a half circle, leading up to the star group. The entrance to each seemed to begin at empty space. The whole system gave an appearance of an enormous spinning shooting-star cluster, especially when it began to revolve.

"What are they, daddy?"

"I have no idea."

"There are more." Kaudy pointed over to the right.

As Nyle followed her motion, he found numerous other groupings spattered equidistant from each other.

Are they spaceships sitting out there in space?

An extremely large bear was approaching beside them, walking upright and faster than the conveyor travelled, apparently in a hurry to get to its destination. As it came abreast of them, it spoke in what sounded like a male voice. They could clearly understand his words.

"I could not but overhear what your female asked," he stated timidly. "What you see, are the different jump stations to other star worlds." He waved pleasantly, and continued on pass.

"Daddy?" questioned Kaudy with astonishment. "There are giant teddy bears in space?"

Nyle chuckled. " 'Peers so, munchkins."

****

When they arrived at Universal Centre after the third transporter jump, they were ushered into the immigration office without delay. By now, they were both very tired, and Nyle hoped this would be the last stop.

He left Kaudy in a chair in the corner behind him, as he took the seat in front of the desk. The attendant behind the table was a cross between a humanoid and some kind of rodent.

After it fed their small identity cards into the base, it studied the readout that appeared on the computer screen. With a fat finger, it seemed to be flipping through the data, as one would browse through the apps on an iPod.

Speaking at last, it did not introduce itself. "I am afraid I have bad news. It appears you have no equity…"

"I had a condo…"

"Of little value. It was under financing; you owed more than its value, therefore your furnishings had to be sold to balance out what was owed. Also, some of that property was also financed."

Nyle couldn't argue with what was fact.

"So where does that leave me? What happens here?"

"It leaves you in limbo. You cannot be trained until you are placed. With nothing to begin with, you must have a sponsor."

"I thought my former employer was my sponsor?"

"It says here, you came of freewill."

Again he couldn't dispute the facts. It was true.

"So…what do I do then? Can I go back home?"

"All ties to the Forbidden planet are cut. You are here now. Must make the best of situation."

"Okay. What happens now?"

"As you have nothing but small property, and no saved currency; also no sponsor, you could remain here, and wait out a year to be accepted on your own merit…"

"What does that mean?"

"If you have a special talent that is in great demand…"

"Such as?"

"Physicians; computer programmers; mechanical repair…"

"I've tinkered with cars most of my life," Nyle supplied hopefully.

The mole-like face frowned in puzzlement. "Oh! No, no! Mechanical repair does not mean what you think. It refers to the repair of the mechanical…sorry. I believe you would call them robots on your world. Also, it includes the boards…computers in your terms. You were scheduled to be trained in that field, but now as you cannot pay your way in, it makes you unacceptable…unless you have a more in demand talent."

"But, you said that was in demand."

"Indeed. However, you must first get off this station and be accepted to another world."

"And how do I do that without any money? I can't even pay for food...or lodging for that matter."

The creature grunted. "Know you not that basic necessities are supplied? You need only do your appointed labour for four days a week, and you will receive what you need."

"But you said I can't work."

"One may take menial task while waiting. The first week's needs for you and young one will be given free bonus."

"Okay, then I'll go that route. How do I get off this station?"

"You can wait out the year to be accepted on your own merit, which is highly unlikely, or you can place yourself on the Universal mating list, and hope some female of another world will have the credits to sponsor you, and be willing to accept you for mate."

Nyle didn't much like the sound of that.

"Why can't a male be my sponsor?"

"Most planets have a ratio of fifty to one..."

"How do mean?"

"Fifty males to every female. Males are unwanted; we have a glut of them."

"Then even a female wouldn't sponsor me?"

"You have other factors in your favour...the little female with you."

"What! You want me to sell my daughter?"

"No sir. Not sell. A widowed female may have a son who does not qualify for mate. This would then make you of interest to her, as some would choose mate from extended or attached family."

"Ho...ly crap! What kind of universe is this?"

For a second the male was silent. At last he spoke carefully. "I am aware, these ideas are hard for you. I am undesired myself. I have been on this station for much of my life. Some worlds are much stricter; males are killed if they indulge in rape, and same-sex relationships are forbidden there. Believe me, this is your best option...think of the young one. Do you wish her to be stranded here? And what will become of her if something should happen to you? Males have been known to kill father or guardian for a female. At least if you are accepted into a family, you have protection for her."

Nyle felt like the wind had been knocked out of him. He bent forward, running his hands over his face in consternation.

What am I going to do? I sure messed up this time! My bridges are burned, and I can't undo the mistake.

Worst of all, I dragged Kaudy along with me, thinking we'd both be free from Seline's controlling vindictiveness. How can I protect my daughter? What kind of life will she have now?

She'll almost be like a hunted animal; never safe. I almost wish I'd left her in the hands of her mother.

Nyle lifted his head. There was only one way to go.

Maybe later when I have a job, I can get out of the marriage, and take Kaudy somewhere safe. For now, I'll have to try the spousal sponsor.

"So, how does the mating thing work?"

"Both you and the young one will be assessed physically, emotionally, mentally, and your history taken. Then you will be placed on the waiting list, compared to available females. Your compatibles will then be notified. I must warn you; new females will not be choosing you. It is set to be age appropriate, as well. But there are many widows denied second mate, and others…forbidden to ever mate…these will be considered also. Then you wait for one willing to sponsor and accept you."

"I'm wondering about something here. Why, if there are so few females, would anyone refuse her a mate?"

"Some are old; others too dangerous to you to be accepted into their clan…"

"You mean, like violent?"

"That too, but with some, it is dangerous for you to be their partner. A threatened or perhaps, mixed species, of which either or both of the parent species consider them outcast. Then you also would be viewed as adversary. But not to worry, not many of those." Going back to his original spiel, he reassured. "There is only one species prohibited from reproduction, and that is because this infected species carries a blood anomaly others do not wish passed on. It is unlikely you are compatible with such a one. They are of the highest intellect…"

Nyle made a rude noise. "So, in other words, you have elitist bigots out here too?"

Silence filled the small chamber. Apparently, he had been understood all too well.

Nyle cleared his throat, wishing he'd kept his thoughts to himself.

That certainly is no way to get out of this darn place.

"Ah…guess…I suppose, we will be placed with any species?"

"It is unlikely you will be compatible to any but a humanoid…or one of mix: part human, and say…cat or such. Do you prefer she look mostly humanoid? It will lower your chances."

"I suppose, any species will do. If she was willing to take us, and…if she can get used to me, I'll get used to her…eventually. When will this all happen?"

"I will put you on assessment for tomorrow. After that, it is simply a waiting game until one replies. I'm certain you must want to rest now, as the little female with you has fallen asleep. Wait one moment; I will call a mechanical to accompany you to your quarters."

CHAPTER 12

"Arf!" thundered Bom, with a bellow that could be heard all through the breeder kennels. "Arf! Where is that beastly cur?"

Trembling visibly, the prison supervisor hurried to the side of his warden.

"Is there a problem, sir?" he asked timidly.

"Problem! Problem? You bet we have a problem! What have you done with Red Toes? She's not in this stall, where I left her."

Arf swallowed back bile.

If something is wrong; if they've mistakenly taken the she to the breed tank, Bom will blame me. My life will be over!

Three of the other sentries joined them.

"I had her put in another section, in a cell by herself," declared the youngest male, Par. "She'd been fighting with a female who'd just given birth, so I thought it best to separate them."

"I don't care what she did!" Bom yelled. "Show me where she is!"

Like a pack on the hunt, Bom and the other three followed, as Par led them through the passages to a remote corner cage.

"In there." he pointed.

Just inside the sliding gate, four bowls filled with food lay still untouched.

"She's not been eating?" Arf observed.

"She doesn't like the gruel, sir; will only eat fruits. When she was with the pregnant cow, she ate, but we don't give fruit to those not carrying."

"Don't care," Bom growled. "Open it up!"

Par slid the door gate back; he and Bom went in to stand over the woman. Arf held back at a distance, while the other two males remained in the hall.

The younger male kicked at the female. "Get up! Your master wants you."

"Turn her over," hissed Bom.

Par nudged her over with his foot, and the human flopped to her side like a rag doll.

Bom growled deep it his throat.

Without warning, he turned, grabbed the young male by the throat with one hand, ramming him against the side of the cage. As the second paw came up driving violently in, his claws came out: vicious, sharp and deadly, penetrating deep, just below the ribcage. Bom mercilessly twisted his wrist, and his victim gasped, went rigid. Then in one swift motion, the razor-sharp weapons were drawn down the belly, slicing his opponent near in half.

Arf stepped back, terrified for his life.

Bom let go of his prey; and Par slid lifeless to the floor. Bom spun toward Arf with venom in his eyes.

"My meat is damaged; you will pay for that! Get this worthless piece of garbage out of here!" he ordered to those watching at the gate.

The two hurried in, fearing his wrath would turn to them, gathering up the bloody pieces, escaping at a near run.

Bom turned again to Arf. "Get out of my sight before I kill you too. Report to gladiator. I will watch you die hideously by another's hand. Be gone with you!" he bellowed.

Arf turned and fled.

****

He ran like a banshee was chasing him.

My life is over, but I'll not die before Bom! I'll not give him that pleasure!

As he passed the weapon's room on his way to the gladiator pens and pit, he turned aside.

Arf stopped, stepped in, surveyed the array of sharp sickles and long cutting swords. He grabbed up one of excessive lethal potential, stood for a mere second, then fell with all the force he could muster upon it.

****

For the second time in a week, Bom came charging into the med bay with a human female slung over his shoulder. He brutally deposited her on the empty bed in front of Loki.

"Can you fix it, Noor?"

He wasn't ordering, he was asking, an unusual attitude for Bom. It was almost as if he cared about this one.

Loki turned her gently over, as the overseer stepped back to give him room.

Her face was skeletal, the body emaciated. She was filthy.

"Did you do this?"

Indignant, Bom bristled. "She's my meat! They abused her in the cells, where I had them keep her, until I was ready."

Loki shook his head. "Don't know as I can do much. She won't be able to run from you; her neck's broken."

Bom hissed like a provoked cat. "I killed the varmint that did this! She would have made such a challenging foe. She had it in her to turn and fight. I could see that."

Loki gave no evidence he had heard. He examined the female more closely; he knew he had to make the effort. His nemeses would punish him if he didn't seem to try.

One eye was blacken, swollen shut. The nose and mouth were blistered; the lips cracked from dehydration. Her naked body was covered in bruises, and in raw patches the skin had been broiled away; the upper legs had at least third degree burns on the inner thighs and buttock. He didn't dare examine in the private area.

What has been done to this she? Have they tried to cook her alive?

Tears sprang to his eyes; Loki swallowed hard with empathy, sympathy adding to the pain of this assessment.

Why does this one affect me so profoundly?

He touched her forehead. "She's burning with fever," he stated with candour. "Something has caused a sickness."

Bom growled disapprovingly. "I won't eat a sick one. Kill it!"

Loki shook his head. "I don't kill, Bom," he said quietly. "I'm a healer, not a butcher."

"Then take it to the kitchen. Feed it to the humans."

"Whatever this disease is, it'll get into your food chain that way."

Bom snorted. "I don't care what you do with it, just dispose of it."

Then, he turned about and stormed from the bay.

Loki sighed.

Maybe she will die on the way to the garbage chute.

Anything I do for her will only prolong her agony...and she'll end up back in the kennels after.

For the first time in his life, he hated that he was a healer.

****

Loki carefully lifted the battered little female. Just at that moment, she gave a small sighed inhalation. He moaned in despair.

You would have to be a fighter, wouldn't you?

Nobody deserves to die like this. Why did they ever take her? She's too old.

I wonder if she has family. Are they in here too?

Carrying her against his chest, so as not to jar her, he headed out of med bay. The garbage chute was near his quarters. Every step felt like he was doing something wrong.

Oh, please, just die, little sweet one. Why do you have to keep taking another breath?

He almost wanted to smother her, to end the misery.

But is the wretchedness I wish to alleviate mine or hers?

He came abreast of the stasis room, and thought of the Essence.

In all this time, it has never given up.

This one is another of like personality. To let her die is like snuffing out the life force of the Essence.

I am in a belt, useless. But...there is a way...

I'd have to hide the fact from Bom.

He did say, he didn't care what I did with her.

A thought occurred to Loki.

Bom said I could take a human pet...from the kitchens. Kitchen, disposal; what is the difference?

He arrived at the disposal chute...and passed on by.

I'll have to make sure he doesn't recognize her.

Loki headed away down the corridor, to his bed nest.

CHAPTER 13

The first thing Loki did was put her on a mat on the floor of his quarters. He would have to leave her alone, while he finished the shift.

I hope she lives until I'm off on sleep break.

He took a sponge, soaked it in water; placed it to her lips. She sucked feebly at it, like a hesitant nursing infant. Having had the moisture to ease her thirst, the frail female drifted off again into a fevered sleep.

Loki went back to work.

****

It was the first wee hours after the Roog had gone to feast. Zaba and Uel had both already left for their sleep chambers; in fact Loki had purposely waited for the bay to be empty, so he could get the supplies he needed without arousing suspicion.

He gathered sponges, syringes, tubing, ointment, disinfectant soap, a portable water pump and douche spray unit, a body brace, an artificial breather, and anything else he thought he might need, then headed off to his own quarters.

When he got there, the little female was still breathing, though with great difficulty.

Hang on little she. You are not alone anymore. Loki is going to help you.

She was so small, not much bigger than half his size. So fragile, so delicate, he cringed at the things he must do to her.

He gathered now from his own stores: an acetone solvent, he'd found in the supply store shortly after he'd arrived, which he had found useful to remove the grime he discovered everywhere in his suite; the shaver, tooth paste, hair shampoo, and a package of cotton balls; another of cu-tips, and last of all, an assortment of small bandages.

I'll need something to clothe her with; maybe later, when she's better, I'll get something from More.

I'll also need a place for her to sleep. For now, when she's clean, she can stay with me on my bed.

What if I can't save her?

He refused to go there. He had committed to it now, and he would see it through.

He lifted her carefully, carried her gently to the shower in the corner, lay her out spread-eagle on the floor, in the one foot high tub-like depression.

Loki suspected some sort of inner contagion had caused her fever, and the most likely area, as he deduced from her burned lower region, was inside the private area.

She tried to deal with it herself. Smart, but ineffective.

He dreaded to violate her so, but if he was right, it must be done.

Loki stood up; left her there; fetched the douche machine, and rolled it near. Filling it with warm water mixed with disinfectant, he took the wand, and inserted it. For a minute or so, the water washed away brown, and he knew he'd been right, but then something seemed to block the flow. He removed the instrument. It came out covered in excrement.

Loki shuddered in revulsion.

Did she do this? Is she suicidal? That doesn't make sense. If she is responsible, why would she try to remove the result with scalding water?

He shook his head, putting the matter to the back of his mind.

First things first!

He tried to reinsert the wand, but it wouldn't go in.

He removed it.

Only one thing to do.

He shivered, not wanting to do this to her.

Loki went for a pair of surgical gloves and a vaginal speculum. Spreading her legs, he inserted the instrument. He slipped one gloved finger deep inside.

And that's when he found the pessary. It had worked deeply inside blocking entry.

If she was conscious, this would cause her extreme agony.

It came out easily, pulled out with a liquid plop, covered in black, green and brown slime. He set it in the disposal tray at his side.

Leaning back, he pondered.

Fallen bladder, easily fixed.

This time he went in with two fingers, and had the procedure done in seconds.

At least, my minor healing ability is still available.

After he had removed the expander, and finished the inner cleansing, Loki sat back, suddenly struck by a thought.

Isn't it a common practice for human physicians to prescribe estrogen cream to lubricate and counteract dryness when a pessary is used?

And didn't Bom say he took this female from breeding...even though she is obviously too old?

Loki almost laughed then.

They misinterpreted her scent! The dogs have been tricked! That no doubt saved her life at the time.

He marvelled at this twist of fate.

But, was this really just providence? Or maybe, like we Noor believe, the Mighty has a hand in guiding the universe after all?

It gave Loki the hope to continue. He went back to his labours.

Taking down the hand-held showerhead, he turned on the water, tested it to make certain it wasn't too hot. Not that she would consciously be aware, but he didn't wish to burn her skin worse than it already was.

Being careful not to jar the damaged neck when he moved her, he soaped and hosed her down back and front. The water easing away contained straw, filth, and grains of sand, as it fled toward the drain.

She is so tiny...compared to my big muscular frame; the breasts are small, like those of my foster sister Twila.

He recalled bathing Twila when she was younger and just beginning to form. She'd put a stop to it once she was mature, preferring rather to do it herself. He was still puzzled by that; he'd been acting as a brother.

Didn't I care for her from the time she was orphaned, because Dia feared water? She is my sister! I am more than twice her age; I thought of her merely as the daughter I cannot have.

Loki cleaned inside the ears.

This she has tiny ears, not cat ears like me, like those I hide beneath my ginger curls.

He gently washed her hair.

She has such fine locks, not coarse like Roog and some of the Feline.

At last he set away the sprayer wand, took a towel and carefully patted her dry. With the human still lying in the depression of the shower, he took his shaver, and began to remove the silver-white curls from her head. When she was completely bald, he gathered the cuttings and placed them in the disposal tray.

He surveyed his work.

One more thing to do...so Bom won't recognize her.

He went for the acetone solvent, knelt again, and with a small cotton ball, began to remove the red nail polish from her toenails.

He had recognized the colour as fake, once again because of Twila. Before his sister had mated, she used to paint her toenails a brilliant green to get the attention of the males.

This little she has delicate feet and toes, just like Twila.

Twila had Noor feet; so did all the half Feline/Noor. It had always bothered momma Dia, so she hadn't liked to wash her Foster's feet.

Remembering that, Loki chuckled.

At last, content he'd done his best inside and out, Loki got his toothpaste. He gently opened her jaw expecting to find discoloured and broken teeth. In shock, he realized the cavity was empty.

No wonder she wouldn't eat! She wasn't able to masticate.

With his finger, and a smudge of paste, he cleaned inside the mouth.

Next Loki went for the body brace. Shifting her gently to her belly, he fitted the flexible transparent binding along her back from just above the base of the skull to the bottom of her tailbone, and clamped it tight.

With this apparatus keeping bones in place, she should heal perfectly…if my plan works.

Through all his ministrations, the small female had laboured to breathe, never giving in to the shadow of death waiting. It was as if she knew she was being cared for by a sensitive, empathetic hand, and would do nothing to defeat the promise of recovery.

Loki fetched the small breather mask, fitted it to her bruised face, and turned on the attached miniature oxygen cylinder. Immediately, her efforts grew less a struggle, and she seemed to relax, dropping into a deep coma.

Don't give up on me, little she. We've only just begun.

He prepared a place on his bed for her, padding it with a catch sheet in case she went incontinent, covering that with an extra soft towel for added comfort.

He lifted her tenderly, placed her on his sleep mat and covered her, then left to clean up his mess: to return the douche machine, empty the trash tray down the disposal chute …and prepare himself.

****

Tubing and implants in his hand, Loki lowered to sit on his sleep mat beside the small female. He went to work immediately, first tying off his left upper arm. Then finding the artery in the indent of his inner elbow, he drove a large bore cannula into it, and attached tubing and clamp to the imbedded bore.

Next he found a vein in the right inner elbow of the human, and inserted a similar but smaller cannula into it, then placed the other end of the tubing over it.

Cautiously, he opened the clamp between them, and watched his life blood seep into the transparent channel, down toward the unconscious female, and into the waiting vein.

He sighed heavily. All seemed good.

Leaning back against the wall, he prepared to wait it out.

He would do this for three more successive nights and hope his Noor blood would do the healing work that he could not.

I can't give you more than that; it will cost my life, and I have others to consider besides myself.

After about an hour, Loki reclamped the tubing, removed his end of the apparatus, and detached from her insert, leaving it in, and covering it with a small bandage. He sat back and watched his own small incision slowly close and heal.

At last, secure in the fact he'd done all he could for one night, he lay down beside his patient, and quickly fell asleep.

It seemed as if he'd only just closed his eyes, when the pounding at the door drove him up from troubled dreams.

"What is it?" he asked in a hoarse whisper.

"You are late, Loki," warned Uel through the barrier. "Zaba has just come in. You'd better get to the bay before he misses you."

Loki groaned.

Is it morning already?

"I'll be right there. I overslept. Sorry."

CHAPTER 14

The Slither appeared out of thin air startling Twila. The snake-like human-cross known as Sith still unnerved her even though she knew it was loyal to Dia's family, sworn to protect the females of her clan.

Twila inhaled slowly to calm herself. "What is it? Is there a threat?"

"No, mistress. Thor wants you at the board. There is a message coming through for you."

Twila frowned.

Who would contact me directly?

Having delivered the missive, Sith vanished as abruptly as he had appeared.

"I'll be at the board," Twila told her foster father Kimon, as she passed by. Then moving at a leisured swinging gait, passed through the beds of the holding ward to the small alcove that held the communication centre with it's many board connections. Every male eye followed her movements, albeit covertly.

****

Thor was a large purebred Feline male with long black fur streaked with grey. He was a distant cousin to momma Dia, and as aged as she. It seemed he'd been around since before Twila was kit, and at the board equally as long.

Having the superior knowledge, when Liam was home he would work first board, but Loki's mirror image and mental half also was a rescue/warrior; when required he could be called away to search for a family or a lost kit, sometimes on some far away outer planet, as was the case today.

Thor usually worked second board, or support, but today, he was alone, and manning all centres. He seemed stressed.

The computer terminals not only connected the med bay to the inter-space communication system, coordinating rescues, incoming casualties, incoming messages, and medical queries from other medical stations, but also linked to the universal data library where all histories and medical knowledge of all registered beings, of any species, was stored. Usually, with his exceptional rapidity at assessment and board skill, Liam had no trouble keeping abreast of the demand, but he did the work of ten, he was half Noor. Thor was a mere Feline, and though he'd been boarding for almost a century, he was still only one male.

As she came up on him, Twila sensed how overtaxed the elder was.

They really need to train another male for these boards. Hasn't Shiveron asked for such training? Maybe poppa Kim should let him?

But then again, Liam is responsible for such instruction.

"I was told, you have an incoming for me?"

Thor hissed in annoyance. "Give me a moment. Silly board stream! I lost it. Let me reconnect."

Twila took a seat at the terminal at the far end.

"There now," Thor said at last. "I've directed to your board, and have placed it private. Don't mind me. I'll just continue going crazy."

Twila laughed. "I'll help you after I'm finished, if you want, male?"

"Naw. Things will settle down soon. Be glad when Liam comes back."

****

Twila turned her attention to the on-screen message. Reading it, her jaw dropped in shock.

What's this? There must be some mistake.

'A compatible has been found that corresponds at ninety-nine percent of requirement. As all other matching females have rejected male, programme has gone to widowed mate rejection list. Thus you are notified, you may take second mate, should you so desire. Male requires sponsorship to enter into outer worlds, has no property. Has young female dependent, fourteen. Male is human with evidence of Noor infection...'

"What! What? That's impossible!"

"Something wrong?" Thor asked from his corner.

"No. No sorry. Just talking to myself."

No way he can be Noor infected! Dia and Kimon know every Noor; we are all in this nest, and none, that we know of, has infected anyone. Surely, an unknown cannot have slipped by my fosters!

Twila read on.

'...age thirty-four, healthy, and has minor training in mechanical repair. Male is immigrant from Forbidden Planet.'

"You're joking! He'll be primitive, a savage!"

"You can tame him," came confidently from across the room.

"Oh, and since when can you read minds, Thor?"

He chuckled. "I smell hormone...and I know message came from mate list site."

"Ha! You keep this to yourself, do you hear?"

"Mum's the word. Are you going to accept?"

"I don't even know all the details yet; haven't even seen what he looks like. Leave me alone, male, and get back to work!"

Chortling to himself, Thor answered an incoming call.

Twila sat back to ponder. She flipped to the dual pictures of the man and his daughter.

Well, at least he's not ugly.

She shivered in spite of herself. It had been a long time since Jabek's father had been tortured and killed.

To be alone is hard.

And my young male is cursed to the no mate list too, because of his Noor blood.

If the human male has the Noor anomaly, so does his young female. She is fourteen, Jabek sixteen, perfect for mating...but will they be allowed to reproduce?

At the very least, he will have a companion.

She had to do this, if not for herself, for her son.

Twila typed in: Will accept; will sponsor. Notify of arrival time, please. And sent the message.

When she stood up and made to leave the room, Thor grinned widely.

"I hear one word of this on the floor, or anywhere on ship," Twila hissed. "I will see you are transferred off our base, so fast you will wonder what Tornado Being caught you unprepared."

"Mum's the word!" Thor agreed stoically.

"Better be!" Twila growled.

CHAPTER 15

Loki stumbled and almost fell. He sat down hard on the floor between two empty beds.

The room swam, gyrating, tilting nauseatingly. He was about to pass out. He hadn't done that since a child.

The next he was aware, the short Root, head physician Zaba, stood over him. "U...e...l!" he bellowed. "Where are you?"

"Here, here," Uel panted joining the irate master. "Oh...dear..."

"Yes. Oh, dear. What is wrong with this stupid Noor?"

Loki couldn't get the words out to tell them he'd be fine in a minute.

He knew what was wrong with him. He'd given too much blood; he hadn't stopped at the fourth night, like he'd planned.

The little she isn't responding as she should, and I am loath to give up in defeat.

"Well?"

"Well," Uel declared. "He's probably low energy. You can't expect to keep him in a belt without effect...and obviously, he's not been getting enough rest."

"Harrumph," grunted Zaba. "So...you think he wants a day off?"

Uel hissed in annoyance at the insensitive Root. "Wouldn't hurt. We could all use a day off once in a while."

"You have sleep period. Casualties never come in until after Roog quit feasting and rutting."

Uel hissed in frustration. "The Noor needs a break. Give him time to heal back."

"From what?"

"He's practically responsible for this whole bay, keeps it running smoothly, tends it by himself mostly; keeps it clean, is on call in the night. Give him a break."

"Harrumph! So...okay, one day. That's all! Get him out of here, before I change my mind." Then the Root turned his back, and stalked away.

"What mind?" grumbled Uel. "Stiff slave driver! Loki, whatever you been doing, you better quit it, before Bom finds out. I'm no dummy; I've covered for you, but soon they are going to realize you've been stealing supplies and using equipment at night. You want us to stay here the rest of our lives?"

Loki licked his lips; croaked out the words. "I'll be fine in a minute. Just help me stand up."

"You're an idiot! If you think this will get you out of here, you're sadly mistaken. Others have tried it before you. Bom has fed them to his dog cousins."

"He wouldn't like my taste. I'm Noor. We have a tingling bitter after flavour."

"Ha! Glad you still have a sense of humour," Uel declared, as he helped Loki to his feet. "But it doesn't impress me. I got you some free time; use it! Go get some rest!"

"Kay." Loki swayed dangerously.

"Need me to help you to your room?"

Loki thought of what he had hidden there. If Uel knew before the she was healed, Loki couldn't trust he wouldn't tell Bom.

"No. No, I'll make it."

"Okay then." Uel gave him a sidelong glance, then turned and walked away in the direction the old Root had gone.

Loki sighed, and stumbled away in the opposite direction.

****

As he passed by the stasis chamber, he stopped short, his thoughts going to his hidden patient. He turned into the room; stood there watching the dim pulsing light.

Wish you could tell me what to do next? All your knowledge stored away in there, and I can't even tap it. She's dying on me anyway. I can't give any more.

His vision narrowed. Swaying in weakness, Loki turned about dejectedly.

If he had been more alert, he might have noticed the light in the case blink out. It then appeared on the ceiling above the case. When Loki left the room, travelled step by weary step to his chamber, it followed, hovering at the ceiling just behind. When he slowly opened the door, stepped in, before he shut it, the transparent creature slipped in, hovering at the ceiling.

It remained there while Loki checked his unresponsive patient, lay down beside her, and gave way to sleep.

An hour passed. The light image moved, shifted, lowered slowly to hover over the small human form…and blended with it.

****

Loki sat bolt upright, as he woke to the thrashing of his diminutive bedmate. Her sounds were almost animalistic, as she tore frantically at the facemask of the breather unit. She was covered in sweat, seemed almost convulsing, yet her actions appeared purposeful.

Loki quickly unlocked the mask from her face, tossed it away to a corner; heard the clank of the empty oxygen cylinder as it hit the floor. Before he could move out of the way, the female turned on her side, gagged, and retched, foam spraying from between parted lips. The light blanket over them was baptized.

Somehow Loki didn't care anymore. He moaned, and slid down beside her. Hopelessly, he lay there, wishing she would just give up and die.

What have I done? I am just prolonging her torture. Hasn't she suffered enough?

A light rap at the door had him worried. "Who's there?"

Has someone heard the commotion? What time was it, anyway? Still day?

"It's Uel," came the voice of his fellow prisoner. "Sorry to disturb you, but…I need to tell you something. I figured you'd want to know."

"Just a minute."

I can't let him inside. Especially not now!

****

Loki opened the door, standing blocking the view into his room. Uel didn't try to enter, but spoke in a whisper.

"Pew! I smell vomit. You sick?" But the Feline didn't wait for an answer. "I told you never to eat the stew.

Human meat doesn't agree with Feline digestion. Get fish from More, rather."

Loki wasn't going to correct his misconception. "What's so important? I haven't been asleep that long, have I?"

"Naw, it's still middle noon. I thought you'd be interested…"

"In what?"

Uel sighed, skirting the issue. "Well…I was dumping trash down the disposal chute, and…well…"

"Spit it out Uel. I'd like to go back to bed."

"Ah, ya sure. Well, as I passed by the stasis room, I noticed it was dark."

Loki frowned. "What are you saying?"

"The Essence…I think, it's died…"

Loki groaned, doubling forward in grief.

Ah, man! Now, I can't even help it.

"Sorry…" Uel seemed at a loss at what to say.

Loki straightened, suddenly resolute.

"Better this way," he declared coldly. "It's time she was released from her bondage. She's been tortured long enough!"

When he spoke the words, Loki had more in mind then just the Essence.

Without thinking, he pushed the door closed, slamming it in Uel's face.

****

I will do one more thing for her before I leave her to die.

Finding an old cooking pail, he filled it with warm water and soapsuds, and brought it to his sleep mat. Leaving it on the floor, he first removed the light sheet he had over the human.

What difference does it make if she is naked for now? This will soon be over.

Setting the thin coverlet in soapy water in the walled bottom of the shower stall, he washed, rinsed, wrung it out, and hung it over the top of the rail to dry.

Kneeling down beside the bed, he turned the female on her back. It struck him then; she had rolled over on her own the first time.

And wasn't she using her hands to try to tear away the mask?

She should have no ability to move! She has been motionless for nearly a week!

Is she healing?

He shook his head.

No, she can't be, all my imagination.

I'm too stressed. I'm seeing things. This needs to end, not just for her, but also for me.

Loki wrung out the cloth he'd placed in the pail of soapsuds, brought it to the gaunt face. The lips were still parted, and she seemed to be breathing easier.

In his mind, he purposely denied the fact.

As he washed carefully at the now green-yellow skin of the shiner, he realized the swelling had lessened. That too he ignored. He washed the second eyelid. Rinsed his cloth, turning back to wash around mouth and nose, and was shocked to find the eyes open.

This he could not ignore.

For a moment the eyes shimmered in rainbow hues, then the irises turned blue with an elongated vertical pupil like that of a cat, and lastly her soul-windows became the cerulean blue human irises with a tiny centre of black.

Loki pulled in his breath.

I have infected her; passed on the curse of the Noor. I sure can't leave her to die now!

The eyes slid shut; she sighed weakly, as she moved off into sleep.

Tears dripped from Loki's eyes, as he finished bathing her.

At least now she will mend. From this point on, I will forever be responsible for her. That is a given!

Loki also determined, he would keep her out of a belt, even if it cost him his life, and someday…he would set her free.

CHAPTER 16

In the Feline society, females went into first heat at fourteen, at which time they were mated. Males were ready at fifteen. When first mate died or was killed, males were delegated to warrior status, and their sentence included all junior male family members under them, as well.

With the lack of available females in their twelve planet system, if warrior males wished to change their societal position, they were left no other recourse but to seek a partner elsewhere. And there was only one place where there was a bounty of such females: the Forbidden planet!

Reon was well past the age of ready mating; both he and his father were delegate warriors. At eighteen, Shiveron's only male offspring was never to be allowed a mate in their society, unless an intervention could be enacted.

Shiveron had gathered a collection of like-minded individuals, each with the thought of acquiring what was not readily available to them. His main purpose was to get a mate for Reon; he never expected a second mate for himself.

However, if he were to find a single mother and daughter of the appropriate ages, it would be much appreciated, and he would indeed take the opportunity.

He vowed he would never take the female from a mated set, even though by Feline order of challenge, many fought and overpowered to take a mate from another.

But, as far as Shiveron was concerned, this human species they preyed upon left much to be desired when it came to protection, sexual prowess, and the tenderness required to keep a partner content.

Tonight, the warriors were going hunting on planet Earth.

Cloaked and invisible to the naked eye, in the bushes many miles from the large city, the group had left hidden the small shuttlecraft that had brought them. It would sit waiting for their return until dawn. The males' intention was to scavenge the area in the dark of night, until they had found what they sought, and had attained their goal.

They took to the surface in slow easy strides, so as not to use up more energy on the going, that returning burdened down the necessary vigour would be at their disposal, available should they be chased and a fight ensue. Keeping to the shadows along the city edge, loping fast, like a pack of primitives, not moving closer in until the houses came in sight, they approached the large urban settlement.

Shiveron led his hunting pride into this alien world. Purposely, as a safety precaution, the destination had been left a long way off, but if they held back their strength, and played it out gradual, they would fair well.

The perceptions of the group were heightened, the Felines in hunting mode. Even Shiveron and Reon though Noor half were disguised by shape-shift as Feline.

The distant city lights shone brightly, reflecting against the dark sky in vertical rainbows. The air was cool. Such a night should have been most enjoyable, would have been, had they not been on a planet in the Roog system, where they would be hunted as enemy, because Roog were dog and Feline cat, adversarial by nature.

But these were not like the Roog: vicious, predatory, and merciless. Felines were cautious, watchful, timid, and benevolent, yet if need be, they could be intimidating.

These were strong males, powerful, warriors. Yet of them, Shiveron was the largest, his assumed black wavy coat blending into the night around them, except should the moonlight reflect back from his normal silver markings, which he'd chosen to retain. The six greys paced beside him coalescing like shadows, huge, cat-like, but still smaller than he, and in the centre, the youngest even shorter.

Only Reon, who had also chosen to keep his white markings, could perhaps be seen from afar, so the others hid the younger kit in the midst of them, protected by the midnight and the grey, confusing the eye, camouflaged as shadows…almost.

With great trepidation, Shiveron had taken his son along, yet he knew the younger male needed to be the one to chose his own. Also, he was the lighter, swifter, in case they were attacked unexpectedly, or pursued. Reon could run ahead, arousing those left at the shuttle, sending back a second wave to deliver those cornered.

The males slowed as they entered the avenues, slinking in between the structures, into the alleyways behind, separating to go their separate ways. They would come back together again at the city's edge, when each had found his chosen.

Now that they were alone, Shiveron stood indecisive, wondering what route to take.

The sudden brightness of the street lamps made his eyes water. In reflex, he squinted. This blinding glare meant, now he needed to depend on his other senses until ocular vision adjusted and returned.

Why must humans persist in chasing away the darkness? Perhaps it is because night is never safe for them.

The air was colder than he was used to. Shiveron had never seen snow before. The white frozen water covered the paved streets everywhere.

Slippery. Hard on the bare feet!

There were puddles of melted moisture, ice-cold liquid! He stood in one; his toes had gotten wet.

The moisture hanging in the air clung to his fur.

Uncomfortable! I am a warrior male; I will not complain!

He felt static energy spit across his shoulders and back, causing the hair of his tail to spike, standing on end. Shiveron wanted to yowl with the discomfort it brought.

How do the pure feline stand this constantly? Maybe it wasn't such a good idea to go in camouflage?

I am a warrior male! This is nothing!

We must wait; somewhere nearby is the one we want. Let Reon sense her.

Shiveron's hair was curling from the condensation, making him appear as a new birthed kit.

Like a female!

I am not meant to be beautiful. I am a male! I am warrior! And proud of it!

What is wrong with me, that I am so distracted?

At last his eyes adjusted to the glow of the street lamps. No longer blinded, Shiveron took his bearings. He stood still listening.

What attracted both males was the angry shouting, as it lacerated the air around them. It sounded like a pair of she-cats fighting, the sounds of home, almost.

And to a Feline, their screaming and yelling meant there was no male at home.

Shiveron turned to Reon. "Do you think you could tame one?

Reon grinned wickedly, and nodded.

****

Prone on the sofa, Moriah fumed, as she cut the connection to the other end.

Where is my mother? How many times now have I tried to call her and received no answer? It must be a month since we've talked.

If I hadn't hurt myself so bad at work this week, I'd go over there tonight and make her let me in. Never mind it is near bedtime, I'd take her to task for ignoring me. Doesn't she even care what happens to us? You aren't the only one who has health problems, mom; accidents happen to others, too!

So what if you are sixty, you should be a mom first and always! You should care, no matter what!

And what is the matter with that brother of mine, that he can't call once in awhile either?

Her daughter, Iora, stomped up the stairs into the living room, roughly slamming the bowl of treats she carried on to the coffee table.

"Why are you so miserable?" Moriah demanded. "You've been short tempered the whole night, like a bee has gotten into your hair or something."

The caramel skinned beauty had gorgeous black curls she kept perfectly, painstaking styled. Iora spent hours and hours primping before the mirror in the bathroom before leaving each day for school. At sixteen, it seemed, the most important thing in her life was to look good; her appearance was even more important than eating.

Because of this, and her fussy eating habits, she was under developed and rail thin. Her height also accentuated the fact; she was taller than Moriah's five foot four.

"I'm tired of handing out candy to these snot-nosed brats," Iora fired back hotly. "I want to go out with my friends! Why do I have to stay; you're here? I'm not some old fogey."

"What was that?" Moriah fired back quickly. "Did you just call me an old fogey?"

At just the right moment, the doorbell at the back door interrupted; Iora grabbed the bowl and fled from her mother, to give out suckers to the costumed halloweeners.

As soon as the girl returned to the upper level, Moriah, from where she lay on the couch, picked up the argument.

"Where do you think you're going this late at night, anyway?"

Iora huffed. "There's a party at Sadie's. Can I go now? The little kids should stop coming now. It's after eight."

"No way are you going!" Moriah shouted. "You are going to clean up this mess! You were suppose to do it when you got home."

"I didn't make all this mess! You did!"

"You made most of it!" Moriah declared hotly. "Do you even care? I work my butt off to feed you, put clothes on your back. I've always given you everything you wanted. The least you can do is to be considerate. But, not only are you not grateful, you treat me like your servant, like you're ashamed of me. I'm not your housemaid, you know! I'm your mother!"

Iora snorted, as if she couldn't find a quick retort, or perhaps doubted Moriah was much of a mother by her standards. It was hard to tell sometimes what she thought. She was either too quiet, or fought Moriah like a she-cat.

It was then Moriah realized the windows were still open. It had been so hot inside when she'd arrived home; she had opened everything up wide.

But her temper was too close to the surface for her to care if anyone heard; Moriah was on a roll, self-pity and pain ruling her words.

"This is not my fault!" she continued. "I never asked for this injury! I can't help it if I can't keep up. I work, and when I have a day off, I cook and clean and wash. When do I get time for myself? You head off to school; get to play with your friends. It's time you get your head out of the sand, pull your own weight around here, start helping with things. I slave all day lifting old people, cleaning up their messes, and what happens? I come home to a house that's worse than the homes I've just left. And they need Home Care!"

Moriah barely took a breath, before she continued with her tirade. "And you think you are hard done by when I ask you to pick up after yourself; you think you're entitled to the things I give you! I am not your personal slave!"

Moriah groaned.

All this arguing is giving me a headache!

"And I'm not your pal either, like you seem to think! I am your mother! Mothers aren't supposed to be best friends with their daughters! I know, I've done that all your life. I admit, I was wrong in that. I did it in the past, because you were too shy to mix with other kids. Being your chum is not normal, you know! I didn't have to do it! You wanted it, so I did it! I was all you had. But I'm not your sister! I'm your mother! I'm not doing it any more!"

Tears formed on the lashes of the teenager. "I thought you liked when we did things together?"

"I don't like shopping with you! Nothing is ever good enough! You get everything; I go without! I'm tired of pretending I like what you do. I hate the things you like! All your life I've bowed to your wishes. I don't even like to eat the way you do, but we always have to favour your tastes; I can never have what I like!"

How did the conversation take this turn? It's just that it's been building for so long, it had to come out, and now I can't stop.

Tears rushed to her own eyes.

"I want my own life for a change," she wailed. "I'm tired of picking up after you, of picking you up from school. I'm fed up with shopping for what you want only. When is it going to be my turn? I need someone to care about me, to take care of me. I can't do this anymore!"

Moriah sat up, cradling her back with her hands, hot tears falling.

"I'm constantly aching, and you couldn't care less. No sympathy at all, no offer to help! Momma, can I go out with my friends? If you want that, from now on you do something to earn it, do something around here! You wouldn't even have friends if I hadn't pushed you to interact!"

Iora finally found her voice, and she had inherited a sizable temper of her own. "I made my own friends! You weren't there. You weren't with me at school! I got invited to the party tonight...because they like me! I could have been at that party, if you hadn't insisted I stay and serve you, hand out these treats to the little squirts! You are not my keeper!"

"Oh, yeah, now that you have friends, you think you're better than me! If I didn't check out your friends' families first, so I knew they were safe for you to go to their sleepovers, you'd just be going off naively with any guy who wanted you!"

"I hate you, mom! I hate you! You've always been so dominating! Nobody else has to put up with this kind of possessiveness! I hate you! You're a bad mother!"

"I'm what?" shouted Moriah. "I'm what? Thanks a lot! That hurts, you know."

"Good! I meant it to hurt you!"

"You go to your room, you hear? And don't you come out until morning! And put out the porch light and lock the door, when you go by. And don't forget to set the alarm!"

Her daughter fled her presence like an angry stomping bear, her countenance like a thundercloud, grumbling in the background.

CHAPTER 17

Shiveron and Reon stood in the jut-in just behind the back door listening to every word, each with sympathy toward the female of their own age.

The older male had never realized a female might feel the burden of responsibility. It had never dawned on him one would even be left on her own. Females of their world were the heads of a family; served and treasured because they were in limited supply. Their word was law; obeyed without question. Females were guarded with great care and possessiveness. He couldn't fathom anyone abandoning one.

And this she did seem to be an alone female.

Who fathered her child, and why does he not take care of them? Has he simply taken her for his own satisfaction?

Such a one, on their world, would have been cornered and torn to pieces.

According to what he had heard, these two had been alone for a very long time.

Shiveron queried by mind projection.

Reon? Have you made a decision?

I will rescue the younger. Leave the mother.

Ah, no. Mother has good in her. Just hurt, angry. You know how females are when they are beside themselves.

Reon nodded.

Sorry, poppa. I was not kind. We take both.

Shiveron grinned.

They settled down to wait. When all was quiet inside, they would enter.

****

The back door of the residence was at the north side. At last, the inside of the building had gone dark, and from the outside appeared silent. Shiveron motioned his son to stay hidden, while he approached the door alone.

He touched the doorjamb cautiously, found the alarm system in the frame; he could feel in his fingers the pulsing energy that ran through the wiring. In his mind, he traced the lead wire back to its source in a room downstairs.

From a hidden pocket on his belt, Shiveron produced the damping device, attaching it over the area where the wire was situated in the middle of the frame. After a second, he heard the click that told him the alarm had been disengaged.

He turned the doorknob slowly; the device not only had disabled the warning, but had also unlocked the door. He removed his appliance from its position, and dropped it back into its hiding pouch.

It seemed safe now for them to enter. But he cautioned Reon to remain where he was, until he could determine if it was indeed hazardless for them inside.

Like a primitive, Shiveron slipped in, sliding, slinking, making himself diminutive, shape-shifting to a smaller version of the cat form he'd chosen as camouflage, laying close to the floor, then moving forward, slowly.

He was in an alcove; the wall high above on both sides of upward leading steps shielding him. Another set of stairs led down, as well.

These females aren't very well protected here; too easy to get in unseen. What if we were Roog? They prey upon

118

the vulnerable. These females would be easy meat to them, if they had discovered them first.

With their advanced technology, Roog and Feline were no match for the human world.

Shiveron made for the lower level first. As he moved down the stairs, his senses detected the position of the occupants: the older female lay dozing on a couch in the room above, the television softly speaking in a hushed tone though the room was darkened. The younger female was down here behind a closed door, working at a muted computer. She was in an Internet chat room site.

Shiveron almost chuckled.

She didn't go to bed; instead she chose to seek solace from another.

We'll have to move with care here.

He had thought both asleep, but even though they weren't, he was in now, and needed to proceed.

No male presence. I was right about that.

Shiveron decided to bring Reon in.

Returning to the side entrance, Shiveron eased open the outer door, beckoning to his young kit. Together they moved into position.

Shiveron moved up; Reon down. They would go to opposite corners of the apartment, the elder to the northeast upper; the junior to the southwest lower quadrant, thus ensuing coverage of all contained in the living space. Here each would set a locator.

The only material unable to be teleported to a transfer station in this manner was a living creature, thus they must manually remove these females before activating the jump sequence so their property would eventually arrive at home in med bay.

The locators placed, Shiveron moved back down. Reon chose to hide in an empty cupboard for the wait; Shiveron decided to step into the open closet of the empty larger bedroom, disappearing among the clothes.

In his mind, he watched the female above. He sent out an unspecified thought warning to awaken her.

She jerked awake, groaned at the sudden movement, and sat up with difficulty. The half-Noor male felt empathy; she seemed in such pain.

Rising from the couch, she moved slowly to the steps.

The female progressed as if injured, her back stiff, as though fearing a sudden jarring. One step at a time, favouring her right leg, setting it down gingerly, as if she were unable to feel it, she inched down the stairs to the basement rooms. She clung to the railing, not letting go between the steps, using it for support, sliding her hand along but not releasing until she reached bottom, and the solid floor of the hallway.

As she passed her daughter's room, she must have noted some evidence of activity within. "Iora! Shut off that computer, and go to bed! Do it now!"

Shiveron grinned in the dark recess of the closet, and he watched in mind vision, as the younger female obeyed. He knew Reon too was aware.

If this female can notice the misdemeanors of her offspring, we had better hope she does not sense us before we can move.

The older female went to relieve herself in the small compartment between the two rooms. The sound of rushing water came to his ears.

Then she moved into the room where he hid. He watched silently as she disrobed, still favouring her back and the one leg. She worked carefully, gingerly.

He cringed at the pain he felt emanating from her, and the lust that should have been aroused at watching her uncover herself was tempered by sympathy.

Stark naked, she turned toward the open closet.

He shivered.

She is beautiful!

Small bosom, body well formed, as good as any Feline, but somehow, in his eyes, she stood above the rest. He hadn't expected that.

Too bad I have to be rough with her.

Her sudden tension alerted him; she had sensed something amiss. He could wait no longer.

Shiveron lunged from the closet, growing in size as he came. He was so quick, her scream died in her throat, as his hand closed over her face. She had seen movement from the corner of her eye, and turned away, just as he jumped.

He didn't expect her to be able to fight, considering her condition, but she struggled, biting and scratching with short-nailed ineffective human hands. He was glad she wasn't Feline; she would have easily matched his aggression, giving him a fight for his life.

Shiveron almost enjoyed it, the challenge of conquest...until she went limp in his arms, slumping like a rag doll between his legs.

Then he felt remorse. He had hurt her. He had not meant to knock her out, not even to fight with her, but she had startled him; surprised him, that even hurting, she would and could fight back. And then his Feline side had burst to the surface with the pleasure of the conquest. Shiveron felt shame, for having overpowered this helpless female.

He eased her to the bed. He knew there was no time to savour victory or rehash past deeds; he couldn't afford further delay.

He searched the closet for something loose fitting to cover her, found what looked like pyjamas hanging on a metal hanger. He slipped them on quickly. Her body was ice cold.

How can I keep her warm? It'll be cold outside.

He took from his pouch the bindings and gag…and tied her hands securely in front, then taped over her lips.

Leaving her, he went to Reon.

****

Reon stepped from the storage compartment, as his father gave a silent order.

It's best to render the young one unconscious. Don't let her see you, or she'll panic. Be gentle, and quick.

Reon nodded.

With Shiveron standing behind watching from the shadows, Reon opened the door. The female he'd chosen lay with her back to the door. Her stunning beauty took his breath away, and for a second distracted him.

She had silken black tresses, long to her mid-back, curled in natural spirals that fell over shoulders and pillow. Her skin was smooth, a light caramel brown, and the side of her face, that he could see, revealed long sweeping lashes against the flawless cheek.

Reon was smitten.

His father hissed in his mind.

Move!

Reon struck quickly, like a viper; one press to the nerve at the side of her neck. With the opposite hand he caught her as she went limp and slid toward him.

Bind her; carry her over your shoulders. I'll get mine.

****

With both females slung over their backs, the bound hands under each male chin, Shiveron and Reon left the building. Standing just outside, Shiveron pressed the button on his belt to activate the teleport locators, and every piece of movable property vanished from inside. Then he left one last gift: turned the dial on a small incendiary device, and rolled it inside.

They were half a block away when the structure exploded, and by the time the emergency vehicles pulled up to the burning house, the four were already out of the city.

CHAPTER 18

When Moriah came to she was riding the back of a longhaired gigantic beast, the wind wild and bitter cold, blowing around her face and back. The rest of her body was suspended, bouncing and jarring as each long stride came down. She didn't stay conscious long.

The next time she awakened, she was stationary; her tormented body screaming its agony, as she lay bound on the dirt floor of an abandoned old shack. Now there were four huge beasts hissing and spitting in low tones to each other near the door-less entrance to the structure, and over in the corner, huddled together with Iora, were two other women bound as they were.

One of the grey cat-like creatures howled a warning; the larger cat-beast turned its head, then rose and came toward her.

Moriah cringed, expecting more ill treatment.

This is the one who attacked me!

He dropped to one knee, slipped an arm beneath her shoulders and gently shifted her to a seated position against the rough wall, so they were level eye to eye. As he withdrew his arm, he pushed her hair tenderly back from her face with a human-like hand. His eyes were blue, like those of a Siamese cat, and held apology mixed with sympathy.

"Are you cold?"

It shocked her to hear the words in her English tongue, and from what appeared to be a savage beast, no less. But her acidic anger arrived quickly.

She couldn't answer him aloud because of the tape across her mouth, but she wouldn't give him the benefit of a nod or shake of the head either, just out of principle.

Why would you care, anyway? You've already manhandled me enough to bruise every part of me.

He grinned, as if he'd heard the thought, but no doubt he merely saw the wrath in her eyes. Hissing something over his shoulder to the others, the big cats seemed to break out laughing.

Is their hissing and spitting a comprehensible language?

Turning back to her, he spoke again in her dialect. "I am sorry; I meant you no hurt. I felt this was the most logical way to get you to come with us."

Puzzled, she wondered what he wanted with her.

Before Moriah could think of a way to communicate, he turned quickly at a commotion in the doorway, as a fifth large cat carrying another woman burst through.

The enormous black beast took the woman from the other, ordering in English as he tossed her toward the corner: "Stay hidden if you value your lives!"

There was no time for further interaction; all hell broke loose out beyond the entrance.

✳✳✳✳

"Shiveron!" yelled the grey Feline, as he appeared in the doorway. "I'm sorry. I couldn't help it. I led them right to you. We didn't see the Roog until we came near the shack, and then it was too late. They've already got Anar and his she. Whatever happens to me, please save my female; give her to another, should I die."

Shiveron moved with speed and purpose, catching the human and tossing her back, yelling in the human tongue so the other females would understand. Then he escaped into the night, his three companions on his heels.

The Roog will not get our hard earned partners, not if I can help it!

But my son need not die in battle yet; he is far too young.

"Run, Reon! Get help! Hurry! We will distract them!"

The young male took off with unprecedented speed. Even with his unequalled youthful prowess, it would take at least twenty minutes to reach the ship.

Shiveron turned into the battle, his claws suddenly out, sharp and vicious. He had no time to count the number of their attackers, only knew the four Feline were out numbered. Suddenly, a sturdy dog bitch was upon him. Snarling, hissing, he met her head on, vengeance in his mood and manner.

At least this time I am allowed a chance to fight. Last time, when they took my mate, I never saw the power wand before it took me down.

****

The noises from outside terrified the five human women in the shack. The new one had fled to the corner out of sheer fright.

It sounded like a ferocious fight between a dog and a cat: snarling, hissing, barking and occasionally, the yelp of an injured victim; the tearing of flesh, and liquid splat of blood.

Moriah, nearer to the door, tried to crawl to her daughter and the others, but realized if she went by the gaping exit, she would be seen. It might bring whatever was out there inside. She couldn't risk that, so she stayed where she was.

Only the new woman might know what was happening, but the tape across their mouths successfully muffled them all. Each was bound hands in front, legs free. If they wanted to run, now would be the best time, yet Moriah knew, she would not get away like the others, she'd be too slow, injured as she was. And Iora, for all her animosity toward her at times, would not leave her mother behind.

First off, they needed to know what they faced. Moriah raised wrist-wrapped hands, and pulled at the tape over her lips. It stung, brought tears to her eyes, but it was easy to rip it away.

There was no point screaming; it might bring worse than the cat men.

"You! The one they brought in last," Moriah whispered. "I need you to take off your gag."

She was just a young girl not much older than Iora; all of them were in their upper teens or early twenties, except for Moriah. She had no time to ponder that. She had already assumed leadership; there was no point in backtracking now.

The young girl removed the tape.

"What happened to you outside?" Moriah asked.

The girl gave a visible shiver. "Great giant dogs! One grabbed the woman on the back of the other cat. When it pulled, it brought the cat thing over on its back. It just bit into its throat so fast, blood spurting everywhere. The girl on its back, I think was knocked out. Then the dog just started eating her."

This brought frightened muffled moans, and squeals of panic from the other girls. Moriah quickly hushed them. "Be quiet! You'll bring them in here."

It's not just Iora, but also the other girls now that are my responsibility. I have to think!

Which is worse, dog or cat? Both are monstrous, and obviously deadly, but at least the cat creatures seem a bit benevolent.

In Moriah's opinion, it was better to go with the feline, to hope they'd win out.

The sounds outside suddenly died. Now all you could hear was what appeared to be the feasting of a wild animal. Moriah shuddered, waited.

After a time, she grew brave. Trembling, she grabbed a nearby rotting three-foot two-by-four, and using it to push herself to a standing position, inched toward the dark opening in the aging structure to see what was going on out there. As she stood in the doorway, the stick now a weapon lifted above her shoulder, she took in the scene.

Bodies were everywhere. Three dogs remained, one eating at a cat creature, another feasting on the trunk of a human woman; the third approaching the still, face up, form of the battered larger black feline. He stirred, and Moriah realized he was still alive.

It went against everything in her, but Moriah knew when the dogs were finished out here, they'd come inside. Her best bet at protection was to help her kidnapper. The dogs had not noticed her, so moving silently, she rashly stepped into the open.

****

Shiveron opened his eyes to find his chosen female approaching him with a large club. He didn't notice the

Roog male just behind him, who was searching the bodies for any still living; all he thought was she meant to finish him off.

But he was still too groggy to move quickly.

The human swung down hard; Shiveron rolled to one side, heard the blow crack against the skull, and saw the Roog dog fall forward across his legs. Before he could free himself, he saw the other two beasts had noticed, and were coming at them from either side.

The female had lost balance with the force of the swing, stumbled against him and sat down jarringly at his side. He knew she wouldn't survive tussled up as she was.

****

The unyielding impact had knocked the wind from Moriah and deadened feeling. For a second she sat stupefied. Then looking at the cat, she saw claws ease out from human-like hands, and dread flooded up her chest.

But instead of the killer cut she expected, he slashed between her bound hands, freeing her.

"Fight little female, like you never have before!"

And then he was on his feet battling with a dog beast.

Forgetting her own pain, Moriah stayed at his back, her own to his, swinging at a second attacker as often as she could. The second blow shattered the beam in her hand, and she was left with only a foot of weapon.

And suddenly in the throws of battle, there were two more beside them. They were not foes, and Moriah gave way to them, sat down in among the bleeding corpses...until she heard the wailing of the smaller cat male.

She looked up, saw the large black feline go to the new arrival.

He must have spoke in her tongue so she would understand.

"Reon! Reon, son, be silent. You will bring more down upon us."

"What was it all for?" the younger admonished, answering in the same language. "All these died for me, and we have lost what we came for."

"None lost, Reon. They gave their lives valiantly; their hope even in death to give what they procured to another. And the females are safe…"

"Mine too?"

"Yes. But were it not for mother, the one you first meant to leave behind, I would not have lived. She is worth much more than her weight in treasure."

The smaller beast turned toward Moriah. "Her beauty is inner, hidden deep."

The elder male laughed, patted his back. "You are exhausted."

"And you are hurt, Poppa. I feel it."

"We must leave this place quickly. No time to waste. Are you able to run back? Did you stop for a break between?"

"Only as long as it took them to leave the ship and follow."

"Huh!" he grunted in disapproval.

****

Shiveron turned to the two new arrivals, as they joined them. "We have five females inside. You left Cam back at the ship?"

"Yes, sir. Figured it best in case we were victorious. He'll have the shuttle ready."

"Let's go then. I will carry two. Each of you pick your choice, she will be yours to keep. Reon will carry the one for Cam."

"Poppa, I carry my she."

"No. I cannot carry two heavy ones. Your she is light."

Reon sighed, surrendering.

****

Moriah followed them inside. The larger male turned to her, and again spoke in her tongue.

"I am Shiveron. My son is Reon. For your benefit, we will speak in your dialect, and translate if need be. We have taken you…to be mates for our males. If you do not accept this, you may go back to the city, but…many Roog are about, now. You will not make it back alive."

He turned to the other girls. "All are free to leave, should they choose…"

Shiveron left the choice hanging in the air. All had heard his words. None moved.

He turned to the other cat men, hissed instructions.

The women didn't flee when the large beasts came toward them. Each male chose a female, slinging it over its back, the bound wrists under their chins.

Shiveron turned to Iora. "Come little she; you will ride my back. I will carry your momma in front." When he had her shifted behind him, he scooped Moriah up into his large arms, and rose. "What is your young one called?"

"Iora."

"Iora, hold in with your knees against my sides, then you will not bounce with every step."

****

The rest of the journey was uneventful. Half way to their destination, Reon stopped, gasping with exhaustion, bending forward panting. They waited till he was able to go on, then continued at a more leisurely pace.

As they entered the inner parts of the spaceship, Shiveron folded to his knees, and fell on his left side. One of the greys was abruptly standing over them. He bent and pulled the girl from Shiveron's back. Moriah slipped from the downed male's limp arms, and stood up, fearful. Then, Reon still panting was beside them.

"Cam, take the ship home!" he ordered, as if he were now in charge. Moriah seemed to hear the words in her mind.

Reon bent to his father's side. "Poppa, can you hear me? You are safe. Go normal."

To Moriah's utter surprise both Reon and Shiveron metamorphed into a combination between a cat and a humanoid. But now Shiveron's body was covered in angry looking puncture holes, bite marks and deep ragged tears.

Moriah took to trembling, as she realized the agony he had endured to get them to safety. She would never again assume this male was what he appeared to be.

Reon examined his father's injures.

"Poppa, I will get water for you to heal."

"No. It can wait," Shiveron objected, without opening his eyes. His breathing was harsh and laboured. "I will heal back when I bath at home. Just…let me lay here a bit."

"Okay, Poppa." Reon stood, beckoned to Moriah and her daughter. "I will take the shes and put them where they are safe."

"No. Leave my she," Shiveron returned weakly.

When Reon had left with Iora, Moriah sat down beside the injured male. Shiveron reached out, took her hand, and pulled her to him. She lay down. He folded her gently against him, sighed, never once opening his eyes.

And that tender needy embrace erased all thoughts Moriah may have had of fleeing from him.

CHAPTER 19

It was raining. Without opening her eyes, Althea stuck out her tongue to catch the moisture, and realized the water was hot.

Her eyelids flashed open.

Where am I?

Warily, she looked about her. She was in an enormous shower stall, propped up, seated against the wet wall, opposite the flowing showerhead.

Then she saw him, and her brutal past experiences came thundering back.

He stood, his back to her, naked, if you could call that nude. His shoulders and back were covered in a short auburn fur, and he had a seven-foot, shorthaired tail, resting limp to the side. As she looked higher, she found a mop of copper curls, wet and pasted against his head, and tiny cat-like ears.

At first Althea thought this might be Bom, but of course, the body colouring didn't fit; also, this one had no dog in him.

How did I get in here? Don't cats hate water?

He seemed to be enjoying the cascade, his eyes closed in pure pleasure, and it appeared his intention, the escaping droplets were to cleanse her on the way down, as well, for he stood slightly to the side so the flow bounced from him to her.

Althea made an attempt to rise, but weakness prevented.

He turned swiftly, sensing her movement.

"Oh, no, little she," he quickly cautioned. "You are far too weak to stand yet. Stay put. Enjoy your wash. I will see to you when I'm done."

Who is this guy? He sure doesn't act like my other captors.

Too wobbly to even crawl away, she just sat watching him.

At last he turned off the water, squatted down to her level. Althea flinched, closed her eyes, and pulled back.

"Oh, little she. Don't be afraid of me. Loki means to help you." He reached out a human-like hand, took her chin in his palm. "Please look at me. Do you not remember Loki caring for you? I am physician; I would never do you harm."

Upon opening her eyes, his groin was directly across from her, and any reply fled from her mind. All Althea saw was the flap of skin where his man tool should have been.

Stunned, she realized he was some sort of cat, not the vicious dog creatures she was accustomed to.

Is it male or female?

Embarrassed, her gaze slid up to his waist, and she realized he was wearing a rusty looking wide spandex belt, with glowing lights along its horizontal length.

Why would anyone wear a belt in the shower?

Uncomfortable, no longer listening to his chatter, Althea licked her dry lips.

"Ah…little one," he said with sympathy. "You must be thirsty."

Suddenly he was gone. Althea relaxed for the moment. And then he was back with a huge cup of water, holding it to her lips.

"Drink it all…"

She didn't need to be told a second time. Althea caught the edge of the cup, sloshing it over her naked skin as she gulped it in.

It is cool. So good.

"Easy. Easy, you will choke, little female. Slowly."

But Althea was afraid he was just teasing, and would take it from her, before she had enough.

When the cup was empty, she sat back exhausted. As he disappeared again, Althea closed her eyes, and immediately fell asleep.

****

She opened her eyes, as Loki turned on the showerhead in his hand. She was covered in soapsuds. Too spent to assist or fight him, Althea let him do the work.

To his credit, he was both gentle and careful, turning her to the side to reach her back. It was then she realized she was in some sort of brace, fitted all along her spine.

And when he sprayed the back of her neck and head, she was aware she was shaved as bald as a baby bird.

He turned off the water, and as the cold hit her, she shivered. Suddenly, a pressure formed in her belly, and she steeled herself.

Need to go.

Althea began to squirm.

Shouldn't have drunk all that water.

He chuckled. "Just let it go, little she," he suggested. "Won't matter in here."

But she was stubborn, and held back.

"It isn't good for you to hold it," Loki warned. "Do I have to make you go?"

How would he do that?

But nature undid her; her legs became wet, and a warm red-brown fluid drizzled out and spread across the bottom of the stall to the centre drain.

"That's better. Don't ever hold it."

When he reached for the wand again, she found her voice.

"Where do I pee?" Althea croaked.

"For now till you're stronger right here in the stall. Or I will lift you to the stool. It's much too high for you to get up there."

Oh, wonderful! I am at his mercy for even basic natural functions.

Loki turned on the water, sprayed off her legs, rolled her, and washed bottom, as well. Althea was beginning to feel considerably mortified.

He patted her dry with a large towel, then cautiously lifted her, and carried her to a large mat in the corner. They appeared to be in a kind of combination bedroom and kitchenette. Rolling her to her stomach, her head away from him, he began fiddling with the back brace.

"I think you are healed enough, we can dispense with this."

A sudden snap-release and Althea was free.

"You can try to move, but do so carefully. Let me know if it hurts."

The first thing Althea did was roll over, and pull the sheet up over her nakedness.

"Ah," he said. "I should find something for you to wear. Don't try to leave the room. You will not be safe outside."

When he left the compartment, Althea dropped into a doze again.

****

It must have been hours later; Loki came with a bowl of broth. He sat behind her for support, and spoon-fed her. At first she made a face, turning away.

Althea remembered what their stew was made from, and she would have none of it.

"It's only fish broth," Loki explained. "I know; I don't much like it either, but it's all that's safe to eat. I promise, if I ever get out of here, I'll never eat fish again."

That made Althea chuckle.

He is a cat; he should like fish. But then he likes water and takes a bath. Is it so unlikely, he'd dislike fish?

As her tongue found the chunks of shredded fish, and she tried to chew, Althea realized she had teeth.

"How'd I get new teeth?" she asked in surprise.

Loki laughed. "I transfused you. My blood has healing properties. You will easily mend yourself now."

Althea looked down at her emaciated arm atop the sheet. "Well, can't be soon enough. I look like a scarecrow."

"Better to look like that, than to have Bom recognize you."

"What did you do, steal me from him?"

"Not quite. He told me to dispose of your body. I hid you in my room instead."

"Won't he kill you for that?"

"He doesn't know, and he needs me. He doesn't dare kill me. The Feline hierarchy would rebel at such an action."

"Why do you stay here then?"

"Unfortunately, I can no more leave than you can."

"Are you a prisoner, too?"

"Indeed." He sighed. "And at the whim and will of the mighty Bom," Loki declared sarcastically. "He said six months, but that remains to be seen."

Althea looked above and behind her head trying to look up at him. Her sight was much improved, as well.

"Why? What did you do?"

He gently pushed her head down with his free hand. "Be careful how you move. I don't want to put you back in the brace."

As Althea relaxed again, and he brought another spoonful of his soup to her lips, he answered her question.

"I defended my sister's honour. Bom meant to defile her."

"But isn't he a dog?"

"Part Feline, part Roog. Two species with great animosity toward each other."

And suddenly, Loki no longer seemed like her adversary. He had become a friend.

CHAPTER 20

"Hey, human, Nyle!"

A scrappy three-foot high weasel-like creature stood a few feet from where Nyle was mopping the hall floor. He quickly checked where Kaudy was; she was polishing brass doorknobs a few feet behind him.

"Human! You hear me?" their visitor squealed impatiently. "You deaf?"

The non-human population had a habit of complaining about his work, so Nyle wasn't too enthused at being approached.

"What you want?" Nyle grumbled, continuing to squeeze out the mop in his pail. "I'm finished here. Not doing it again!"

The small being grunted. "Not about work."

"What then?"

"Sent to call you. Report to claim desk."

"What did I do now?"

It just grunted again, and turned and fled.

I'm sure sick of being on this station. I'd do just about anything to get to another planet, but there has been no word that a compatible female wants me. It's probably because I have a young daughter.

****

Nyle stepped into the complaint office, Kaudy right behind him. He left her seated in the corner, and parked himself down before the interview clerk.

"I was told to report…"

This time the being behind the desk was a large cat creature. It spit in annoyance at him, produced a miniature Plexiglas square and plugged it into the slot on the console. He pondered the screen for a moment, then finally gave Nyle his attention.

"One of our females has accepted to sponsor you."

Nyle pulled in his breath.

Finally! I am so ready to be gone from here!

"So what happens now?"

The Feline looked down at him, hissed again in aggravation. "If you want to stay alive in our culture, you'd best be more submissive. Obedience to your female is imperative! For that matter, males must obey any female. Is that understood?" He narrowed his eyes in warning. "In my world, if you fail to do so, the male relatives have the right to kill you; they will kill you! I could kill you, if I choose! Simply because I do not like you."

What is the matter with this guy? Is he envious because this woman has chosen an outsider, or did he just have it in for humans?

"You are fortunate to be chosen at all," the Feline went on. "We have twelve planets with fifty trillion inhabitants on each, three quarters of which are male. She could have chosen anyone of us, but no, she accepts this petty excuse for a human. But then, why would we even want her?"

He seemed to rumble in that way a Feline approached humour, a deep in the chest guttural sound ending on a hiss.

Is he laughing at me? What's the big joke?

"You have the misfortune of being chosen by the only female Noor-half in existence. Her Noor side makes her deadly to any mate; they say she could fry your brains, should you displease her. And we mate for life, human! Understand?"

Oh, wonderful! How is this any better than staying here, a work slave mopping floors?

But he had Kaudy to think about. He'd gotten her into this, and she had long ago realized she wasn't going back home. Nyle had had trouble placating her with promises of a better life, should they ever get a sponsor.

The young girl now treated, what she thought were his imaginings, with apathy, viewing the prospects as only imaginary. She had resigned herself to the condition they were in, as if the state was permanent.

The Feline broke into his reverie. "You have one hour to pack up your belongings, and report to ship dock five. You must go by shuttle rather than through jump station. Be gone from my sight, human. And take your young she with you, before I decide to take her from you."

****

As they approached their destination, a colossal space station as big as the entire province where he'd been born, Nyle peered though the window of the craft. A gaping hole opened in the side of the larger vessel, and appeared to swallow the small shuttlecraft whole. The miniature transport eased inside, coming to a stop within an enormous steel, bare-joisted cavern.

The outer doors descended; darkness enveloped, and Nyle and Kaudy waited for the next action. The small craft they were in had been automated; no one was there to give them instructions.

The outer room brightened; the side door of their prison slid up. Nyle rose, took Kaudy's hand, and stepped outside.

Waiting just ten feet away was a seven-foot tall brown bear, with human-like face and hands. It stepped forward to greet them.

"I am Wadi, guardian to the Dia nest. I am to escort you to Twila who has chosen you. Come please. Your property will be transported by mechanical."

He led them to a small platform suspended six inches off the metal floor. Standing on this was a second bear-like humanoid with fur colouring of a dark shade of black. This one was about six foot five, an inch or two taller than Nyle.

As they stepped up, Wadi introduced his companion. "This is my she, Rimu. We are mated, but she also stands guardian with me. Sit you down. As you are unfamiliar with travel by platform, you may be unstable; we wish no harm to come to you."

There were no seats, so Nyle eased to the floor of the hover-sheet pulling Kaudy to his lap. Almost immediately, the twelve by ten foot metal floor rose up to about six feet in the air. It began moving slowly off over a lip into a chasm with a sheer drop below of thousands of feet. As they moved along, Nyle could see other platforms carrying freight or passengers in opposite directions. Far below, the busyness of workers intent on their labours was evident: small shuttlecrafts on the bottom being serviced, others disgorging their contents, still others leaving through open portals like the one they'd arrived through.

"Daddy, we could fall," Kaudy whispered fearfully.

Wadi answered her. "There is a gravity field about us to protect."

After about ten minutes, a small door on their right slid up, and the platform docked, attaching like a ramp to the floor of the tunnel beyond.

Wadi stepped out. Nyle and Kaudy followed, while Rimu took up the rear guard. The outer entrance slid back down.

"Follow please," Wadi ordered.

A short walk of about twenty feet brought them to a second door. Here they were challenged.

The snake-like creature with a human face appeared out of nowhere; hissed a warning that made Kaudy scamper behind her father.

"We bring to Twila," Wadi explained. "They are safe, Sith."

"I am not Sith. I am Serene, and I'll decide if they are safe."

A red forked tongue shot from her mouth, tasting the air. She moved around Nyle, following Kaudy, as she rounded her father to get away from the frightening creature.

"Okay. Safe!" Then the being simply vanished.

CHAPTER 21

The woman turned toward the four, as they entered the receiving office. Her eyes found them: a bright turquoise blue with the black vertical slit of a cat's eye. Her colouring was the tan-flesh tint of a Caucasian human, and her hair was short, white-blond and curly, parting only slightly for the tiny cat ears. She stood approximately five foot seven, and if he were to guess her age, it would be around thirty.

"I will take them from here, Wadi," she said, and Nyle understood her, even though she wore no translator.

"Yes, mistress. Should we remain on guard outside?"

"Unnecessary. I can defend myself."

Nyle cringed, remembering what he'd been told about this female.

Wadi and Rimu left the room, leaving Nyle and his daughter alone with the supposed formidable half-Noor.

"I am Twila, your sponsor. One moment while I attend to a matter. Please take seats."

When she turned away, as it swept the floor behind, Nyle saw the swish of a near invisible white bushy tail. Except for short white-blond fur, peeking out at the top of her collarless, long-sleeved top, and travelling up her neck, one would never guess she was a Feline. Should she hide her ears with her hair, except for the eyes, you would think her a humanoid...until of course, you saw that tail.

She wore a loose fitting tunic, which had a short, pleated skirt that came just below the knees. Her legs and feet were not like those of a Feline, but more that of a human. The delicate feet were unshod.

She walked with a grace not unlike some human women he knew; a seductive movement that caught the male eye. He could not but appreciate her form, for it too was quite curvaceous.

Twila went to a wall unit much like that of an intercom on Earth, pressed a button, and in a tone of scolding, demanded: "Jabek, where are you? You will attend me! Now!"

A sixteen-year-old male suddenly materialized beside the two humans, giving them a start, so they stepped back in shock. The adolescent was the spitting image of his mother, but taller by at least four inches.

"You cannot use the door?" scolded Twila. "So you do not scare the bejebbies out of our guests."

Nyle hid his smile.

So, did he use a transporter, or can he teleport manually by mental energy?

"Sorry, I'm late, momma. Poppa Kimon had me busy."

She hissed in frustration. "Whom are you to obey first and foremost?"

The male seemed at a loss as how to answer. "Momma Dia, then you...and Poppa Kim last?"

"Remember that next time. I know that puts you in a bad place between us, but refer him to me next time, and I will placate him. Now, to the matter at hand. Turn, you may look at the female."

As the boy obeyed, his image began to fade.

"Jabek!" Twila reprimanded softly. "How will she know you, if you go invisible every time you are with her?"

"Sorry, momma. Only females I know are you and momma Dia. I am..." He faded once again.

"Ah, Jabek," she said quietly with sympathy. "You are handsome male. No need to be embarrassed."

Jabek came fully visible, as his mother continued. "I have chosen this she for you, but you must gain her trust and love. As with us, she must choose you. Do you understand? You will be her guardian, until she accepts promise, and mate only when you are ready…"

Until that moment, Nyle had let Twila have her say, but the last words brought apprehension for his daughter, and a protective anger that focused quickly on the adult female.

"Oh, wait just a minute here! My daughter's not some bawd for sale…"

Twila spun on him, livid anger evident on her features. The action had Nyle stepping back cringing.

"What was that male?" Her voice dripped venom. "What world are you on at this moment?"

"She's my daughter!" Nyle answered bravely, though he quaked in his shoes. "She's my responsibility…"

"Correction! You are my sponsored male; therefore she becomes my responsibility!" Twila let the silence continue for several beats, as her temper visibly cooled. "I realize you are unfamiliar with our customs, and I will take that into account. We will speak later."

As the female turned back to the young ones, Nyle tried a second time, not caring that he was risking his own life. He was not prepared to let things go just yet. "She's too young! And on my world, she gets a choice in the matter."

"As does she on this world. And we mate for life, at age fourteen. Now! Male! Be silent! Or you will not be around to see their children."

Nyle almost tried again, but the warning look in her eye, and the memory of the statement 'they say, she could fry your brain, should you displease her', had him wisely backing down.

"Now then," Twila continued. "Jabek, from now on you are this female's caregiver, defender, and teacher. She will accompany you in your duties, and do her share along side you, until we know her capabilities. For now, take her home. You may show her the sights along the way."

"I know not her name?" the young male requested.

"She is Kaudy. And she is greatly fearful. Soothe her trepidation."

"Daa…ddy?"

"Go with him, munchkins. It'll be okay."

As the two turned to go, Twila added one more instruction. "And Jabek, see that you always give the proper respect to her poppa."

The boy bowed from the waist, then caught Kaudy's hand, and scampered from the room with her.

****

Nyle fully expected to be punished. The words he heard were totally unexpected.

"I am pleased with you human. But…though I will need you to keep me from dominating you, and will sometimes need your adjustment, you are to do it gently, and never in front of the children, or in public. The Feline law requires I kill you if you do."

Nyle's jaw dropped, and Twila smiled for the first time.

"I live in a world that I may not always agree with, where I too must obey rules. I am not fully Feline…and in

Dia's nest we have been given the freedom to be different, but out in public, we must keep up appearances."

He was speechless. Nyle had not expected to be taken into her confidence.

She sighed. "Now, where do I begin? As your sponsor, do you realize it is considered, that I am taking you for mate?"

Nyle nodded. "That has been explained."

"Okay. There is a process. As the female, I must accept you. It is not as on your world. Here the male asks if the female will have him. If she accepts, they are then considered promised, until such time, as she feels comfortable for him to fill her needs…"

Nyle had no difficulty following her implication, and it had him feeling a sudden embarrassed warmth.

"There is no marriage ceremony performed in Feline culture; male and female simply go away and consummate. After that first time, they are then considered mated for life. As any male can then be challenged; he may be attacked…even before the mating. The female may defend him, should she not wish the attention of the second male, but mostly, it is the responsibility of the male to protect her from such attentions."

Twila took a breath. "We will skip courtship, unless you decide at a later date, you wish it. By law, we will now be promised, and proceed from there."

Twila stood up. "We will go to our quarters, as I'm sure you must be weary. The custom is for the male to become part of the female's nest. Felines live in family groups with the oldest female as the ultimate authority. Dia, a pure Feline, fosters my brothers and I. Head physician Kimon is her mate. On the way, I will explain more."

****

So, I guess I'm more or less attached to this woman, and there's no getting out of it.

Nyle had to admit, he wouldn't find it difficult to make love with her, but it was hard to come to grips with the cat part.

Will she be feral or gentle in her demands?

Nyle couldn't help seeing her in the guise of a domesticated cat.

He'd once had a pet kitten he'd treasured tremendously. It had appeared as if Shifera were talking to him, scolding when he stayed away too long; her meows had seemed to make sense.

Nyle had gotten the kitten from a household, where she had been abominably misused and neglected. The former owner had five dogs and three other cats, and the poor creature had needed to fight just to get food. At first she spit and clawed him, not liking his attention, especially when he'd had to treat her infections and injuries. When he first brought her home, she was infested with worms and fleas, but Nyle had treated her with the medicated powder, forced medicine down her throat, waited out the day until she was healthy, and coddled her thereafter, cuddling her each night until she'd had enough of him, and wanted down.

Her favourite spot to curl up had been beneath him in the mechanism of his recliner chair, and no matter how often he scolded, she would still slip in unbeknownst by him.

One night he had fallen asleep in his chair, and when he woke in the wee hours of the next morning, without thinking, he'd moved the chair to the sit position.

In memory, Nyle could still hear the agonizing howls, as Shifera died, caught in the mechanized works. Though he'd made a valiant effort, he could not free her.

He'd bawled like a broken child, as he placed her mangled body in the freezer to preserve her, then scrubbed and disinfected where the mess inevitably had spread. To this day he would never again use a recliner.

When he lost that cherished companion, his grief had been unrelenting, his loss profound, as he blamed himself for the sin of carelessness. For days he had been inconsolable.

At last, after a week of mourning, he had wrapped Shifera in a blanket, taken her toys, and ridden on his bike to the top of a hill on nearby crown land, dug a deep, deep hole, and buried her there at the top of the hill. Placing a large flat stone above her to mark the grave, Nyle had said his goodbye.

It was disconcerting that Twila's markings reminded Nyle of his lost kitten. He hoped if he became fond of Twila at some point, he would never have to part with her in parallel circumstance.

He'd been deep in thought for so long, Nyle hadn't realized Twila was silent until she broke into his reverie, making him start.

"I must warn you, human," she cautioned softly. "I can read your every thought."

CHAPTER 22

He looked so enduring, his pupils going large with shock, as he turned to look at her. "How can I…"

"Ward against it?" Twila finished for him. "Right now you cannot." She took his hand, and led him into the bed-nest rooms. "Liam will be back tomorrow. I'll have him teach you to block, and to send your thoughts out to me, so we can communicate silently without others being aware."

Nyle stood there, where she left him, pondering what he'd just learned. Twila went to the closet for her nightwear.

He'll need night garments also. Humans get cold in the night.

Twila went to the replicator. "Let me see? I'd say you are a large size in male human?"

"Medium. Why?"

"You will need what you call pyjamas."

"I have clothes I brought along…"

"I doubt they will be warm enough. We sleep without coverings, and Dia likes the heat turned down during sleep cycle." Twila motioned toward the enormous padded sleep mat that covered near half the room. "We also sleep cuddled all together. It is a Feline practice Dia has indulged in since we first came to her."

"You sleep on that?" Nyle inquired. "All together."

"Yes."

"Every night? Together?"

Twila nodded.

"But…what about when…ah, you go…intimate?"

Twila laughed. "Oh, human. Nyle. You will need to become less inhibited. You are as bad a Jabek."

His mind had gone to the very act.

"Bu…but," stuttered Nyle. "In front of the kids?"

"No, of course not. Momma Dia and Kimon have a sound proof ante, a room into which they go when they need to be apart, but…sometimes when a female goes into heat unexpectedly, things can happen…elsewhere."

Nyle turned a beet red. "Ah…ah, can't we sleep in the ante?"

"What for? No, Dia would not permit that. When there are multiple mated couples in a nest, only then do they take turns."

Nyle was saved further embarrassing discussion, when Jabek and Kaudy scampered excitedly into the room.

"Daddy!" exclaimed Kaudy exuberantly. "They have gardens! Right here on the ship! And a park…and a running track…and hydroponics' sheds…flowers, and large fruit trees from the Noor planet, and…"

"Okay, munchkins. Calm down," Nyle laughed. "So you like it here?'

"Oh, yes, daddy! I never want to go back."

"Not even to…"

"No way! Momma's a cruel devil compared to Jabek's mom."

Twila suddenly came alert.

What is this?

"Her mother lives?"

"We've been divorced for years. She kicked me out before Kaudy was born."

"And usually my mom won't even let us see each other," Kaudy broke in.

"Then how did you come to be with your father?"

"Daddy stole me away from her," Kaudy said proudly. "We escaped!"

When Twila turned on him, Nyle was looking decidedly uncomfortable.

"You stole her from her mother!"

"You don't understand. She's kept her isolated; punishes her for things she does when with me. If we have fun together, Seline keeps her in her room for weeks after."

Twila frowned. "She is bad momma?" she questioned, shocked beyond measure. Never in her wildest dreams would a Feline abuse a female, let alone a young one.

She watched as memories of past goings on sped rapidly through Nyle's mind. It had her turning, and probing the thoughts of the young girl to verify.

"Beast of a female!" Twila spat harshly, after reading the girls unpleasant experiences. "She shall never again see you! This I promise!"

At her outburst, she felt Nyle relax. And Twila quickly changed the subject to prevent further tension. She had quickly realized Kaudy wasn't the only one who had been battered.

I will need to tread lightly with this one. He will expect ill treatment from me.

****

"Jabek, time to bathe," his mother ordered. "Take Nyle with you into the male pool. I will care for Kaudy."

"Don't you want to bath together?"

"Jabek, you know the rules. We have not yet mated, so we cannot bathe together. And you are only guardian to your female. Now go."

Twila pushed the garments she'd gotten from the replicator into his hands. "These are for the human. Go."

"Yes, momma."

Jabek reached out and took the human by the hand, led Nyle toward the far wall where the door slid open to admit them to his side of the baths.

This male was only slightly taller than he was. To Jabek, Nyle seemed more like a teen companion than an adult. He had seldom had another, other than his mother's brothers, to bathe with, and this was an experience he was looking forward to.

He was also excited at being the teacher here.

When the panel slid shut, Nyle stood where he'd left him. The man was gazing about in obvious surprise at his surroundings.

"I thought cats don't like water?"

Jabek growled deep in his throat. "Never call us cats, human. Cats are primitives! We the Feline are the civilized species."

"Oh...kay. What do I call you then? Noor?"

"Noor is a derogatory term."

Nyle huffed. "Just what am I to call your mother, then?"

"Momma, is to be called 'Mistress' by you. And any male is 'sir'."

"Even you?"

"You may call me by my name. Jabek."

"Okay. And how does this work in here? I don't see any showers."

We don't need showers!

The huge, treated, recycling, water-filled, rectangular basin was twenty feet across, forty feet wide, and ten feet deep. The side platforms were tiled and circled the enclosure, except for at the far end where a five-foot waterfall poured from the back wall.

Jabek shrugged.

Why would you need showers? I suppose that's a human thing.

"First, we disrobe," he explained, as if the man were simple. "We soap up, then enter the pool, make our way to the waterfall, and rinse off. Some prefer to swim over…"

"Felines swim?"

Jabek shook his head. "Most Felines hate water. Momma Dia had this made just for us. She and poppa Kim won't touch the pools. Her fosters are mixed Noor; we love the water. We heal with it. Our injuries quickly close when washed with water. When Dia realized this, she immediately did research into the nature of Noors; then had the pools made, but always from the first, she does not like to take part in our cleansing ritual."

"So…you have the capacity to instantly heal yourself?" clarified Nyle. "Wish I could do that. Okay. So, I strip first. And I take it, none of you are the least bit self-conscious?"

That made Jabek laugh. He'd been bathing with his uncles since he was born.

Saying nothing, he slowly began removing his leggings, all the while watching the human take off one piece of clothing at a time.

Gosh, but they wear a lot of unnecessary garments. All Feline males need are leggings.

"You are different," Jabek noted. "Your manhood is on the outside."

Nyle's features turned a darker hue. "I guess. So, where are yours?"

"Inside; seed sacks to each side; tool under the flap of skin. See."

Jabek unabashedly pressed with both hands on either side of the slight lump on his abdomen, causing his instrument to peek out. "And when we satisfy the female, being a shape-shifter Noor, I will be able to lengthen or shorten as the she needs. I'm told, humans are inadequate in this respect."

This time Nyle went completely red in the face, but it didn't stop his next question.

"I know you're just a kid and all, but would you know…are the females different than a human woman?"

Jabek took offence at the first part of the enquiry. "As soon as we reach fifteen, we are all fully educated on pleasure techniques, and the anatomy of the female. And yes, both females that are pure Feline, and those of Noor-half, resemble a human female."

"But do they have…multiple nipples?"

Jabek grinned. He was watching the man's mind. "Feline or Noor-half have only two. They are small chested, and most Feline males are not attracted to the size; only when she goes into heat does his imagination seek to picture her. The Feline females will often bear twins. My twin was miscarried, before we were born. It was a female. The Roog had momma and poppa captive…"

"Ja…bek! That will be enough!" came Twila's voice from the air about them. "When Nyle is educated tomorrow, his knowledge will surpass yours, so you have no need to elaborate. And…when we are mated, he will become your new poppa. He will then be the teacher, not the other way around. Show respect, male! Or I will be forced to punish."

Nyle grinned. Jabek faded for a second, but his indignation brought him back swiftly.

"Momma!" he scolded. "Stop watching! I'm an adult male!"

"Then act like it. Adults do not manipulate themselves, nor do they discuss the using of a female."

Nyle's grin widened. "Pretty hard to hide, when she can keep track of you so well," he observed, tongue in cheek.

Jabek hissed. "Momma, stay out of my mind!"

"And you stay out of the human's. Give him privacy!"

****

When they left the bath, Twila had a light lunch of sandwiches already prepared for them. She and Kaudy were now in pyjamas: leggings with a loose fitting top.

They ate sitting cross-legged on the floor.

"My brothers are all away at the moment," Twila excused. "And momma Dia and poppa Kim have decided to eat elsewhere to give us time to get acquainted somewhat before they introduce themselves. They will join us during rest period."

"Dia is the head of your nest? I understand Feline are matriarchal, are the Noor as well?"

"They were, but as there are so few of us, and no pure Noor among us, or even in existence, we remain under Feline headship. By universal law, a species is not permitted a distinction unless there are at least ten individuals, and even then, depending upon their ability and age, they do not pick a ruler."

"So, how does the Feline system work?"

"Tomorrow my elder foster will teach you, but...I suppose I can give you a quick overview. Our queen matriarch, Kei, rules all twelve planets with some fifty trillion subjects on each. She has underling males, who carry out and enforce the rules, laws, and see to the functions of society; also close associate males who mete out discipline and protect her. She has a mate, and he may disagree with her, give her suggestions, or correct her, but of course, again, that would be done in private."

"How can she possibly oversee and police so many, and be certain total justice is received by all?"

Twila chuckled. "You think of us according to your human societal experience, but the planet you come from is one of the most undisciplined in the universe. In our world we have integrity and accountability, no crime is tolerated, none exists. All are honest...well most are. Bom is our one exception, as he refuses to be a part of either Feline or Roog worlds, of which, he is of both...I fear I've gone off track. It would be best if Liam were to give you this summary."

"How does your immediate family discipline work? Who's responsible for that?"

"Dia, mostly, but Kimon, or eldest male present, will discipline the males…"

"So, right now, is that me? Or Jabek?"

"Jabek is youngest male in the nest. He may never correct…unless he were to have a family of his own. Liam will teach you this. Allow the females to discipline if it should be necessary. That is the safest."

"But…what if there is abuse within the family?"

"One hiss from Dia and no one crosses her. But you speak of physical and sexual." Twila shook her head. "Such things are none existent in our society. These crimes are instantly punished by death, meted out by the adult males of the nest. That is why it is essential all males be trained in diplomacy, the laws, and defence protection procedure."

"Sounds very harsh to me."

"You have grown up in a very violent society. To balance our strict rules, Felines are very affectionate creatures. We cuddle a lot, interact and do things together. We use touch for comfort, and as a Noor-half this is crucial to me. Noor means light, the good side of creation, and they were well named. As for the act of procreation, it is permitted only to those who are mated."

"So what are you saying; there is no hitting, fighting, child abuse or say, incest?"

Twila visibly shivered. "Not in a Feline family. Sometimes rape from outside the nest, but the males of the family punish that with instant death…unless the female intercedes and will have him. Our efforts go to keeping each other protected, and happy with an agape type love."

"So you have no criminals?"

Twila sighed. "Nyle, you are most hard to appease. I grow tired of your constant questions. In any society there are those who break the rules in a minor way…Now, I would very much like to retire, for I am very weary. I've worked a full shift. Tomorrow Liam will educate you, and there will be no further need for questions."

Twila rose, and stowed away their dishware. Jabek and Kaudy lay down on the bed mat. Enfolding her with his arms and legs about her, the boy slipped behind her. Kaudy fit perfectly, they were like two spoons in a drawer, but the action made Nyle extremely nervous.

"Do not fret so, Nyle," Twila admonished. "He is well behaved. In spite of his actions in the bath, he has been trained in self-control, and he will have me to deal with should he do wrong."

Nyle sighed.

Will I ever get used to their way of doing things?

"I suppose you expect the same from me? I mean, the self-control bit…"

"Yes. Until heat takes me, or I willingly give myself to you. And advances will be futile, so do not attempt them."

Oh, boy. How am I ever going to do that?

"Remember, rape is punishable by death," Twila added, as an additional incentive.

She lay down upon the mat. "I know you are human and your body temperature is less than mine, so I will extend my Noor aura of warmth to include you. Usually, the male keeps the female warm, but I will be the one tonight to see we remain comfortable. Any other time, the heat of the others will do it for you."

"You still want me behind you, like Jabek?"

"Yes, please. It is a comfort thing."

For Nyle, the night was a long one, and he was surprised he slept at all, but he must have dozed off eventually, as he started awake, when the two pure Felines joined them. By then, he was sleepy enough, that he drifted quickly out again.

CHAPTER 23

After many days of dozing and being pampered by Loki, Althea became strong enough to wander about the room and explore while he was away. Usually, she wrapped the sheet about her, but one day when he returned, Loki brought a small shift with him.

He lifted her up on the counter by the sink, and proceeded to draw it over her head. When she had slipped her arms in the tattered sleeves, he set her on the floor, and stepped back to examine her.

Disappointment mirrored on his face.

Althea knew she was skinny, still just skin and bones. Self-consciously, she pulled at the shirttail; it barely covered her bottom.

"Too small," observed Loki.

****

It is more than too small. It's also too tight, showing every curve. And those naked pale legs will easily attract the males in the medical wards. I don't need to be fending them off.

This just won't do. She needs leggings.

He was a poor judge of size, having had only experience with Twila when she was small.

More said, 'bring your pet to me,' and he'll give me anything I want.

More was partial toward Loki, but still he was only a Root, and could not be trusted.

However, Loki decided to take the chance.

"Come with me," he ordered. "They will consider you my pet, so walk behind me. They'd wonder if I were to carry you. Stay real close on my heels. Where we are going isn't safe."

I'd better not take her through the female breeding stalls; a human might recognize her. The shorter route through the stud cells is quicker, though it is no safer. But, surely the male humans have had no experience with her. They won't be likely to recognize.

****

Althea could feel their eyes following her. The men in the cages were muscular and well fed, but their thoughts and motions were lascivious: one at the fringes of her sight was doing something unmentionable through the bars; and two others were like engaged, one positioned behind the other. All the men were naked.

She did her best not to look at them.

"Hey, Healer. You got a pet now? Give her to me. I know what to do with her. Don't you want little ones?"

A second objected. "She's too skinny. No tits to her."

"Better if the top is flat; more fire underneath," laughed another.

Althea could feel their lust, their arousal. She shivered, tried to fight the tears, but they betray her, falling hot and fast, until she was sobbing brokenly. Against all her efforts, her body began to shake uncontrollably. And Loki was getting farther and farther away, as he sped up to get passed the area more quickly.

There's no way I can keep up!

So, she grabbed at the tip of his long sweeping tail, as it swung back and forth. For a second Althea thought she had stopped him, for Loki halted abruptly. Suddenly, like a rope, his powerful tail circled her waist; a second later she was rising through the air, and next, was in his arms.

In her ear, Loki hissed. "Sometimes, I am glad I am in this belt. It dulls my abilities, so I feel less of their hunger, but oh, oh, I forgot, your senses are enhanced. I am so sorry, little she. We will never come this way again."

Althea clung to him, sobbing into his shoulder. Her trembling hadn't quite stopped, as they entered the storerooms.

****

"Huh!" thundered the Root. "So this little mite is your new pet. The garment did not fit?"

"Little tight; little small," Loki rumbled. As her face was buried against him, it sounded much more formidable, almost angry.

"Set it down; let it choose. I give it whatever it want."

She clung to him, not wanting to be set free, but Loki insisted on putting her down. After being placed on the dirt floor, Althea gazed about at the counters of produce.

"Bring her in here," the Root ordered, and headed off in another direction. Althea made certain she followed close on Loki's heels. "Just got new shipment of property," the large tree creature revealed. "The human can have anything it want."

"More...will that be docked from my food ration?"

"Nah, nah, More's in a good mood. Store closed; it sleep break now; dogs go away. Ha! In good mood. Yes! Healer can have anything; my treat."

"Go for it, little she," Loki encouraged with a gesture. "I'll look too, seeing More is being generous."

Althea circled the tables, until suddenly something caught her eye.

From a distance away, Loki suggested: "Look for leggings, little she. You need leggings. And something more loose for top."

But Althea was more interested in what she saw on a table by the wall, and she kept it in sight, as she searched the garments at her disposal, looking for what Loki wanted.

It took mere minutes for her to find jeans that fit her, and a top much looser than the one she wore. After all, these were her things. Everything was here: clothing and bedding, furniture; ornaments and pictures, kitchen pots, spices, and dishes, all her property. How they had come by it, Althea didn't know.

As far as I'm concerned, they can have it all, but I will not leave behind the family picture in the corner.

When she had donned the clothing, she made a bee line for the snapshot, slipped it from the frame, folded it, and hid it in the pocket of her slacks. Then she joined Loki, and stayed at his side, until he was ready to go.

He carried her back through the darkened hallway. The stalls brought back memories of Lana and Beth.

Where are they now? Are they dead?

That night as Loki lay sleeping, she slipped from the sleep mat, got the photograph from her jeans, and sat gazing longingly at the picture.

I will never again see my daughter and son, my granddaughters; they are lost to me forever.

And Althea cried, silently and bitterly, letting go of that chapter of her life regretfully.

CHAPTER 24

"Shiveron! Attend me!" the irate voice of Dia came from the intercom. "In my office!"

Barely healed, he hadn't even been back to the home nest. When he'd entered the hospital central ward, Shiveron had sent Reon on ahead to present Moriah and Iora to Dia. He'd expected the matriarch to train the females, and heal his new she, but though Shiveron and his son had remained in the medical wing awaiting word, until now he had heard nothing.

And it did not bode well that his foster mother was angry.

Where is Reon?

"Coming, momma Dia."

When Shiveron arrived, he knew why he hadn't been able to find Reon. He was met by him at the office door. The boy slunk away, as if he'd betrayed his father, or had been roundly reprimanded...or both.

Dia got to him first.

Shiveron hated when she went around him to get the facts. It always meant he had no time to prepare her, and she took the tainted view as gospel.

Steeling himself, Shiveron went inside.

Indeed, momma was in a scolding mood, livid as a cat on a hot tin roof. Though all her foster children now stood much taller than the five foot Feline, when she was enraged, they cowed. In spite of being ninety, Dia was powerful and vicious when it was needed. But Shiveron knew her as both harsh, and gentle. From past experience, he also knew to wait her out.

"Whatever possessed you?" Dia spit. "What were you thinking? To risk young Reon, yet! Is to have a female so important? You both could have been lost! There are so few of you; did you consider your Noor heritage? You are the preservation of that species!"

Shiveron hung his head, letting the tirade wash over him. He knew until she wound down, he'd never get a word in edge ways.

Finally, silence reigned in the room.

"I sent Reon away from the battle..." he ventured, assuming Reon had spilled the evidence of the Roog encounter.

"Oh, yes! So he could come back to find he was orphaned completely...or perhaps, his poppa, a prisoner. Well...at least I'll give you this much. You did keep him safe."

"He has a beautiful she, chose her himself..."

Dia hissed. "Little spitfire, she is. Talks back; I had to scruff her, and she would not give quarter easily."

Oh, great. Could it get any worse?

Shiveron remembered his first discipline. He couldn't recall the circumstance, only the uncomfortable, terrified feeling of being powerless beneath the formidable Feline, who at that time was three times his size.

At his arrogant disrespect, Dia had pounced from behind, catching him by the back of the neck just below his ears, her deadly teeth just barely breaking skin. She held him face to the side against the hard floor, straddling his back, hissing viciously. One wrong move on his part, and she could have snapped his neck.

All she had wanted from him was submission and an apology, no back talk, no challenge, just, as she called it, 'quarter'. When he surrendered beneath her, and admitted his fault, apologized, Dia had rolled him over, and cuddled him, rubbing her face against his, her scent glands marking him as her own.

None of her children would ever fight her after such an encounter. They much preferred the reassurance of her arms, the feline smell of her silken, long black fur, as her scent went from feral to loving. Her body heat created comfort, the soft coat arousing against their bare skin; the purr of contented acceptance that followed, made them feel protected.

No, not one would cross her again after that first scruffing and cuddle…not even her mate, Kimon.

"She is submissive now," Dia declared. "And, both females have now been trained to know our ways, and their place. It did not help that you took them by force."

"It was the only way, momma. You know that. They won't let me take second mate, and that leaves Reon in limbo. I just wanted him to have a chance."

"What chance? By the ruling put forth by that Roog moderator, no Noor or Noor-half may have offspring. We are to kill them before or at birth, according to that usurper."

"But you won't, momma. I know that."

Dia sighed. "No I would not. Have I killed my fosters? Did I do away with Reon or Jabek when they were birthed? No! Nor will I any other, even should they put the whole healer nest in prison." She hissed a Feline curse word, and spat. "Wish there was just one pure Noor living. They policed this universe with compassion and justice. If the Roog had not eradicated them all, our Space would be quite different. The Roog would be the ones under discipline for their practices!"

"If we could just get moderator Clio off the universal council…"

"Aye. Someday…there will come a Noor leader again. Noor prophecy foretells of a two and two, a four ruler, and they will govern the twelve Feline planets plus one of their own, and expand to include all the civilized universe. It is said this will come to pass in our generation. Many have thought Liam Loki is the male of that four…"

"Ah, momma. How? He is forbidden to mate…and in his case, the mental must choose. Liam has no flesh inclination to fall into physical love…"

"Ha! And, you have sidetracked me, haven't you? So…you apparently have such a physical need."

Shiveron faded abruptly. As he fazed in again, he declared: "I could not leave the momma. The she was alone…and momma Dia, she is a warrior princess!"

"Is she now? Is that how she came to be so broken?"

"Ah, momma. She was broken before…and still she fought at my side. If it had not been for her, Reon would have indeed found me dead."

"I like her, but like her daughter, she needed to learn her place."

"Did you have to scruff her, as well?"

"I only needed to warn, and when she saw I could handle the young one, she willingly gave quarter to me. Moriah had not learned the trick of discipline, surrender followed by love. She gave in too easily; spoiled the kit when young. It will be different now."

"Are you still mad with me?"

"You know my anger is short lived. I like your she. Fact is I approve of both choices. I have told Reon he must teach his she to trust, by giving her kindness. Mother and daughter have it beneath, but have fallen into the habit of battling for supremacy. With leadership taken from them, they will learn by example."

Dia sighed. "But now we must face your problem. Your little she is too hurt to be healed. I have taught her female ways, so now you must take her to Liam to teach and train in a task that suits her, but handicapped, she will never be able to fill her mate duty, nor will she be strong enough for much work. Without healing, you will never have a lover; she will die of her pain. I am sorry, Shiveron. Perhaps, Kimon has a solution…"

"There is another way…"

"Discuss that with your poppa. You know that is forbidden."

"Where have you put her momma?"

"She rests in the ante off my office. It is in your hands now."

****

"I wish Loki were free," Kimon bemoaned. "He could have instantly healed this."

Shiveron and Kimon had stepped away to discuss the prognosis, leaving Moriah alone on the examination cot.

"Use me, poppa," Shiveron pleaded. "I too have the Noor blood."

Kimon hissed in vexation. "Your infection is minimal, yet…still deadly. As soon as the principal has been corrupted, the Noor blood virus spreads unperceived through all consecutive living relatives, and even to succeeding generations; they don't even need to be in contact. It is like it spreads by thought… That is why they disallow carriers mate status. We do this, we are breaking the law!"

"I don't care! This she is mine; I am responsible for her. If you won't help me, I'll do it on my own."

"And what of Reon's she?"

"He already has the anomaly. If the daughter will have him, and they are both carriers, none can object if they are mated. No harm; no fowl. Is your nest not already all Noor-half?"

Insult was immediately evident.

"You forget! I am not! Dia is not!"

"If you could be infected, it would already have happened. Never mind. I'll do it on my own. If Dia wishes to expel us for that, we will go out on our own."

"Dia does not condemn your idea, you know that."

Shiveron turned to go back to his hurting female.

"Wait, Shiveron," pleaded Kimon. "I will help. You are my foster, and I see she is very important to you."

****

Moriah cried out as he undressed her, not because she thought he meant to violate her, but because every movement brought pulsing livid fire up the length of her spine. Her neck was so stiff and unyielding it had numbed everything from there down, and as Shiveron moved her, the tears of agony came.

He moaned in empathic sympathy along with her, but still proceeded.

It is necessary.

CHAPTER 25

Moriah half woke on a bed of straw. Still too sleepy to realize where she was, she stretched to ease the pain in her back, but kept her eyes shut, aware of the bright lights above, through translucent lids.

The stench of feces, urine and blood assaulted her senses.

Did I pass out at work?

Yet still, her eyelids felt so heavy, she couldn't raise them, and Moriah remained unmoving, not making the effort to open them.

With a sight beyond herself, Moriah became aware of the room in which she lay; though her lids remained closed, she could see her surroundings: a sheet over her body, the wall across the way, and bars to the left side.

Bars? As in a prison cell? How did I get here?

I must be dreaming. Right?

Like a turntable carousel, the wall opposite began to revolve, until what was on the back of it was facing front. When it stopped turning, Moriah saw the large, black and silver, shorthaired, cat-like humanoid strapped against the wall, his legs and arms spread-eagle in the shape of an x. She heard the click, as the bands across wrists and ankles released.

For a second his image dimmed. Then he dropped to a crouch, rubbed blood from his hands along the straw on the floor, and suddenly he was beside her, crawling under the sheet with her.

He ran his one hand along her sore back, then across to her waist, and she realized she was naked. He cuddled, surrounding her shoulders, forming a comfort of warmth, like a second blanket from behind.

That feels so good.

His other hand passed over her breast to settle on her belly, and she realized she was heavy with child. She drifted off to sleep again feeling loved and safe.

****

The second dream came much more harsh.

She awoke, but did not open her eyes. She realized she was once again alone, and the pains of birthing were in progress.

As before, even with eyes closed, she could see the room about her, the bright light, the wall across from her. It was empty.

And once again, it began to rotate.

Shocked by what she saw, a scream escaped her.

Shiveron hung against the wall, this time unconscious. His body was slashed with deep bleeding cuts, up the legs, thighs, belly and arms. On his right cheek was an ugly oozing cut.

Tears sprang unnoticed, coursing down her cheeks and dropping from her chin. She choked back a second scream, knowing it would bring back the cruel tormentors.

All she wanted now was to go to him, get him down, and wash him.

Without opening her eyes, as if in a dream, she rose from the floor, moved over to a pail of water that contained a cloth. Moriah had a sense of de-ja vu, as if they were repeating an on going torture ritual, as she carried the bucket toward her male, and set it down to the side.

She was limping, as if she too had been hurt. Not looking down to see why her feet would not properly obey her, Moriah only had eyes for her male. As she stood beneath him, she wondered how to get him down.

Suddenly, one at a time, the upper bands on the wall released, and Shiveron slumped forward, first hanging by only one hand, then his ankles. At last, dropping completely, drunkenly toward her, as the second set of cuffs let go, he fell.

Moriah reached out to catch him. He landed heavily against her, covering her with his battered body, dragging her down with him. With much effort, she flipped him, moving out from beneath him, leaving him resting on his side.

Tears crawled her cheeks, melding with the water, as she wrung out the rag, and gently washed his forehead, then his eyes.

Coming to, he sighed softly, but did not open his eyes to look at her. Instead, tears slipped from beneath his lids.

This is my fault. I wouldn't cooperate with them, so they've tortured my male.

But, for the life of her, she couldn't recall what they wanted of her, or who they even were. Then she remembered: she and Shiveron had been attacked. One captor wanted her to give herself to him and she'd refused.

She carefully washed the angry cut on her male's face. He winced when first she touched it.

On down the body: arms, chest, belly, she proceeded to wash. His broad beautiful chest was banded with the deep gashes, stopped only in the region of the drain-belt they had fastened around his waist.

How did they do this to him? Do they have a new weapon? One that only hurts a Noor?

When she reached his groin, she realized how close they'd come to damaging the vital hidden manhood within. Though the genitals were not visible exteriorly, the cruel cuts were inches away from the small slit opening concealing his tool. Just a little more to the side, and they would have castrated her male.

She shook as she worked, silent tears travelling still, her own labour forgotten for the moment. He lay quiet, sighing with the pain of her ministrations, but not a word of complaint escaped him. He would take death itself for her and their kit.

She inched back away from him, watched as he began to heal.

"Now," came a harsh voice on the air. "You will give me what I want!"

As they came to take her, Moriah began to scream again, thrashing out at them blindly, fearing.

Why can't I see?

Then a fleeting jump forward brought to another moment: the aftermath. When haemorrhaging profusely, she'd given birth to a son.

Yet no, that was another.

After accomplishing their fiendish task, the Roog had left Shiveron and his mate to die, not bothering even to watch, as the Feline female had bled out. And after the mother had escaped in death, Shiveron had hid the newborn kit beneath him, until days later rescue from home had come.

But, it had been too late...too late...too late for that beloved first love. And consequently, the infant Reon had grown up without her.

After all these years, Shiveron still grieved, howling mournfully in a private corner when he could, away from the prying eyes of others. But his brother knew, and did not reprimand, though his comfort often was rejected.

Only she, Moriah could end that cycle.

****

It was common practice in Feline society for a parent or male guardian to share the bed with a sick kit or mate while they underwent hospital care. Shiveron had dozed off, sheltering from behind, when he first felt Moriah tense in his arms. Before he realized it, with her new telepathic abilities, she had joined his mind, through a dream-like state, entering his memories.

When she began screaming, it was already too late. He couldn't shut her out in time. Shiveron brought his arms up around her to ease, held Moriah until she stopped thrashing. In a desire for additional comfort, she turned front into him. He was shocked at the unexpected acceptance.

Whether the action was intentional or not, Moriah was aware of the Feline custom, as Dia had sleep-schooled her. For a female to turn face to the male and straddle him, as she was doing, meant she accepted him as her mate; it was an unspoken invitation for him to take her.

And from her mind, Shiveron realized, Moriah was serious in her action.

But he also knew, physically, she was not healthy enough yet for the offer to be enacted, so instead, he cuddled her deep; she moulded against him, basking in their closeness, falling asleep again instantly.

Suddenly, Kimon was beside them.

"I heard the she screaming," he whispered. "Is she in pain? I thought she was responding to the treatment."

"She was dreaming."

Shiveron felt it was useless to explain.

Kimon will not understand the full depth of a telepathic relationship. How can he? He is merely Feline.

"She will be fine, healing well. No need to worry."

Kimon nodded, appeased for the moment, and disappeared the way he had come.

Rejoicing in his acquired new status, Shiveron eased back into slumber himself, content to know he was now promised to his female, and nothing could change the fact of it.

CHAPTER 26

Arriving at the cubicle just as a young human woman was leaving it, and expecting to be the only one to be trained, Nyle was brought up short. He hadn't realized there were full humans on staff in the med ship.

He hesitated in the doorway.

"Come in. I'll be right with you."

Nyle stepped in, and stood waiting. The programmer had his back to him, and because Nyle saw the short fur travelling up the neck above the long-sleeved, collarless shirt the individual wore, he immediately assumed he was a pure Feline.

When the being turned, Nyle was shocked to see the humanoid features. The male's straight black hair was silver at the temples, and covered the tiny cat-like ears; the eyes were Feline with the dark vertical slit in a field of turquoise blue, but his face, hands and feet were decidedly human-like. It dawned on Nyle then, he'd seen no tail, and as most of the staff went barefoot, he knew a Feline foot when he saw it. This male had toes as human looking as Twila's.

Nyle's eyes travelled back up the full height of the being.

Man! How tall is he?

"I am eight foot three; nine feet when I am together with my physical," the creature disclosed.

Nyle's jaw dropped with the intrusion into his mind. He had believed Twila the only one able to do that.

"Sorry to have invaded your privacy. As a telepath, it is not only my duty to train, but also to oversee others, so there is no breach in security. I did it from force of habit. My apology. I am called Liam."

"Twila's brother?"

"Yes. We are fosters."

"Ahh...I'm Nyle; she's sponsoring my daughter and I."

Liam grinned broadly. "This I know."

"Ah...do you mind if I ask you a question?"

Liam nodded, so Nyle went for it. "Are you two some sort of humanoid mix?"

"No. We are Noor infected."

Nyle frowned.

Infected?

"What exactly does that mean?"

"Infected is a term others use for our blood line. They call the Noor gene an infection because the Roog have taught the younger generation to fear the Noor species. Our parent species was once a very powerful force, policing the universe with powers of unmatched paranormal abilities."

Nyle latched onto the age bit.

"And, you are how old, then?"

Liam laughed. "Only sixty-five. I am of two species: one, the Feline, can live to an age of two thousand; and Noor, which had unlimited lifespan, but could still lose its essence if drained of energy."

"You said, the Noor were the police of the universe?"

"Were, yes. The Roog killed off all pure Noor. There are now only five Feline Noor-half in existence..."

"Twila, Jabek..."

"Shiveron, Reon, and myself, Liam Loki. Have a seat; we should commence with your training."

"So, how does this work?" Nyle asked, as he sat down.

"Please remove your translator."

"But," objected Nyle. "Then I won't be able to understand you."

"I will speak your tongue, until you have been educated; after that you will not need the device."

Unclipping the band from his neck, Nyle held it in his lap, because he feared he might be left without a means of communication, but Liam reached across, and took it from him.

"Do not fear, human. Noors are known for their inability to lie, and I am seldom wrong with an assessment," Liam declared candidly, placing the instrument out of sight. "Let's see now. According to your first evaluation at the jump station, they thought your blood contained the Noor anomaly…"

"What?" exclaimed Nyle, turning around to look behind at Liam. "How'd that happen? I've never been near aliens until now."

"First off, their tests could be faulty. Second, one does not need to be near a Noor to be infected; it passes from generation to generation, down through the family of a parent. If indeed the reading was correct, it would mean one of your ancestors was the blood recipient or was born a Noor."

Nyle gave a disbelieving laugh. "Don't you think we'd know if one of our relatives was an alien? I grew up on Earth. Aliens don't live there."

"Truly?" Liam said, tongue-in-cheek.

"Well…especially a Noor. They'd have…powers, wouldn't they?"

Liam grinned. "Shall we just see if it is true first?"

Nyle turned back around, and sunk into the padded seat back behind him.

"If you are part Noor, you should train easily, for they have an incredible ability to process and retain knowledge…"

"I have to go to school?"

"No. First off, Nyle, discard all preconceptions regarding gaining an education. This is a new life with different ways of doing things. In the outer universe, we teach by sleep programming. The device I will attach interfaces directly with your brain. Within a short space of time you will have what you need at your disposal. It works when awake, but best when you are in sleep cycle. Please close your eyes and relax; it will speed the process."

Liam attached a small round metal disk to the left side of Nyle's head just above the ear.

"Let's see. You'll need languages, defence, board and repair training. Of course, the basic Feline customs and history, some Noor knowledge, and as Twila has chosen you in promise, you will need pleasure training."

Nyle frowned. "You mean sex? I know how to do it. I got a child, you know."

Liam chuckled. "Yes, well…with us, it is done a little different. As I've stressed before, forget previous misconceptions. Now, just sit back, and close your eyes. I'll be here to monitor, making certain the feed doesn't move too fast, but if indeed, you have Noor blood in your make up that shouldn't be a problem. And when you are done, I will be testing you."

****

Nyle woke with a start when Liam removed the teaching appliance.

"Well, it seems you are infected with the Noor anomaly," Liam admitted. "You would not have retained as much or as quickly as you did, if you were not."

"But, how did it happen?"

"More important is are there others out there like you? We thought that we knew all Noor-half. Are your grandparents or parents living? Do you have siblings?"

"My grandparents on both sides are dead, so are most of their older family members. My dad's dead, too, but my mom's alive, and I have an older sister with a daughter."

"Your sister…is she mated?"

"No, never was. If I'm infected, what about Kaudy, my daughter?"

"The anomaly proceeds down the blood line. You are Noor; that means she also will be."

"Could I have gotten it through my older sister?"

"Not likely. To be as receptive as you are means it comes through the older generation, but as most of those in your family tree are dead, it must come through your mother."

"Why wouldn't it come through dad?"

"How did poppa die?"

"Blood clot started in the lung…they think. Then, went to his heart."

"You see if he were Noor that couldn't happen. Noor are self-healing."

"My mom's mom also died of a heart attack…"

"And the other grandparents?"

"All died of old age related conditions."

"Then it must come from momma."

"Whoa. Mom got sick lots of times too; she even was being treated for something female, last I heard."

Liam shook his head. "Interesting. This must be a new infection...unfortunately we do not have all the facts, so until we do, we must wait to solve the puzzle. How about we test you instead of worrying about it?"

"Okay. What do you want?"

"Stand up." Nyle obliged. "Now, you are Human-Noor; most will think you merely human..."

Nyle grinned. "That's good, right?"

"It is to your advantage to keep it hidden, yes. You do realize you are able to obtain weapons to defend yourself?" Nyle nodded. "You are in a mostly Feline society; show me what you would use were you attacked."

"I'd use manipulation, give myself claws."

"Do so then. Show me!"

This is going to be fun.

Nyle raised his hands, willed the nails to extend, then withdrew the claws back to normal human length.

"Good. Can you shape-shift?"

Nyle metamorphed into a large longhaired Feline.

"Good! Excellent!" Liam said pleased. "Now, come back."

Nyle was laughing gleefully, as he returned to his man form.

"I caution you, Nyle. You need to be careful. It is best that those outside our family nest not know your abilities. Sometimes it is even wise to keep it from Dia and Kimon. They would be exceedingly frightened if they knew all our capabilities."

Nyle sobered, knowing immediately there was danger just in being Noor.

"Now, let's test your board skills."

He brought forth a portable, transparent, paper-thin, ten inch by two-foot wide rectangle; a computer screen. Then had Nyle return to his seat, and placed it in his lap.

"I presume you left your family back on planet?"

"Yes."

Nyle immediately knew how to operate the board. He activated it and it rose into the air to suspend, top just level with his shoulders.

"I want you to look for your family. Tap into the human grid." As Nyle obeyed, touching the screen to do each task, Liam continued instructions, watching over Nyle's shoulder. "Next, select the Forbidden Planet system. Remember it is slower and more primitive than ours…last known address of each…"

Nyle was both amazed and fascinated at what came up on the screen. Not only was there the residential address, but also birth date, driver's licence, place of work and associated history, along with articles of news coverage relating to the subjects he sought.

His jaw dropped. "Holy crap!"

"Inappropriate language, Nyle," Liam rebuked. "Watch that. As a Noor, you are expected to display exemplary behaviour."

"But…don't you see? My sister and her kid are dead!"

"Always remember; just because their media says so, does not make it fact."

"But the whole building blew up!"

"Never assume. Were their bodies found?"

Nyle searched the article. "No. No bodies."

"Well, then; there you are." As if he had no empathy, Liam gave an order, deftly sidetracking Nyle. "Next, I want you to find what they have on you."

Nyle obeyed. What came up had him equally disconcerted, even though he had expected it.

"Man! Oh, man! Seline has the police looking for me. I'm wanted for kidnapping, and my mom, for questioning. They think she's an accomplice. Mom didn't know anything! Bet that's why it said, no known address for her. She must be on the run…"

"As I stated previously: never assume."

Nyle laughed. "Yeah; guess you're right. On earth we have this saying, 'assume makes an a s s of you'."

As he translated and understood the meaning of the spelled word, Liam fought not to smile. "I quite agree."

"So, maybe they're all together, then? How do we find them?"

"Do you have pictures?"

"Sorry, I lost them in the transfer when they sold my property."

"With their driver's Id, we can put a search out on the stream. It will take time, but if they are on surface, we will find them. One or another should turn up eventually. So…I think I am satisfied as to your testing. You have retained considerable, and the rest is simply practice. So...why don't you report to Thor in communication. He is quite overworked, and will be glad to put you to a task."

Liam took the board from his hand, and turned away. Nyle knew he had been dismissed.

****

Deep in thought, upset by the findings of his board search, Nyle mulled them over, as he threaded his way through the beds in the med bay.

Will Liam execute the search for my family, or am I supposed to do it? Maybe, because Twila and I are not yet intimate, they will just leave it slide? Also, there is entry to the area. It is forbidden. We can't just go down there and get them.

Nyle wished he'd gone about things differently.

I never meant to get mom in trouble. Maybe that explosion wasn't an accident either?

All kinds of scenarios fled through his mind.

Did someone deliberately hurt my sister because of what I did?

Nyle was so intent on his own thoughts, he took no note of his surroundings. He failed even to hear the envious hiss of disapproval, as he passed beside the cot of an injured Feline warrior. Nor did he see the male reach for his heavy weapon bar, which lay beside him on the bedside table.

Nor was Nyle aware of the stealthy approach of his malicious challenger. The killer blow whomped heavy striking just above the neck; felling him instantly. Nyle plunged forward, landed eagle-spread on his face, bleeding profusely from the wide gash where the skull had cracked open.

Pandemonium broke out above his inert body.

CHAPTER 27

The next morning, Loki decided to take the chance and bring his little she with him into the prison medical bay.

"Stay very close beside me," he warned. "Hide behind me, if there is trouble."

Uel was first to notice. "What's this? You've found a pet human?" He followed her around, as she hid behind her benefactor. "This she is ugly as sin. Did you shave her so she wouldn't attract attention?"

Loki said nothing. After a time, Uel let it go, and returned to his own work.

****

Althea was enthralled and excited at being permitted to leave Loki's quarters, but out here, she felt like the smallest of creatures. At five foot three, she was not much more than half Loki's size, and though the other attendants were a little shorter, they still were larger than she.

Loki went to an area that seemed to be an examination room, with a cot that was closer to the floor, low enough for a human to shift up on it. There was a shelf just above, and he lifted Althea to it, putting her out of harms way. The perch was sturdy, and wide enough that she could lie on her belly, and watch what took place.

Through the day, a long line of human women came through his station, all in various stages of pregnancy. Loki examined each in a tender, modest and caring fashion. Althea realized he was physician to the bred females.

When his day came to an end, Loki again made his way to More's establishment. This time, they both walked, and he took a shorter, more circuitous route past empty cells reeking of urine and excrement.

At More's, he gathered the makings for a meal: fish, bread and half a dozen apples. Althea tugged on his sleeve to get his attention.

"Can I have something?" she whispered, when he turned to look at her.

Loki looked up at More questioningly. "Did you understand?"

"She wears no translator, but she wants, right? More likes her; let her take whatever she want."

"Go," Loki encouraged. "But only small things."

Althea scampered into the back, where her belongings lay stored, still untouched. She knew what she wanted, and found it in the kitchenware: her spices. She quickly found a box of salt, and a container of lemon pepper. She also found her store of candy bars. Slipping three of the bars into her front jean pocket, she picked up the other two items, but as she turned to go, Althea spied her electric frying pan.

Her arms loaded, she went to where the two males were talking, hoping Loki would not reject the appliance.

Loki looked down at what she'd brought. "Seems my she is better at shopping than I," he commented, putting her acquisitions with his. "I'll need a bottle of oil, as well."

Althea had forgotten that item.

More put all articles into a sack, and Loki headed out of the store, Althea close behind him. No currency had changed hands, and she wondered at that.

Preoccupied with her thoughts, when the large black and tan cat with the bulldog face appeared in their path, she let out an involuntary squeal. Too startled to move, Althea stood there shaking.

I recognize this male! This is my nemesis, Bom.

The large beast laughed. "Found yourself a pet, after all, did you?"

"You told me too," Loki returned, as if the formidable creature was not to be feared.

Bom snarled at the insolence, but seemed to think it not worth his while to carry the encounter to violence.

"If you intend to keep that ugly, scrawny thing, make sure you tag it. When it fattens up, someone might want to eat it."

Loki said nothing.

"You hear me?"

"Yes."

Bom turned, and disappeared down another corridor.

****

After they had dined on fried fish, Loki brought her out into the empty med centre again. He sat her down at a table and got out a metal tube with an attachment at the end, a box of fittings for the machine, and a sheet of miniature pictures.

"Which one? You pick." He handed her the sheet.

There were pictures of cats and dogs; pigs and goats; dragonflies, ladybugs, and butterflies, among other things. Althea pointed to a blue butterfly with wings resting back against each other.

"A tusha, eh. I like tushas, also."

"Tusha?" questioned Althea. "It means butterfly in your language?"

"Yes. In Noor." Loki grinned. "I think I'll call you that. You do need a name."

Althea wasn't going to tell him she already had one.

Well, that chapter of my life is over anyway, I might as well have a new name.

As Loki went about fitting the appropriate end to the tag instrument, he began enunciating different words, as if to teach her.

"Titer…"

"That's not the Noor tongue," she returned resolutely.

"Tell me what dialect…from Earth."

Althea had never learned any other language but English. But suddenly, it was as if she could read Loki's mind.

"Titer…butterfly in Armenian."

"Lapia?"

"Burma…Burmese."

"Vlinder?"

"Dutch."

"Motyl?"

"Czech."

"Bebe?"

"Fijian…Fiji."

"Kupu?"

"Indonesian…more correctly, Javanese."

"Titili?"

"Kashmiri…India…Pakistan, to be exact."

"Now, tell me how you did that?"

"I see it in your mind."

Loki grinned, then suddenly, brutally, he stabbed the back of her left hand with the tattooing tool. She gasped in shock as pain radiated up her wrist from the outside edge of her hand. The instrument had gone deep into bone.

"Sorry," Loki said apologetically. "I had to distract you. I knew it would hurt."

"You're mean!" Althea hissed at him.

"Ah, Tusha. If I had done it any other way, it would have hurt you more. I have to do this..."

Althea hissed at him again; it was like she had an angry cat inside her. That was when he pulled her close, and cuddled her.

For a minute she fought, then subsided.

"That's better. Let's see your hand."

She let him cradle it in his bigger one. He turned it over. Where he'd pierce her was a tiny blue butterfly so real it almost looked like it might fly away.

And Althea laughed delighted, her pain forgotten.

****

The next morning, the day repeated the one before. Tusha watched Loki from her shelf, sometimes taking time to admire her new delightful butterfly tattoo.

Finally, at one point, she shifted and inched down from the shelf to sit beside a young teen that Loki had just declared pregnant. The girl was in tears.

Tusha encircled her shoulder to comfort her, reached into her pocket and retrieved one of the chocolate bars. Breaking off a small piece, she offered it to the youth.

Stunned, the girl's mouth dropped open, and as if she feared the proffered candy would be withdrawn, snatched it from Tusha's hand, greedily gulping it down.

"You should savour it," Tusha reprimanded. "That's all you get. I need some for others."

****

Loki had watched all this in awe. He chuckled to himself, as he shooed his patient away to the guard that had brought her, and resolved to let Tusha remain near to appease the distraught patients.

They were nearing the end of his patient schedule, on the last one of the day. Tusha had just given another square of chocolate away, when a paw reached out to snatch her other hand.

They had been so intent upon what they were doing; neither had noticed Bom's arrival. The hand he caught was the one on which Loki had placed her tattoo. Tusha yelped, more from shock than from hurt. Their patient jumped from the bed, and scampered toward the door, where her guard caught her.

Bom growled deep in his throat. "The cows are not to be fed!"

Then his other fist came up and smashed Tusha in the face. She lost her balance, and fell from cot to floor. For just a second, in her anger, her eyes flashed multi rainbow hues, and then the phenomenon abruptly vanished.

Loki had seen it; Bom had not...because, he was looking up at his prisoner physician.

"Where did it get that?"

Loki didn't want to lie, so he stayed silent.

Bom growled angrily. "Keep your pet in line! Or I'll have it killed!"

With that Bom spun on his heel, and stormed from the room.

Tusha's face was rapidly bruising and she shook visibly. At that moment, Loki wished with all that was in him that his healer abilities were not curtailed.

He lifted her to his arms, and angrily carried her from the bay.

CHAPTER 28

That night, after they had eaten, Loki took a cup and a small spoon, sat down on his mat, and encouraged Tusha to come sit on his lap.

"I am going to teach you to protect yourself," he told her. "Today was too close."

Tusha turned to look at him questioningly.

He must have something other than the norm in mind.

Warily, she wondered:

Is this another lesson like the butterfly names?

"I am in a belt, so I can't show you how to do this."

What is that belt for?

"You have my Noor blood now; it will give you...talents, not possible to others."

"The belt keeps you from doing things? What things?"

"Normally I can teleport, manipulate...heal others instantly, and...shape-change."

"Will I be able to do those things?"

"I do not know the depth of your power; I cannot test you. I had to learn how, and I cannot show you..."

"The belt holds you back? Then take it off!"

Loki grunted. "Sounds so simple, doesn't it? But the truth is, it is designed so it can only open with the key...anyway, point here is this: The belt would do the same to you. Whatever happens, if you can prevent it without giving yourself away, never let them put you in a belt."

Tusha nodded.

"And, whatever you do, don't let anyone see you practicing. If you discover you have other talents I have not shown you, don't even tell me. No one must ever know you have the Noor anomaly, or see what you are and can do…"

"Why?"

"Because in here…even should you ever get out, the fact of what you are: Noor and female, will cost you your life. Trust no one. Even back home, we are forced to hide abilities because of the fear in others. My mental has untold talents he is forbidden to use, and must hold himself in check, hide them, as others are not ready for the mind shocking things we can do."

Tusha was astounded. All this was hard to take in. She had always been so powerless and vulnerable in life's storms; it hardly registered that she could be any different. She saw the reasoning in hiding such abilities in here, but elsewhere, seemed unreasonable.

What is that universe out there like that a mighty creature such as Loki fears to reveal what he really is?

"Teach me," she finally pleaded. "I will be careful."

"I can only ask you to try," Loki admitted. "I may be wrong, and you may have little mental strength, as is the case with this physical side in which I dwell."

"What do you mean, Loki? Explain, please."

"Another time. Now, we must try…" He placed the spoon at arms length on the floor. "Bring it to me," he ordered. "Use your mind and will it."

Tusha's jaw dropped. "Telekinesis?"

Loki nodded. "We call it manipulation. Relax, concentrate…no pressure."

As with the thought reading, Tusha simply wished the spoon into her hand. Immediately, it was there.

"Holy man! I can do it!"

"Indeed. Much power is there; you have a mental."

She wasn't going to ask him to explain this time.

"Okay, now see if you can do the same with the cup. This time, put it in my hand."

The cup shot to his hand.

"Easy. Don't let it shoot across like that. Dematerialize and rematerialize at the second location."

The cup and spoon were suddenly sitting at arms length.

Loki laughed. "Two at once. Excellent."

"Is that the same method you use to teleport?"

"Aw, be careful, little Tusha. To use your jump ability, especially in here, will get you in great trouble…and, it takes much physical energy to master it. I warn you; not enough light source to do large or prolonged use of powers in these prison facilities. Another drawback, to anyone who may take it upon themselves to rescue any Noor inside."

"They thought of everything, eh?"

Loki nodded. "Almost everything." He grinned, and winked. "We have a secret weapon, but we must be wise."

Tusha smiled.

I am his secret weapon.

"Now, we will try you with another side channel. Turn the cup a different colour."

Tusha liked blue, so she turned the copper mug a shade of turquoise, the colour of Loki's eyes.

"Now, can you change the molecular structure?"

"You mean like this?" Tusha turned the metal cup to porcelain.

"Okay, see how large you can make it."

The vessel grew and grew, until it near touched the ceiling.

"Better stop," Loki cautioned. "Put it back to its original size and form."

It became a small battered copper mug again.

"Try making something living…"

"It won't be real," Tusha reasoned. "I can't create life…"

"And how did you come to that conclusion?"

"I'm not a God."

Loki grinned.

"Nor, would I want to be."

"Remember that…when you feel the need to kill."

Tusha gave him a look of disbelief. "We can…"

"My mental can. You forgot to carry out my last request."

A small yellow and black bird replaced the cup. As it hopped about looking for crumbs, it emitted a warbling frantic tweet.

"Ummm." Loki licked his lips. "Haven't seen one of those in a long time. The cat in me wants to swallow it, and I feel the urge to stalk. Better turn it back to cup."

Tusha laughed teasingly. "It would turn back to metal in your belly."

And abruptly, the cup was back, spoon protruding above the edge.

Tusha sighed heavily, and leaned her head back against Loki's chest. Suddenly, she felt so very, very tired.

"Aww," he said sympathetically. "You've done too much; drained your energy. Time to rest. One more thing: be careful to keep a reserve of energy. Never let yourself get this weary again. You are never safe in this place."

Tusha sighed again; she could hardly keep her eyes open. Immediately, sleep crept in around her.

****

Loki held her close until she was deep in slumber, reluctant to put her down. She felt so good against his chest, he wanted to go to sleep like that, but he knew it wasn't wise.

Never the less, he sat there thinking.

I was right. At first I thought it was my imagination when I saw her eyes revert, but this time...I know for sure.

The Essence isn't dead; it has simply relocated. The mental-Noor she has found a surrogate to replace its physical. It stays sleeper most of the time because of the lack of energy. It's not apparent unless needed. The introvert personality has no substance, but it's inside this new Noor human. And its physical was unaware. But it won't be long and they will know each other, their strengths, how to work together. The mental will school the physical.

My teaching work is done! But from now on, I need to protect Tusha at all costs...as long as I am able.

This she is the long lost Noor queen! And whether she is unaware at the moment, her knowledge is as old as the universe. When they have their union accomplished, this mighty creature will turn the cosmos on its back. The added personality and experience of the human's existence will make the younger being more insightful.

CHAPTER 29

Shiveron was helping Moriah to dress. Kimon had finally agreed she was fit enough to go to the bed-nest.

"He said, according to the scans, you are healing well," Shiveron encouraged. "The shattered vertebra has reformed whole; the one that was tipped, and pinching the sciatic nerve, has shifted back firmly in place."

"I know the pain is gone. Your blood has healing properties."

"Not just my blood, but now yours, as well. I've passed on the Noor anomaly to you. You are now half human, half Noor."

Moriah realized she had that information stored in her mind. Liam had come and sleep-fed information, while she was recovering. Along with that, and the female teaching programme Dia had prepared her with, she now understood most of what was going on, and what was expected of her.

"My neck is no longer a problem either. It has strengthened and gone back to normal. It doesn't slip out of alignment, the way it always use to, before."

Shiveron took the liberty of gently kissing the nape of her neck. She permitted the tender embrace, knowing, now that they were promised, it was allowed by the rules of courtship. She turned around, and moved into him, face forward, a gesture of acceptance.

"I'd better get you home," he said huskily, and moved to arm's length.

Taking her by the hand, Shiveron guided her out of her private room, to an elevator in the hallway. Here he used his palm to activate the sensor pad at the right of the door.

When the private family conveyance arrived, and opened to them, they stepped in together.

Shiveron slipped his arm about her waist, and once again, Moriah allowed the intimate action.

When the door opened on the near empty quarters, she was not surprised at its sparseness. This nest did not consist of normal Feline, and most of those belonging to it, were seldom home together, as they served the med centre, and were on call continuously.

Only the one corner held anything resembling furniture: a large-sized soft mat that spread over two-thirds of the room; everything else was hidden from view by panels in the walls.

Shiveron turned to her. "I don't know about you," he declared. "But, being in med bay so long, gives me a feeling of utter uncleanliness. Surely, you would like to bathe?"

Moriah too felt almost crawly. The med bay was manned by mostly Felines who disliked water, and saw no need to use it to wash.

"I'd love nothing better."

Shiveron slid open a panel, revealing two sides of the bath pool.

"Will you be okay on your own?" he asked, assuming she'd rather bathe alone this first time.

Moriah grinned. "Come into the female side with me," she suggested coyly. "We are promised."

She felt the excitement in him at her invitation; also felt him steel his needs, as was the custom of the male.

They are so controlled!

This time she took his hand, and as she led him inside, she heard the panel behind them slide shut and lock, as he willed it to seal for their privacy.

Moriah looked at the enormous recycling pool, the five-foot high waterfall above, on the far wall. It wasn't a carnal need that made her shiver, but a Noor desperate requirement to touch the water. She almost jumped in with her clothes on.

"What's wrong with me?" she gasped, turning to him. "I feel like my flesh will crawl off me, and leap into the water on its own."

"A Noor needs bathing like other creatures need food. Come, we'll take it slow, so you enjoy every minute of your first encounter with the healing sensation of liquid."

Moriah trembled with anticipation, as he removed her clothing. When he slipped from his own, she could wait no longer. She started for the edge to step in.

Shiveron caught her by the arm. "We need to lather up first."

Moriah moaned with a longing that came deep from within. But she obeyed him, following his action, covering her skin with soft cream. Then he led her to the pool's edge, and they slid in together.

She had never felt such a feeling: like silk against the skin. It almost burned, like an antiseptic, penetrating deep into the pores.

He pulled her down into the depth, until the water was over their heads. His voice came inside her head. Telepathic communication!

"Open your mouth; swallow some, drink it…take it inside to heal deep. Open your eyes."

When she did as she was told, she saw clearly, all around her. As an example, he opened his mouth, gasping in deep gulps of the liquid surrounding them. She followed his actions…and marvelled.

She didn't choke, nor was she unable to breathe.

I haven't been taught this! Noors are like fish under the water!

She laughed delightedly. Unable to resist, Shiveron placed his mouth over hers.

"We need to wash away the soap," she objected by thought, pulling away.

And when he took her hand; they dived, and swam, until they were under the waterfall. Here they let the cascade wash over them, until their skin was clean and shimmering.

They turned from the falls, swam and dived. His lips found hers, and teasingly, she slipped away again. He chased her, and she let him catch her.

This time she initiated the kiss. It grew deeper.

And suddenly they were making love in the water.

****

Shiveron drew her to the edge of the pool, laughing. "Now, we'll have to bathe again," he half-heartedly complained.

Taking him seriously, she slipped out of the water and made for the soap bottles. He laughed, went after her, and caught her by a dainty foot, felling her gently. She rolled to her back.

They made love again on the tiles, both too absorbed in each other to care if anyone came upon them.

At least, I locked the door.

For a time, they fell asleep in each other's arms. When they awakened, they did soap up again; repeating all that had gone before…right down to the last interaction.

Shiveron had long since forgotten his dead mate, the mother of Reon.

Toward mid-afternoon, they donned pyjamas, and made it onto the sleep mat. He coaxed her to eat something before they cuddled face forward, and both slipped into much needed rest.

Waking briefly in the night, Shiveron realized no one had joined them on the bed mat.

Must be some sort of crisis in the med bay. Nothing else would keep everyone away. Even Reon and Iora have stayed out, and that can only mean extra warriors have been needed in the centre.

CHAPTER 30

Shiveron and Moriah had just polished off huge plates of poached eggs on toast, with bacon on the side, when the outer door to the home nest slid open with a shushing sound.

Reon stepped in with Iora, followed by Liam.

"There you are," Shiveron reprimanded Reon. "Where have you been all this time?"

"No need to scold them," Liam cautioned tiredly. "For their safety, we kept them in momma Dia's ante for this sleep break."

"What's happened?" Shiveron demanded apprehensively.

"Reon," Liam ordered. "Go bathe."

"But...my she?" the younger male objected.

Realizing that was her cue, Moriah got to her feet. "We'll go bathe, as well, okay?" she suggested. At an assenting nod from Shiveron, she took her daughter's hand. "Come Iora."

"Yes. Good idea," Liam agreed. "I need to talk to Shiveron, alone."

When all three had disappeared into their perspective sides of the bathhouse, and the doors slid shut, Shiveron turned to Liam, and again repeated his question.

"What happened?"

Liam evaded. "I see you're mated?" he observed.

"How can you tell?"

Liam chuckled. "Your she is glowing. Litterly."

Shiveron grinned, but sobered immediately, knowing something serious was going on. Before he could ask a third time, Liam lowered to sit on the bed mat. Shiveron joined him.

"I want you and Reon to keep the females here in the nest for the next couple of days."

"Why?" Shiveron asked warily. "Are you going to tell me what's been going on, or must I invade your privacy?"

"As if you could," Liam challenged. Then seemed to think better of his attitude. "Twila's male was attacked by a disgruntle warrior."

Shiveron frowned. "Did I miss something here? When did Twila accept a male?"

"Oh, huh!" Liam exclaimed. "That's right, you've been away, too. So you don't know. The mating bank called her a while back; a male with a young female, just the right age for Jabek, was compatible to them."

"Of what species?"

"He's human, with Noor anomaly."

"You jest!"

"No. Checked him myself."

"Incredible." Shiveron shook his head in disbelief at the good fortune.

"We need to stay at arms length from her for a bit. She's already attaching. If we go give her comfort or protection…"

Shiveron nodded. "We need to give him a chance. I understand. He's been schooled?"

"Aye."

With awe, Shiveron digested the information for a second, then what had been said prior to the revelation, came to his mind.

"You said the male had been attacked. He wasn't killed?"

"Near."

"How bad? Did his Noor self-healing kick in?"

"Yes. But Twila is near frantic."

"Man! And we can give no comfort?"

"Best not to. Let nature take its course."

Shiveron hissed in vexation. "And the warrior? What became of him?"

"The Slither, Sith, was upon him before anyone could stop him. Killed him before he could strike a second blow."

Shiveron growled deep in his chest. "If I'd been there, he'd not gotten in the first."

"Easy to boast, young male, but one never knows how circumstances play."

"I would have sensed the warrior's mind set. I too am warrior. Why didn't Twila's male feel his danger?"

"He had just come by bad news about those he left behind."

"Wish I had been there to alert him."

"Tell me, Shiveron; would you have killed?"

Shiveron frowned, realizing what he had been saying.

"We Noor are peaceful," challenged Liam. "Healers!"

In the silence that followed, Liam changed the subject. "Besides, you obviously were needed elsewhere, otherwise occupied. Congratulations."

Shiveron grinned. "She's been ready since the first day after the transfusion."

"None of my business, male. Private," Liam reminded. "You will keep your shes safe in house? There might be others like-minded. Jealousy toward us is rampart among warriors."

"You don't need to remind me. Do you not need at least one of us to help stand guard in med bay?"

"You are mated now; no more a Warrior guardian. I'll talk to Poppa to reassign you. How would you like training in board?"

Shiveron's heart leapt in his breast. He had long wanted such placement. "Would I!" he exclaimed with fervour. "All my dreams are coming true."

"See me later, then. For now, you and Reon guard our family. Reon needs sleep, by the way. He was too on edge through the break to relax."

"I'll see he rests. I'll take first watch."

Liam nodded agreement. "Then let us join your young male in the bath."

****

Nyle opened his eyes feeling disoriented, and realized he was laying on a cot, on his side, facing the wall. When he tried to roll to his back, excruciating pain shot down his neck to his shoulders.

"Best not move too much, human," cautioned the voice of the guardian Bear, Wadi. "Wait for Kimon. He is coming shortly."

But Nyle needed to see what was causing the hurt. Carefully, he moved his hand to the back of his skull, where he found his head shaved and swathed in bandages.

Without thinking, in one fluid motion, he turned around and sat up. The sudden movement made the world swim, and brought him to gagging from the nausea it caused.

Dangerously, he swayed, and would have fallen from the bed, if not for Wadi reaching out and steadying him.

"Lie back," the bear creature growled. He pushed Nyle down until he lay back on his side.

Nyle had no fight left in him, and he was quite willing to comply. But at least, now he could see where he was, and what was going on. He no longer felt defenceless.

Wadi patted his shoulder in approval. "Nice human. No need to fight."

Nyle grunted. "I'm not your pet, Bear," he growled.

Wadi only laughed. "Your fight's there, at least. You know, we all thought you were dead."

"Take's more to kill me than most. Where's my Kaudy?"

The giant bear grunted disparagingly. "You should be asking of Twila; she's your promised."

"I take it someone attacked me; they wouldn't hurt Twila. They want me dead, so they can have her."

"Yeah, but she never wanted him before…She was just livid when she saw, so angry, we thought she'd kill someone. If the Slither hadn't got there first, that warrior would have had his brain fried."

Nyle frowned. "What warrior?"

"The one who attacked you has wanted Twila for a long time; kept deliberately getting hurt just so he could be in the bay near her. Infuriated him that she'd chosen a human when she's been raised Feline. Now, Twila's so distraught you've been hurt, she's been glued to your side every moment since it happened, bathing your wound herself every two hours. Kimon finally ordered her away to Dia's ante for some rest. She'll sure be upset she wasn't here when you came to."

"Enough!" thundered Kimon disapprovingly, as he came toward the bed. "Guardians aren't meant to be chattering on protection duty, especially not about the private lives of my fosters."

But Wadi was confident enough of his acceptance in med bay, so certain he could not jeopardize his place that he dared to answer back.

"He moved too sudden, needed my help...and reassurance."

"Then, I praise your consideration," Kimon conceded. "Now, be silent! And let me see to the patient."

Wadi stepped back in a dignified manner. It was apparent he was used to the physician's fowl temper and curt reprimands, and took them in stride. The guardian assumed a position of easy alert.

"How are you feeling?" Kimon asked of Nyle.

Nyle swallowed back the weakness. At least the room had stopped spinning. "Like I died and came back too soon," he admitted, tongue-in-cheek.

Kimon grunted appreciatively. "Humour is good. Quickens the healing. Rest a while longer." He peered up at the beeping screen behind and above Nyle's head. "You are mending well, but...such a blow will take time to heal."

"Where is my daughter?"

"With Dia. She is safe. Dia comforts; the little she was quite frightened. Dia reassures... She is good at that."

"Bring her here; I'll…"

"No! You will rest! She is in good hands. Do not worry. We will see no harm comes to her."

CHAPTER 31

As was the usual routine each day, Loki and Tusha were in the prison medical bay.

Loki knew, even though it was a risk, Tusha still kept a bit of chocolate in her pocket at all times, being careful not to let the guards, or anyone else, see her slip it to a girl. Usually, when she was doing it, he tried to hide the two with his much larger frame. Both he and his little companion knew, if they got caught, there would be consequences to pay.

Today the guards were bringing the patients in two at a time. These were the newly pregnant younger ones, and a sentry accompanied each.

"This one can't keep nothing down," the first Roog declared.

"And this one won't stop bawling," the second guard admonished, as if speaking to the female.

"I'll take the second first," Loki said, lifting the young teen to the table. Tusha moved in beside the girl to offer reassurance with her presence.

Loki could see; the female was near to term. At this stage, weeping was a common occurrence in those carrying.

"Now, what are all these tears for?" Loki reproached softly, gently stroking her dishevelled limp tresses. He had little control over nutrition or their living conditions; they were mainly brought in when they were noticed, because they'd become an annoyance. Otherwise, the pregnant ones were left to themselves to fight over the food.

The young teen looked up at him, her soul in her eyes. "I want to keep my baby," she whispered, tears brimming and ready to spill. "I want to raise it. I feel it kicking; I love it. Don't let them kill it. Please."

Much as he wanted to, there was no use giving her false hope. He was powerless to stop this cycle in the prison; if one got away with its infant, the Roog would hunt her down and kill both.

Tears of sympathy filled his eyes.

How many others are like-minded?

Tusha gave action to her empathy. She moved closer. Knowing what she was about to do, Loki moved to block the view of the guards, who had stepped back to give him space.

"Love it with all your heart, as long as you can. It's the best that can be done in here," Tusha advised quietly, slipping a sliver of chocolate into her palm. "Eat it when they aren't looking," she whispered in her ear.

When that one had been sent away, to ease the tension, Loki turned to Uel, working nearby with another set of females. "Uel, when you first came, didn't you tell me, your sentence was near its end? Why are you not being sent home?"

"Ha!" declared the Feline. "Didn't I tell you, we never get out of here? My sentence ended a week ago. But there is no one to miss me out there; no one will force my release. I'll be here 'till I die..."

Loki shook his head.

Surely something can be done about that.

He lifted his second patient to the cot. She was just beginning to show, though she was extraordinarily thin.

"Beth?" Tusha gasped in shock, and Loki turned to look at her.

"You know this one?"

Tusha nodded. "We were brought in at the same time."

Loki looked more closely at his patient. She was lethargic, like a distant wounded animal, her mind far away, somewhere deep inside her. This was traumatized withdrawal here, abuse of the worst kind, which had not been perpetrated by the guards alone.

That's when Loki remembered Tusha's condition when she'd first been brought to him.

Was Beth with Tusha when my little female received that mistreatment? I never asked what happened.

"Did this one see what happened to you?" he asked of Tusha.

His cellmate nodded quietly.

"And who was responsible, Roog or human?"

Tusha would not meet his eyes, though he knew she knew to what he referred.

"The inner damage, Tusha," he clarified.

"Human," she reluctantly admitted.

"And, do you know if this one and the she beast are still together?"

With her hand, Tusha gently turned Beth to face her, searching deep into those empty eyes. "Yes," she said at last. "They remain together. Lana is a cruel one...allows her little food."

"How far along is this Lana?"

"By what I see in Beth's mind, they were both bred at about the same time."

Loki grunted with disgust, and turned to the guard behind. "You watch the cage this female is in?"

"Yeah, it's my station. Why?"

"This one receives no food. How do you expect her to produce if not fed?"

"And how do you know this? It doesn't talk."

"I have my ways."

"Neither you nor your pet has a translator. You understand their speech without?"

"Yes."

"It's gibberish to me."

Loki brought the conversation back to the matter at hand. "Separate the she from the others."

The Roog growled. "There are only three in there. We never keep them single."

"There is another that you did not bring?"

"Yes, an older cow. Gives us less trouble then these two put together."

"Perhaps, the real trouble maker is the seasoned one?"

The guard frowned, pondering the words. "I'll watch more closely, from now on."

"See this one gets dry bread; it will stop the nausea."

****

Just before Loki was finished with Beth, a commotion in the doorway behind made all turn to see what caused it.

When Loki stepped away to meet the new arrivals, Tusha saw it was a huge Roog guard carrying a very pregnant older woman by the neck. All his captive wore was a thin shift, which was wet from the waist down.

Yellow-brown fluid dripped from between her legs, as if she had let go her water in fright…or her water had broken!

"This one is already delivering," growled her warden, indignantly. "She was trying to hide the fact. More and more these stupid things are hiding their labour until it's almost too late. You'd almost think they were intelligent."

He jarringly plunked the hapless woman on the nearby bed, and stepped back out of the way, joining his companion enforcer.

Neither Roog seemed to consider there was any danger their charges might flee, and so stood at ease, simply waiting for the physician to complete his task.

Though each guard was relaxed, they had suddenly become excited, their jaws slightly open, slavering with anticipation…as if they expected to be fed.

Loki pushed his new patient back against the cot, bent her legs toward her belly, and spread the knees wide apart, revealing her lower naked private area. Tusha could now see, the baby's head was already crowning.

With one last scream and a forceful push on the part of the mother, the infant escaped its inner safe haven. Loki expediently caught it, placed it between the woman's feet, tied off the cord, and cut between the sections. He then lifted the squalling newborn, and placed it between the breasts of the mother to ensure it quieted. The tiny creature was a girl, and it immediately sought a place to comfortingly suckle.

Loki turned to fill a basin with water to wash the blood from his new patient. The guard who had brought them in stepped forward, and the Noor hissed a warning.

"Stay back. You know, if there was any sense to your methods," he complained. "You'd at least save some of those birthed as new stock. This one's female. You could let it be raised..."

The guard growled low in his chest, as if being denied his conquered kill. "It goes to the kitchen. That's our orders."

As both male guards came forward to answer Loki's challenge, the occupant of the bed saw her chance. In one fluid motion, cradling her treasured baby, she rolled from the table and dropped.

Trailing a river of blood, as the afterbirth had as yet not expelled, she fled for the entrance to the tunnels...right into the arms of Bom!

The giant Roog/Feline caught her up by the hair, and with the other hand on her shoulder, soundly snapped her neck, abruptly ending her life. The bawling infant suddenly dropped from her limp arms, hit the floor with a liquid thud, cracking its back with an audible crunch, ending a strident scream in mid scale, mercifully silencing the ill-fated baby girl in death.

In disgust, Bom tossed away the carcass of the mother, and headed angrily toward Loki. Loki hissed, and backed up, attempting to shield Tusha and Beth on the other cot behind him.

"You dare defy me, Noor?" growled Bom. "This time I have a torture wand with me. Do I need to use it?"

Tusha enveloped Beth in her arms; both were now visibly trembling, fear flooding every fibre. To them, the whole episode was reminiscent of when Lana gave birth in the stalls.

Wisely, Loki eased his stance, but said nothing.

"You have been lax, Noor. That cow should not have had the opportunity to escape in the first place. I hold you responsible; I've lost a valuable commodity. And that means I must punish you, or lose face."

Loki moaned, sensing what was coming.

"Two more months will be added to your sentence!" Then dismissing the matter, Bom turned on his heel, and barked an order to his sentries. "Take this dead meat to the kitchen, and return the other shes to their stalls."

In a near whisper, Loki dared to object. "The one is my...pet."

Bom turned back, laughing. "Oh, that's right. She's the old one: no good to breed, and of little use."

As the one guard grabbed for Beth, reached for Tusha with his other hand, Bom stayed his action.

"Leave that one. We'll wait for it to fatten."

For the first time since the delivery had begun, Tusha allowed herself time to think. If Bom had heard what went through her mind, he would have done more than just growl.

But it was Tilk who had the venomous thoughts:

Beware, Demon Roog Cat! You would not like the taste of us, and should our blood infect you, and I have the choice, I will never include your carcass in the assembly of my Noor peoples!

And Tusha vowed, as well:

If ever I have it within my power, I will hold this cruel creature, accountable for his crimes.

****

When the bay shut down for sleep cycle, Loki sent Tusha alone to his night room, while he went for the fixings for supper on his own. He needed time to privately lick his wounds from the day's events.

Dejectedly, but not reluctantly, the human Noor disappeared around the corner. Loki also knew, after all that had happened that day, the little female also would need time alone to process.

****

Tusha sat thinking, awaiting Loki's return. But her thoughts were not on the countless women down here, as might be expected. They were in the world above, on her past.

Through no fault of her own, she had also once lost a fetus, at nine weeks in. Her drunken husband had caused the miscarriage by violently shoving her against a wall. Even then the miniature creature had been a recognizable human being, with eyes and ears, feet and arms, even a tiny mouth. It had been a real complete child! She had mourned, even given it a name…

She couldn't help thinking about the many women up there, who wanted to conceive but could not. Countless millions would give anything to have a child; yet there were equally as many others, who wilfully terminated their pregnancies because of selfish, narcissistic egocentricity and blatant ambition. Like the Roog, they unfeelingly considered the unfortunate creature within a mere blob of flesh to be exploited or exterminated.

What difference is there between the Roog and the race to which I once belonged?

And someday soon these Roog predators from below will not be content to forage cautiously only at night. They will break onto the surface, and...

Maybe some of the human race deserves what is coming!

But not the young ones, the babies, no not these...nor the unborn!

Quietly, Tusha began to weep for the millions maliciously lost. Uncontrolled sobs soon wracked her emaciated frame, so taking over that she was completely unaware that Loki had returned...until his hand gently travelled down her back in an attempt to soothe her.

She went into his comforting arms for solace, giving as well as taking.

CHAPTER 32

Shiveron slipped up beside Moriah, as she was putting away sterilized equipment, in preparation for leaving for the bed-nest for sleep break.

"Will you take a walk with me before we head home?" he asked, slipping his arm around the waist of his newly acquired lover.

"Sure. Why not? What did you have in mind?"

He slipped his hand in hers, pulling her toward the private family elevator. Once they were safely shut inside, and the vehicle was on the way down, he took Moriah in his arms, and they indulged themselves in a long tender kiss. When the doors slid open, both were reluctant to break apart, but Shiveron again took Moriah's hand.

Leading her into the huge storage cavern beneath the family bed-nest, he pulled her toward a rectangle container the size of a small house. As he led her inside, and stepped aside for her to view the contents, he self-consciously excused his actions.

"I tried very hard to set it up in just the way you had it..."

His new mate gasped in surprise. "My things! It looks just like our house on Earth. How did you get them here?"

"Jump transfer. We set beacons the night we left. Did you think I would rob you of your treasures?"

"Oh, Shiveron!" In awe, she traversed the rooms, laughed when she found drying jeans thrown over the barrier blocking the stairs leading down to the bedrooms. "Oh, gosh!" she said. "Half this stuff is useless to us now. What am I going to do with it?"

"How about we go through it; you keep what you do want, and we could put the rest for sale as souvenirs from the Forbidden planet?"

Moriah laughed at that. "Or," she said coyly. "We could keep this place as our hideaway for when we want a private time…"

The delighted grin spread across his face before he could prevent it.

****

Nyle was so glad to get out of the hospital; he was actually looking forward to sleeping with his promised on the communal sleep mat in the home nest. She had mentioned Liam and Kimon would bring Kaudy and Jabek with them when they came later, so he and Twila were heading home alone.

He expected momma Dia would be there, as Twila had also said the matriarch had gone ahead to prepare the supper meal from scratch. Dia didn't like the replicator for family meals, but preferred to actually cook.

Twila had admitted tonight was special, that almost the whole family would be home together for this sleep break, and it had Nyle quaking inside.

He knew Liam and Kimon, he'd also previously met Dia, but it was the other brother and family Nyle was wary to meet.

Will they accept me?

As the two stepped into the nest, and the panel slid closed behind them, Dia called from the kitchen. "That you, Twila?"

"Yes, momma."

A young Noor Feline teen sat in the corner of the bed mat playing on a small screen device in his hand.

"Ock, Reon," Twila reprimanded. "Put that away, and come meet my promised."

Obediently, the instrument vanished, and the male arose and came forward.

"Nyle, this is Reon. He is my brother's son. He's still young and learning, only eighteen…"

Reon hissed disapprovingly. "I am warrior; no ignorant," he defended. "I am honoured, master Nyle." The boy gave a slight nod of respect, and stepped back.

For a junior male, Reon was well muscled and tall. Nyle supposed that was due to his half Noor breeding, which was apparent, as he had the face, hands and feet of a humanoid. His manner, however, surprised Nyle. There was none of the subservient fear most Feline males displayed.

"He's been raised without a mother, and sometimes lacks respect," Twila chided teasingly. "But perhaps that will change…so, where is your father and new stepmother?"

"Poppa said they had an errand first. They should be here soon."

Wiping her hands on the apron at her waist, Dia came around the corner of the kitchen alcove, followed by a human female. When she moved aside, and Nyle caught a glimpse of the young girl, the words just slipped out before he realized the error of his action.

"Iora! Where did you come from?"

Both Dia and Twila hissed a warning, and Reon suddenly went rigid, as if ready to pounce.

Nyle stepped back, and dropped his head in submission.

In the heat of the moment, Nyle had not heard the outside panel slide open, nor had he seen the entry of Liam with Kaudy and Jabek in tow. Only when Liam reprimanded him, did he notice Jabek had also taken a stance of attack alert.

"Nyle!" Liam warned. "Remember your place. The eldest female is to be addressed first."

Nyle swallowed.

I knew that. I was just caught off guard.

"Sorry, momma Dia."

"But, momma Dia," objected Iora from behind her. "He's my uncle."

"Eh, what?" Dia broke into a chuckle. "And how came this about? Liam?"

Liam shrugged. "I had no foreknowledge. I am as surprised as you."

At just that moment, Shiveron entered, Moriah preceding him.

Moriah's jaw dropped in surprise. "Nyle! Holy cow! How did you get here?" All propriety forgotten, she ran toward Nyle and wrapped her arms about him, giving him such an exuberant hug it could have cracked bone.

All the while, the stunned Noor Feline members stood dumbfounded.

****

Liam began to laugh.

Shiveron frowned, annoyed.

"Glad you think this is so funny."

Liam grinned good-naturedly. "It is amusing when you think on it. Here both you and Twila have chosen mates, and they turn out to be brother and sister. What's funny is that you didn't even know about it…and for how long have they been here? How can that happen? Were you just never in the nest together? And did your paths never cross in the med bay? Talk about predestined; it brings to mind that old Noor belief: nothing happens by chance."

"And, here's another to knock you off kilter," Liam added. "If Nyle already had the Noor anomaly, it must have come down through this older sister. And you, Shiveron, didn't even check her blood before you transfused her. So, now that she has the anomaly from two sources, does that make her whole Noor? And if so, does it spread both forward and backward to Nyle one way and their momma the other?"

When he watched their faces go from puzzlement to awe and back again, as he presented the probabilities, Liam could keep his merriment at bay no longer. He broke into uncontrolled laughter at this quandary, and they joined in, realizing the improbability this had all happened by chance.

Finally, Shiveron slugged him on the shoulder to stop his hysterical hilarity, and gasping to contain his own mirth, rebuked Liam.

"Oh, yes! My stupidity is so often amusing to you, Mental. If you are so smart, where is their momma? And, for that matter, who infected her? It had to be recent, for them not to know of it? As none of us did it, who was it then? The Roog? Loki?"

Liam sobered. "You have me there; that is the puzzle," he agreed, quickly rejecting in his mind, that Loki would do such a thing unless forced by a desperate situation. "But first order of business is, we need to find her. This family needs completion!"

CHAPTER 33

Bom came striding into the prison med bay in the middle of the afternoon shift. He made straight for Loki's corner. At the moment, Loki was without a patient, not idle exactly, but cleaning his equipment with Tusha's help.

"Send your pet away," Bom growled. "Don't want it hearing what is said."

He walked away, as if he were broiling over something and couldn't stand still. Waiting impatiently, Bom paced the floor beyond. Loki knew he'd better be quick.

Reaching up above his head, he grabbed a small translator for a human, and fitted it to Tusha's throat. Before turning it on, he gave her instructions.

"Go to More, get the fixings for a meal."

"By myself?" Loki nodded. "Can I make it, when I get home?" Again Loki nodded.

"When I turn on your translator, be careful what you say. Those around will understand. When you don't want that, push the centre in to deactivate."

"I know how."

"Good. Go now, before Bom chooses to do something to you."

Loki pressed the translator activator, lifted her down, and she fled toward the tunnels. As she disappeared, Bom again joined him.

"Come with me; we will walk."

As the Roog Feline headed the opposite direction from where Tusha had gone, Loki fell into step with him. They proceeded toward the empty halls leading to Bom's own quarters.

"Your grandmere, Kei, has contacted my father, Clio. She has convinced him, it is in our best interests to set you free; she wants you released...now."

Loki said nothing.

Let the bureaucrats fight it out.

"Kei gave him an ultimatum: if you are not set free immediately, at the completion of the original sentence passed, the Feline will bring war to this sector, and topple his empire."

Loki tried not the grin.

Way to go grandmere!

There were twelve Feline planets to the Roog's sparsely populated three, and though the dogs were more brutal, the Feline, when cornered, did not lack in ferocity.

"And I suppose, Clio has given you instructions? I'm sure neither he, nor you, would want your little cattle farm exposed..."

Bom growled deep in his throat.

Loki knew the male was caught between his father's desires, and his own wants.

"I am to use whatever means necessary to end your sentence."

The unspoken implication was not lost on Loki.

"If you kill me, the result will be the same."

Bom growled again, incensed by the truth of his quandary.

"This is how it will go down. You will obey my every whim for the remainder of the month, and if you still live at its end, you will be sent home…in chains…the same as the day you arrived."

Loki again said nothing, neither agreeing nor disproving.

"Every whim, Noor!" Bom reiterated. "When I summon you, you come! Without argument! You do what I ask; I'll brook no more rebellion!"

Loki couldn't promise he'd obey to the letter, so he remained silent. Bom took it as consent.

"When you go, you leave behind your human pet. Set her loose; put her back among the kitchen workers where you found her…"

Loki wasn't about to correct his misconception.

"And for today, you will serve until the midnight revelry is over. If you fail to be available, and I find out your failure, you will be punished."

Loki hissed in rebellion at this.

Tusha will be planning a meal, and if I must remain in the bay, short of sending Uel to my quarters to tell her, I have no way of informing her I'll be delayed. Maybe I can send Uel to More.

But if he weren't careful, Bom would misinterpret his annoyance. Thinking quickly, Loki redirected the conversation.

"If I survive the month, I get to ask something from you, at my departure."

Bom laughed at his daring. "You bargain with me, Noor? Challenge me?"

"You are not the only one with power…"

Bom harrumphed. "I agree," he said after some thought. "But two things: you cannot ask for the life, nor the freedom of your little she, and second…you must survive…" The warning of confrontation was just under the words. "…until the day of your release. Now, get back to the bay; get out of my sight, before I bring up what I had at lunch."

Loki turned, and as he fled the violent warden, he was already mulling in his mind how he might free Tusha.

****

Tusha was so happy at the thought of preparing a meal for Loki; she breezed through the tunnels of meat cages without seeing the hapless faces of those behind the bars. She burst into the store excitedly, and without thinking demanded of More.

"Can I have whatever I want today?"

More chuckled. "Well now, it makes sounds I can understand. At last Loki has blessed you with a translator. Yes, yes, More likes this little she. What do they call you?"

"Loki calls me Tusha. Can I have anything I choose? He said I could make him a special meal."

"Ha! For Loki! Special; yes, we make special. Tusha may take anything."

And Tusha knew exactly what she would use to trundle it all home.

Once in the excess storage, Tusha hunted through the property she knew to be hers until she found the cart she'd always used to lug groceries home on the bus. She began filling it with her spices, pasta jars, and some canned goods. She needed a can opener…

As she was searching, she heard Uel come into the food area, and engage More in conversation, but she did not try to hear what they said. As Uel made no attempt to seek her out, she went on with her hunt, picking up small things she could use, like a cutting board, larger knives, wooden stirring spoons, and a soup ladle, along with extra plates, glasses, and cutlery.

When at last, she entered the food counter area Uel was gone. Tusha stood before the large vegetable display:

Wilted celery, onions, raw carrots, bags of defrosted frozen peas and corn...is that fresh tomatoes?

"Nobody want those," More revealed. "Felines no like fruits and vegetables; prefer meat, and the fish. Take all you want."

"Loki likes veggies."

"Loki different. Him Noor. Those beings were like human; eat garbage."

Maybe to him, it is garbage. He's a tree that can think.

Tusha was almost tempted to drop into his native tongue, just to shock him, but she kept her peace.

"You remember the Noor?"

"Aye. There was peace when they peopled the universe; not like now under dog."

That's when Tusha made the mistake of trusting a Root. She did twist her tongue to the speech of his species. Shutting off her translator, Tusha addressed him directly.

"Are you friend or foe, Root? Are you for Roog or against?"

He grunted, taken aback at the question, not realizing she was using his tongue on her own. "Had I a choice, I'd go against any to get from this place," he returned bitterly. "But, little female better beware; she be heard by another."

Tusha switched her translator back on, and turned again to the fruit stacks. "Doesn't this fruit go to the pregnant?"

"They get enough. You want? Take all."

"We have no way to keep it. But I'll take a bunch of celery, a bundle of carrots, a tomato, and an onion…"

As More took down, and handed her what she asked for, he delivered the message Uel had brought.

"Uel talk me. Tell you, Loki confined to med bay by order, until orgy over tonight. No allow home."

"But he will come to his sleep room after? Right?"

More bent his head in acknowledgement.

"Well, what I plan to make will take time, and will keep, even cold, so I can still make it. Do you have any meat?"

"I have meat…all kind," More said eagerly, moving behind the meat counter. "See here …fish, human, pig…beef."

"Real beef…from four legged cows in the world above?"

"Aye."

"How old?"

"Get during this night…only hour ago. Just before you come."

"Okay. Give me two big scoops."

"Ha! Loki will like this meal!"

When she was all packed up, and about to head out the door, More called her back. He reached beneath the vegetable counter and pulled out a flask, handing it to her.

"What's this?"

"I save…long time. Noor juice fruit; very popular with Noor male. You serve Loki…celebrate. Okay?"

"Okay!"

****

When Tusha got into the sleep chamber, she put everything she needed out on the counter, took out the big cooking pot, and put the first ingredients to simmer: she chopped the onion, celery and sliced the carrots. With oil on the bottom, she set that to cook until the onion was transparent, while she opened cans of tomatoes, mushrooms and baked beans. When the sautéing vegetables were ready, she browned the meat, added chili powder and garlic. At last, she dumped in the contents of the cans; when this came to a boil, she turned the temperature on the hot plate down.

It can simmer safely now for hours. Loki will have sloppy Joes and pasta, whenever he gets home.

CHAPTER 34

When Loki opened the door, the aroma hit him full force, and made his stomach clench with abrupt agonizing hunger. It was as if he'd stepped from the prison into the home nest, and momma Dia had made his most favorite meal. And Loki loved to eat!

He moaned in anticipation, slavering despite every effort not to.

Where did the she get such ingredients here?

To fend off his desperate need, he went to the shower in the corner, stripped and turned on the hot water. The steam kept the tantalizing smell at bay, for the moment.

By the time he had finished, and was fully clad again, Tusha had spread a small cloth on the floor, complete with plates heaped with mounds of spaghetti hidden beneath gravy, meat chunks, carrot slices and cooked beans. Utensils he'd only seen at the tables of humans…he thought they were called knives and forks, had been placed to the side of each serving, and there was juice in clear glasses.

Where did she get all this? Did she even squeeze the juice from the fruit?

"Did More give you these things?"

"He likes me. Said I could take what I wanted. He even had fresh real beef."

"Human?"

"No. From beef cows, on the surface…the kind with four legs. He just got it in before I got there."

Loki laughed delighted. He sniffed the air again.

"You've used tomatoes…and onions."

She nodded excitedly. "Dig in!"

"There is something I should tell you before we eat. Felines do not digest vegetables well; they cannot eat onions and garlic. It is toxic to them…"

Tusha's face fell, and he thought she would cry. Loki knew what was going through her mind even though he didn't read the thoughts:

I did all that work, and he can't eat it.

He regretted instantly, he'd had to hurt her with his warning.

"But…you are fortunate I am also half Noor. The Noor palette can tolerate any food. My momma Dia and her mate Kimon are pure Feline…"

"She would never make this…I've made such a mistake…"

"Not so. Momma makes this on special days, but when she does, she makes separate meal for Kimon and her. It is my favorite."

That brought a smile back to her face. "Eat!" she ordered. "Before it gets cold."

He dug in without any more argument.

****

He was so full he could barely move. Loki had eaten two plates full before he'd ever touched his drink. Now, he sat back sipping the juice, as he watched Tusha clear away the leftovers.

It suddenly dawned on him; this juice had an unusual flavour. "Where did you get this?"

"More said it's juice from a Noor fruit. He'd been saving it for a long time."

Oh, spit! It's a Noor aphrodisiac! How do I tell her?

Loki set his glass aside. He'd only drunk half.

Will it affect me, too?

And oh, gosh! How much did she have? She is so little, and with her Noor blood mix ...this is going to send her into heat!

"Don't you like the juice? If you don't want it, I'll drink it."

"I'd rather have water. How much is left?"

She looked a bit sheepish. "I drank most of it...sorry. I was thirsty, and it tasted real good to me. I'll get you the water..."

Spit! Spit! Spit! What am I going to do now? Maybe she will just sleep it off?"

"Come," he said, patting the mat on which he sat. "I don't need the water; we sleep now."

Tusha yawned largely, and slumped down beside him willingly. She was asleep in an instant. And Loki followed her just as quickly.

****

He awoke with a start; the little she was on top of him, her legs spread-eagle over his hips. Sometime in her sleep she had slipped off her sheath, and was now naked on top of him. Loki knew what that meant. Her need was unbearable, and he couldn't just leave her in such agony.

That stupid drink awakened her physical Noor! Oh, Almighty...I can't leave her to bear this torture! She'll go mad if I don't do something.

In her sleep, she did not know what she was doing. Her body moved against him, over his hidden sensitive place. The return arousal shot through him, and will power faded. He too had had enough drink to bring undeniable desire.

He kissed her tiny human ear, and need became immense hunger, with nature's response following.

Half awake now, she let him in. His ability to stop was non-existent.

And so he loved her, gently, tenderly, carefully, his huge hands caressing soft skin, the minute breasts, relieving the intense desperate yearning inside both of them. His pleasure equaled hers.

She slept again…and so did he.

****

When he woke fully refreshed, she lay wide-awake beside him.

As her eyes turned to him, he felt sudden shame. He had never meant it to go this far; never intended to be intimate. He blamed the drink; but the beverage had merely done what it was meant to do. Even though, when he'd realized its potent nature, and would take not another swallow, it had already been too late.

Now, he blamed More.

He surely knew what he was giving Tusha.

Perhaps, by some misguided desire to help them, the Root had generously parted with that prize possession, thinking it beneficial for all.

But it isn't! It has unbelievably complicated things. Tusha and I can't be together!

And that means; I have violated her.

If this had happened back home, it would be considered rape, punishable by a quick violent death at the hands of her male family members.

Perhaps, Tusha would defend me...and then we would be mated for life.

But here, even though the fact was hidden, and no punishment meted out...he couldn't be hers...and she couldn't come with him.

"I am sorry," he whispered softly in his Noor tongue. He knew she understood the meaning of his words, and to what he referred. She had the Noor blood; it made her a linguist.

He shifted to sit, rose up, stepped over her, and fled to the shower.

****

She watched his every move, as he clothed himself. At last Tusha broke the silence.

"Do you have a wife, then? Is that why you don't want me?"

Loki shook his head in denial. He answered her in Noor, telepathically.

"I am a conjunctive twin male; I cannot reproduce on my own."

She returned, also by mental voice. "There are two parts to you?"

"Yes. This is not all of me; I am only half here."

She didn't doubt him. "You are the physical part, the part that can make love?"

He groaned at being reminded. "I am the physical, yes, but we both can satisfy…my other is the thinker, the mind capacity. We need to be together to procreate."

"Besides," he added. "By law, a conjunctive male is forbidden to take a mate…I am Noor…"

"Why?" she asked bluntly.

"The reasoning is, we might infect our partner…"

Tusha laughed. "Didn't you already do that some time ago?"

His ire rose up. "I did that to save your life! Would you rather I had not?"

She shook her head.

I would much sooner live than die.

But she meant to bring him to task for his actions, to make him squirm.

"You are more than Noor; you are also Feline. Aren't Felines allowed to mate? Why don't you want me?" she challenged again.

Once more, he was evasive. "I alone cannot procreate; my mental and I must join …junction, to be fertile. I cannot choose our mate wisely…because I go by my feelings. He must want the female…first…" His eyes tracked away to the side, guiltily.

Tusha knew there was something more to this, an underlying misdirection, but she did not probe for his other reasons, let it go, and tackled the matter at hand. "So, being Feline, in your opinion, this was for mere gratification?"

She felt it, as the blunt assessment shocked him; his heart slammed against his ribs, beating faster.

Is that fear? Of me?

Loki sucked a breath, tears forming in his eyes, as if she'd cut him to the very quick.

What is he hiding?

She tried to enter his mind to see, but somehow, he had blocked the reading.

He's never done that before!

He said nothing more, finished dressing, and finally, escaped to go to work.

But, she wasn't about to let him have the last say. Just as he left the room, she fired after him: "Go then, you coward! See if I care!"

Her tears came hot and heavy then, both from the loss she felt, and regret at being so cruel to him. She knew she had used him as a scapegoat. She had needed someone to blame, and he had been the easy victim, when all he'd meant to do was help her.

****

"Where's your little she today?" asked Uel.

"She is mad at me?" hissed Loki, the words slipping out before he'd given them thought. He sighed.

Too late to take them back.

Uel chuckled. "What did you do? Were you unsatisfactory, or did you mate to her?"

Loki frowned, turned to stare at the Feline male.

What is this? Did Uel put More up to his tricks?

Loki growled, knowing his suspicions were correct.

"Why don't you find a female for yourself?" he hissed. "That's what Bom has ordered."

242

He glared at the male until Uel dropped his eyes, and slunk away.

****

That night Loki brought home another smaller pallet, prepared it with padding and a small soft blanket, lifted Tusha from his own bed, and placed her on her own.

The fact that he was separating them cut her more deeply than anything else he might do. By such an action, it was as if he was saying:

You are just a servant, a pet, something to use. Stay away from me, unless I need you.

He gave no explanation, only turned over, and went to sleep.

That night Tusha cried, softly and quietly, so he wouldn't hear.

****

Through the next few days she went obediently with him to the med bay again. In quiet submission, she followed after. He made no effort to engage in conversation, either outwardly or by thought. It seemed, he was regretful and subdued, as well.

Every night Tusha cried; each time she became more uncontrolled. Rejection hurt more than death.

Then on the third night, unable to watch her suffer, Loki relented. He came to her, gently gathered her in his arms, and took her into bed with him, where he cuddled behind her, until they were deep again in slumber.

He had realized, life was too cruel of its own, to have them spend their last days, apart in disagreement.

And so they slept together each night from then on.

CHAPTER 35

"She's just not there, anywhere on the surface!" Liam exploded in frustration. "Even using the sensor to attach to a Noor gleam, there is nothing! Where is she? She couldn't just up and vanish!"

Leaning over his shoulder to see the screen better, Nyle asked: "Did you check if she's been on the world's social media sites? She usually keeps in contact with us that way."

"Yes, I've checked them all, but it's entirely possible she's avoiding those, because the police are looking for her. I've also checked the available vid-cameras in the areas where she might be. I did find something strange." Liam sat back, and whirled his chair around to face his brother and Nyle.

"What did you find?" asked Nyle, slipping into another chair.

"The last time she was in the building where she lived, on the camera downstairs, a neighbor let someone in, that was obviously in disguise…"

"Disguised, how?" Shiveron asked suspiciously.

"It was wearing a camouflage belt."

"One like ours?"

Liam nodded.

"What are you saying?" Nyle asked.

"He's implying, your momma might be in the hands of the Roog," Shiveron supplied.

"Liam?" Nyle demanded. "How is that possible?"

"It's not good to jump to conclusions. Anyway, I've put a tag on her web site. If she ever checks it, we'll know immediately. If she doesn't, I'll have to make a trip to the surface of the Forbidden planet to search for her."

"Don't side track me, Liam," Nyle commanded. "I'm not a stupid, uneducated human any longer."

Liam and Shiveron exchanged a look of regret.

"Okay," Liam yielded. "But as I said before; it's not good to assume anything…"

"Just tell me what you suspect."

"The Roog have a prison facility in the bowels of the planet…"

"Inside Earth? How come we don't know about that?"

Liam laughed mirthlessly. "If humans knew…well, at the very least, there would be worldwide panic. Anyway…we are pretty sure the Roog hunt humans. Now, why a human would let one into a building is puzzling…"

"What do they want with humans?" Nyle interrupted.

"Aw, Nyle," Liam reproached. "You don't really want to know…"

"Stop beating around the bush. Just tell me!"

"They eat humans," Shiveron said quietly.

"Oh shit! Oh shit!" Nyle covered his eyes with his hands, as if that might end the image that came to mind. "Why? Why'd he take my mother? Any other would be a better choice if they wanted…gosh! Mom's build wasn't big; she was average. There were plenty of grossly obese women in her building. Why her?"

"We don't know that's what happened, Nyle. I should never, even, have suggested it."

"Then explain to me, why was that thing in her building at all the night she disappeared? And how come she's the only one now missing?"

Just at that moment, one of the Feline orderlies from the med floor stuck his head in the door of the communication centre. "Hey, human. Nyle."

Nyle spun, annoyed by the interruption. "What?"

"Everyone out here is wondering whether you are stupid or something. Didn't they train you?"

Both Liam and Shiveron hissed at the disrespect to Twila's new promised.

"Spit it out, male!" Liam ordered viciously. "If you have something to say to him, speak plainly, or we will have your carcass for your insolence."

The male immediately took a docile attitude, dropping his eyes. "Aww...Twila..."

"What about Twila?" Nyle enquired, obviously, immediately expecting trouble.

"Twila is..."

"Is what?" Liam demanded, suspicious now, as well.

"She's...cursing and fighting with us all...we know what that means...just thought you should know."

It wasn't like their sister to be even argumentative; she was usually mild mannered, and gentle with both patients and staff. This could only signify one thing.

Nyle's jaw dropped in stupefied reaction. "You don't mean..."

"Yeah..." The male grinned lecherously. "You don't see to her soon, one of us will, and that'll cost you your place with her..."

All three Noor males hissed menacingly, but it was Nyle who spit out an answer. "You so much as try, you'll forfeit your life. I guarantee, she won't have anyone of you. It's me she has chosen!"

"Then you'd better get her to an ante, before she kills someone!"

"Go, Nyle!" Liam growled. "We'll deal with this insubordinate."

And the human-Noor took off, as if fire had lit the tail he didn't have.

****

Twila could hear the plaintive whining, as if from a distance. She knew it was her own voice, but she neither recognized she was doing it, nor understood why. She felt detached, as if outside her body.

So angry, I so want to tear at the faces of those around me, to bite, to claw.

And indeed, she realized, her weapons were out.

What is wrong with me?

She was tearing at the sheets on the cot she stood by, throwing things, sending the tray of instruments across the room. Yelling, growling, hissing awful words at the leering faces of the watching males.

What is the matter with me? I'm never like this. I'm making a fool of myself, before the entire contender Feline population.

For years, she had held at bay this needful madness, kept herself sane and in restraint.

Why is this happening now, at this moment?

Outside of her body, with her mind near absent, above reality, she had lost control. The insanity had taken her over.

Not since she had reached first maturity, had she ever felt such fever.

Heat! Hot. Angry. Pulsing need!

Oh, man! Where is Nyle! I need so badly!

Gasping, skin burning; flesh crawling. Driving urgent hunger!

"Get me Nyle!" she screamed. "I need my Nyle! I need him...I need him," Twila moaned, beside herself.

Tears flooded, knees buckled; next came sobbing incoherency.

"Male...man...Nyle...help me!" escaped the kneeling, in mumbled stutters.

No wonder they call being Noor an infection!

And then alleviating solace, he was there, catching her up into his arms, flying through the aisles, carrying her...to Dia's ante.

****

Nyle opened his eyes, still very exhausted. Twila lay beside him, softly crying. He reached over to take her into his arms but...she withdrew from him.

"Twila," he pleaded. "Was I not...good enough. Didn't I do it right?"

She sobbed all the harder. Once more, he made the effort to bring her close. And at last, she went into him, weeping piteously.

After she had calmed a bit, Nyle again whispered his question.

"Why are you crying? Did I maybe hurt you?"

Against his shoulder, Twila shook her head.

"I am so ashamed. I never meant it to happen like this. I haven't had heat, since my first mating...I wanted our first time to be special...a willful encounter. Instead, I shamed myself...us, before the entire med bay. And, oh Nyle...it is I who should ask: did I hurt you?"

Nyle laughed, both relieved and self-conscious. "Well...it was definitely a wild ride. I've never known anyone quite like you."

For a second, Twila faded in embarrassment.

"Hey," he chided. "Come back, girl. I'm certainly not sorry. But, next time we'll take it more slow and easy. It will be even better than this time."

"You are not angry, that I waited too long?"

"Never. How could I be mad at you? It's just, the whole thing caught me off guard."

"It must have been all the stress," Twila excused. "You're being attacked; the thought of losing you...I'm sorry."

"I'm not," he repeated. "This means, I'm yours now, for life. Right?"

"Yep!" She squirmed tight up against him, and he relished the closeness. "And you are stuck with me!"

"Oh, I like that, female!"

Twila laughed, and hugged him harder.

CHAPTER 36

Tusha had no more chocolate to give away, but she still always sat up on the examining cot, as Loki tended his pregnant patients. It was more difficult to encourage and comfort them now, as Tusha felt just as despondent as they. The full realization of her situation had finally hit home.

She had guessed the real purpose behind Loki's actions: she had heard Bom say it, give Loki two more months to serve, but the actuality of it, brought home the fact that eventually, he was going home. And no doubt, she couldn't come with.

Was that what Bom told him, when he sent me away to talk privately with Loki? Did he give some alternative, Loki has no power to refute?

She was certain that had been why he had tried to distance himself.

Tusha had gathered; Loki didn't want her to probe for the answers in his mind, so she did not try again. One thing she had learned from his blocking her was how to do the same to another, and so their silences were truly excluding, their minds barred to each other, the severance complete.

The fact that Loki had done this with her caused Tusha to wonder if he wasn't already on his way out of prison.

Where will that leave me? Back where I was at the beginning?

It made her shudder with dread for the future.

Behind Loki, at the entrance to the tunnel that led to the cells, an aged human black man appeared.

"I need the one called Loki," he shouted timidly.

Everyone ignored him. Loki was preoccupied, and the man wore no translator, so the others did not understand his words. Only Uel reacted.

"What does that human want?" he hissed in annoyance. "Why can't they give them a communication device so we can understand them?"

Tusha pulled at Loki's hand. Apparently preoccupied with his own thoughts, he looked at her in puzzlement.

"The man behind, in the doorway, wants you…"

Loki turned around.

"What would you like?"

Uel hissed in frustration. "You, too. Do you have to cater to them by conversing in that stupid gibberish?"

"I speak your tongue…to the annoyance of other kinds," Loki rebuked.

Again, he addressed the old man. "What do you want, human? Do you have a name?"

The senior was shaking visibly. "I am called Norris, but none have used my given name for years…The master, Bom, has said, if I do not bring you quickly to the kitchens, I will lose my life by his hand."

Without further consideration, Loki turned to Uel, and switched to the Feline tongue. "I am needed in the kitchens. Take over my patients."

Tusha was somewhat shocked.

Why is Loki not objecting? It isn't like him to leave a patient, even at Bom's bidding.

Perhaps, he thinks to save the old man a violent death? We all know the warden could inflict it.

With the human leading, Loki took off so quickly Tusha almost got left behind. At the last minute, before they disappeared, she jumped from the exam table, and hurried after the pair.

****

Norris flew toward the kitchens fearing for his life. There had been way too much delay.

Life was always preferable to death, no matter how gruesome existence in the kitchens was. And even though he was near seventy, he'd been spared the hellish death of those called 'meat'. Along with his Caucasian wife, Downy, he'd been given the pleasant chore of baking the endless loaves of bread for the population, and the pair, in turn, fed well off their labours. They were much better off than most.

Breathless, he arrived in the kitchens, leading the physician, Loki, and as he turned around, he realized another human had followed. This one had been sitting on the cot, watching the Noor work. He took her by the arm, and pulled her back.

But Bom noticed.

"Ha! Finally! And you bring his she-pet with you. Good! She can watch! Come here, male!"

Trembling, almost unable to breathe for fear of the giant cat-like dog, Norris moved forward, alone.

"Stand before me, in the middle," ordered Bom.

As Norris obeyed, Loki objected, challenging Bom. "Leave him be. If we are tardy, it is my fault. What is your whim, this time?"

"Ha! So you mock me, do you Noor? What have I told you about that?"

"Just tell me what you want, and I'll do your bidding, without question."

"Will you now?" Bom pointed to Norris. "Put it down!"

Loki was suddenly silent. Norris began to moan. He heard Downy, behind the scenes; go to softly keening with dread.

And then the physician spoke, giving respite.

"I am healer, Bom. I've told you many times, I do not kill."

"Put it down!"

"No!"

"Then it is your life, I will take!"

****

Tusha watched in horror, as Bom raised the weapon wand. She had never seen it used, never fully understood the vulnerable position the belt placed Loki in.

Bom pressed the handle of the stick-like apparatus; Loki folded to his knees, gasping.

Tusha felt a hand upon her arm once again, directing her to go into hiding with the other humans. Using a habit she'd acquired from the Roog guards, she growled under her breath, as she fled beneath the cutting counters in the room, out of the way of Bom's anger, leaving the centre to the two would be combatants.

If Loki can just fight back! Surely, Bom doesn't fully have the upper hand; Loki must have some defense.

Tusha watched as Bom changed the setting on the wand, raised it again, and the instrument shot out a black ray toward Loki.

254

She almost screamed when she saw the result.

Blood spurted; a deep jagged gash appeared across his chest from shoulder to opposite hip. And then came another, and another…

Tusha's eyes flashed a rainbow hue, but no one else saw. Suddenly Loki's words were in her head.

He'll put you in a belt too. Be wise, female. Don't reveal yourself.

She trembled with the effort to hold back. Instead of fighting for him, as she was inclined to do, she remained in obscurity, knowing he was right, and this was not the time to challenge.

Even in his agony, Loki is protecting me.

Tears sprang to her eyes, as they went back to the normal hue of blue again.

I was so angry with Loki, and all along, he's known this moment would come!

Bom continued, strike after strike…until Loki fell forward on his belly, unconscious.

The Roog/cat moved forward, kicked at the prostrate form, rolled the Noor to his back with one foot. Bom was facing away from her; Tusha could easily have taken him…

Maybe?

The doubt, and Loki's warning, caused her to hold back.

"Are you dead yet, Noor?" Bom laughed. "Well, if you aren't, we'll just turn your belt up a notch." He reached over, a key in his hand, pushed it into a slot she had never noticed on the belt before; then adjusted the setting.

When he stepped back, Bom pressed the wand again. Loki began convulsing; frothing at the mouth, chewing his extended tongue, blood mingling with the foam sliding from his lips. Moisture spread across his leggings, as his body released the bodily waste.

Tusha closed her eyes, disturbed by his violent treatment and imposed shame. She could no longer watch.

****

When the Noor male finally stilled, Bom turned and peered about him. "Where are you, humans? Come out; come out, wherever you are. Where is that head male? Darren! Where are you?" His voice took on the thunder of command. "Get out here!"

As a frightened Asian human crawled out into the open, Bom snarled at him. "You will not tend to this one's wounds; do you hear? He is to be left to die a slow, painful death, lying in his own filth!"

When the kitchen overseer nodded that he understood, Bom growled back at the small human man. "Get these creatures back to work! The feasting begins soon, and we hunger. Git!"

The thin human fled, calling out, as he went, for his other workers to join him.

Bom turned on his heel, and strode from the enormous cavern of a kitchen, to join his comrades in orgy.

I am so looking forward to this night; I am going to celebrate!

It seems, he had already forgotten his victim, and equally, the small, supposedly human pet that followed after Loki, considering her of little consequence.

A mistake he had now repeated twice, one that would eventually come back to plague him...if she had any hidden skill at all.

CHAPTER 37

Tusha didn't crawl out from under the counter until the sounds of Roog revelry beyond the kitchen had died down. The entire time, Loki had not moved.

She was certain he was dead. And when she approached his side, she felt sure of it. His body looked like a steak on which a tenderizer mallet had been used. It was crisscrossed with ugly cuts, some deep enough to expose the bone.

Loki lay on his back, his arms at his sides, the hands open, as if he were paralyzed, and couldn't move them had he wanted. His eyes were closed; mouth slightly open, dried spittle and blood on his chin, and at the corners of his lips.

At his waist, the traitorous weapon, the deadly belt, still held him captive.

If he is able to recover at all, that must be removed!

But it appeared too late for that.

Tusha knelt beside him. Then suddenly overcome with the loss of him, she gently lay down spread-eagle across his chest, hugging him with all her might. The tears came hot and heavy.

The kitchen workers around them did not stop their constant labors, simply stepped around them, carrying out tasks. While others worked, some took turns in pairs to go to a corner and sleep. Obviously, there were mouths, other than Roog, to feed after sleep break, and in here, the preparation of food never stopped.

Loki's body was cold, but as she lay over him, Tusha felt the shallow ragged breaths. When she realized how near to death he was, she could not check her sobs. Weeping shook her form. She placed her cheek next to his.

It wasn't until she felt movement against her face that Tusha became aware of where her tears were travelling. Loki had widened the gap of his lips so his tongue could escape, and as the moisture made its way from the corner of her eyes to his lips, he was licking across his teeth to take in the wetness.

With sudden clarity, Tusha knew what to do.

****

She was on her feet in a second, searching the room for a water tap. Over in a corner, a facet was dripping silently, one drop at a time, on the floor. Beside it was a ladle.

Tusha fled to the waterspout, filled the dipper with fresh water, and brought it to Loki. But then, she was faced with a dilemma.

How am I going to lift his head, and give the water at the same time? Loki is twice my size.

And then, of all people, Darren stood beside her. He did not speak, simply went around behind Loki's head, and slipped his arms beneath the shoulders, raising him, so Loki could drink.

"You will get in trouble," Tusha cautioned, as she tipped the dipper up, so Loki could imbibe the liquid.

The Asian grunted. "If I, a human man, have become so cold as to not give water to a dying man, I am no better than these dogs, and I do deserve my fate."

Tusha liked this Asian.

Loki did not open his eyes, and when he sipped the water, he needed to gasp for air between, as if he were damaged deep inside. Nonetheless, he would not stop until all the liquid had been drained from the container. When the task was accomplished, Loki went limp, and Darren eased him down on his side, so if what he had taken in decided to come back up, Loki wouldn't choke. Then the human went back to what he'd been doing.

Tusha decided, first order of business was to get Loki out of the drain-belt. Leaving him to rest, she began to search the nearby drawers for some utensil to jimmy the lock.

Suddenly, a pleasantly plump white woman stood at her side.

"I think I have what you need," she said, slipping a straight small piece of metal into Tusha's hand. "It was in a drawer at the back that holds cast-off keys."

"You have a key for the drain-belt?" Tusha challenged suspiciously. "How did you just happen to have such a thing here in the kitchen?"

"It was before my arrival here," the woman explained. "From when they killed the Noor queen. The story passed down is, after her physical died, they brought the carcass to us to prepare it, and gave us a key to unlock her belt. The Roog never reclaimed it, because of what happened after."

"What did happen?"

"When the Roog ate her meat, they got very sick. Those that had eaten it died a horrible death, rotting from the inside. That's why the Roog consider the Noor a contamination. The virus was incompatible with their systems, and killed them instead of giving them the anomaly."

This explanation gave Tusha new insight, and the truth of it was both fascinating and disconcerting, considering how she had been infected. It could have gone either way, even with her.

The story put the Roog/Feline warden in an entirely different light.

Is this why Bom hates Loki so much?

But Tusha had a more immediate question she wanted answered.

"And…why are you helping me, when you know Bom warned against it?"

"Your male saved my Norris. I am Downy, his partner. We owe you…him. If there is anything else we can do, just ask. Oh, yes. And when you've turned the key, you need to press two points at the back of the belt to make it open in the front."

Then Downy faded back into the shadows, to return to the work she'd been doing.

****

Tusha went to work on the belt immediately. The key did fit the lock, and turned easily, but when she eased her hands to the back of the instrument, Tusha could only touch one small pressure oval at a time; she could not reach around Loki's entire girth.

She sat back to think.

I can get help from Norris or Darren, but, they are in enough jeopardy already. Why risk them further, when it is not necessary?

Tusha looked around her, made sure all eyes were turned away. Then with her mind, she willed the small round buttons on the back of the belt to depress. There was a quiet click as both disks released, and then, the front of the belt parted in the middle and slid open.

Loki's eyes flew open. He had realized, what she had done. The astonishment that she could manipulate to that extent was written in his eyes. Then weakly, he surrendered to the silent waiting, closing his eyes once again.

She pulled at the offending item, trying to rip it away, but it was somehow sticking to his skin.

Loki gasped, as the quick pull set him free. It was then she realized, there were spike-like probes inserted into the flesh on the other side.

Oh man! What new agony have I inflicted upon him? If I had known that belt had barbs imbedded in his flesh, I would not have yanked so hard.

Loki reassured by thought.

To pull away slow, would have been far more excruciating.

She looked at him annoyed.

You could have warned me.

Too much effort to thought project.

He never once opened his eyes.

She harrumphed aloud.

****

He seemed to sleep after that, absorbing the energy from the bare light fixtures hanging everywhere. Tusha went for a basin and water, and though the water had come from the lava heated underground beneath them, it was only pleasantly warm.

And so she bathed his wounds, while he slumbered.

CHAPTER 38

Loki opened his eyes, and gazed around him. His sight was returning; hearing, as well, and with feeling, he was also aware of many aches, and...his nakedness. His clothing had been shredded in the vicious attack.

Tusha lay asleep in the crook of his left arm, weary from emotional battle, and physical ministrations on his behalf done during the many days that had passed.

The kitchens continued to be an active place. He still lay at the centre of the enormous cavern; he'd been too heavy, and in too much pain to be moved, and his little she would leave his side only for the bare necessity and only to a short distance away.

Bom had not come back to gloat, nor had he sent any of his sentries to check the progress of his dying nemesis.

Loki could now see to the walls far away in the shadows. The room was as big as the storage area beneath his home nest back on the med ship of his foster mother, Dia. The cavern had obviously, long ago, once been a large granite grotto, complete with an excessively high ceiling, reaching beyond the vision range of most.

Though of a primitive nature, it amazed him how well equipped the facility was. All along the walls, forming a circle, the monster ovens sat, their stacks reaching and disappearing into the expanse above. There was no smoke in the dimly lit room, so Loki assumed there must be an escape hole above, through which the acrid vapour passed out and away.

Closer into the room were the cutting tables, also in a circle, and then the empty space in which he and Tusha lay. At junctions, breaks between tables existed, these each leading out, one to the feasting area of the Roog, another to the storage rooms, and a third and fourth and fifth, accessing the tunnels to other parts of the prison, such as the meat cages, the med bay, and the sleeping area of the prisoners. Loki assumed the Roog had another access, beyond their eating area, which lead into their own sleep quarters, though he had been to that area only from another direction.

Ignoring the constant activity around him, he gazed up to the high, impenetrable gloom above, pondering, wondering.

Is there a way out up there?

It was so high above, and the walls were like sheer cliffs, no human could ever climb out, as was attested to by the fact, no one had ever escaped, and apparently had not even tried.

If that was the way out, the Roog seemed confident, it could not be gotten to…not even by a Feline.

Maybe a Slither could? But, none are in captivity in here.

And then Loki's thoughts went to what Tusha had done with his belt.

Can she maybe find a way up?

At thoughts of her, almost as if Tusha sensed her companion wished to talk, the small female at his side stirred, stretched, and yawned.

He waited until she opened her eyes; let her lay there for a time until she awakened fully.

Finally, motioning upward with his chin, he directed her to look. "See the ceiling?"

"Yes."

"Notice the smoke?"

After looking at the different blackened metal chimneys, she returned her eyes to the large overhead dome. "There is none."

"So, where does it go?"

Again, she pondered the dark recesses above them. For long moments she said nothing. "You think, there's a way out up there?" she finally asked.

Loki didn't have to voice it; such a prospect was the desire of everyone in the facility.

"Do you think you could get up there to find out?"

"Not sure…"

"Will you try? For me?"

****

Tusha stood at the wall, back in a shadowy corner away from the constant bustle. Here it was the darkest, and mostly hidden from the view of those coming through the tunnels on the far side of the kitchens.

The storage rooms that held extra supplies like flour and the bread makings, the fruit that came in, and other things, were just beyond, around the curve of a closer tunnel.

This location was where they mixed the dough for the loaves that were continually being prepared. It was also the noisiest place in the kitchen, because either the giant dough machine was rocking and shaking as it stirred its load, or the machine was being cleaned out with strong smelling detergents in preparation of receiving another batch.

Those with these duties kept mostly to themselves, not only excluded, but isolated from the rest by choice; they preferred to feed themselves, often sneaking some of what they prepared on the sly.

It was the perfect spot to search out a path to the top.

Tusha looked up at the sheer granite face.

How can anyone climb that?

There was a way...but it meant she must use manipulation. Loki, she was certain, had considered that.

And, if I make a path up, is there any way out at the top?

She looked back at the activity out in the kitchen centre. Only Loki was watching her.

Okay. I promised to try to find a way out, if there is one. That smoke, up above, gets out somehow. But is the opening big enough to crawl through, and what is on the other side?

Tusha touched the wall at her shoulder level, and willed the indentation. A slit big enough to place a toe or a hand appeared.

But, though that would do for an agile person, those of lesser ability, such as all the aged in here, would have difficulty boosting up to the mark. So, she made another just at knee level. Then placing foot and hand in the appropriate holds, Tusha began to climb.

Again, an opening appeared just where it was needed for her other foot, and another above the handhold, each gap emerging at a comfortable distance, so that a small human person could mount the wall...all in shadow, out of sight, not visible from below, unless you stood right inside the corner and searched.

They need to place a piece of equipment just out from this wall to block sight, so no one can see the coming or going.

It seemed her actions had been noted by Darren, and he had been struck with the same idea, for he ordered Norris to help him, and they began moving the gigantic dough mixer over to the corner to hide what she was doing.

It was a good thing the two men were so focused on their purpose; neither realized she wasn't just finding the handholds, but was actually making them.

Once she had reached the area above their heads, Tusha blended with the shadows.

****

Tusha had reached the top, and just even with her chin was a hole big enough for two people to crawl through...large enough for someone the size of Loki to fit through easily.

She peered inside. There was a ledge on the other side, so she pulled herself over the lip, and dropped into what appeared to be a narrow tunnel, leading away into the darkness. The only problem, it was filled with acrid smoke.

And, she could not stand upright in it.

Tusha tried not to cough, but she couldn't hold her breath for long, so she crawled rapidly forward and around a bend. Here the space became less congested; it widened and also increased in height.

She stood up, made her way along, until the wall on one side suddenly disappeared, dropped into endless, black space.

Tusha proceeded, carefully now, less she fall to her death, along the ledge, until she found a second enclosed tunnel large enough for her to walk upright. As she progressed, she realized there was no smoke here, and even better, there was fresh air gently blowing passed her cheek.

There is a way out! We just needed to travel the course.

It suddenly dawn on her she'd been gone a long time. She could not examine the rest of the way. It was time to get back to Loki.

If Bom comes, finds him out of the belt, there is no telling what he might do.

CHAPTER 39

Darren, and Norris, Tusha and Downy, and Loki were gathered in a corner debating the best means to go about the escape attempt.

"Someone needs to stay behind," Darren decided. "We can't all go at once. It's better if only a few go this time, make sure there is a way out. When we hear back, we can plan for another group to leave then."

"Just a few, would be wise," Loki concurred. "That way they won't be so easily missed, and the route out can be kept secret."

Tusha was thinking ahead. "When we get up there, we should set up safe places to go for those coming out…like the safe houses used for refugees."

"That is a good suggestion," Norris agreed. "Many will be unfamiliar with life up there. Most of us have been down here a long time."

"And probably, many things have changed," Downy added.

"Also, we don't want them to find us, and recapture us again," Norris pointed out.

"These are all good suggestions," Loki admitted. "So, who will be the first?"

Downy and Norris looked at one another; a silent agreement seemed to pass between them. "We'll go. I don't know how we'll do it, but we're willing to set up and maintain a halfway place, but you'll have to give us time to do that."

"Won't you be missed quicker than anyone else?" asked Loki. "Isn't your duty to see to the bread?"

"Those under us are trained to take over if something were to happen to us," Downy supplied. "We'd like to be first, if that's okay with you, Darren?"

"As I said, I prefer to stay behind. There's nothing up there for me. I can more easily cover for those that disappear. I'm the only one in here with a translator, and it's me the Roog usually deal with. Like Downy says, things are set up so both she and Norris can easily be replaced."

"Okay then," Loki agreed. "Who else? Tusha goes, for certain. Bom will be seeking to take her life."

Darren nodded. "And you must go, Noor."

Tusha broke in. "I want to take Beth…"

Loki hissed in rejection of that. "That will not be easy. That means we must delay until another night when the Roog are in stupor."

Tusha frowned. "But…isn't the purpose to set those in the cages free? I'd like to take those left in the meat cages, as well. The Roog will simply think they'd all been eaten."

"She has a point there," Darren agreed.

Loki sighed. He had hoped to set Tusha free this night, but he surrendered, seeing the wisdom in waiting.

"Well then, let's set the date to go as of two nights from now. That will also give me more time to get back on my feet."

Consensus was unanimous.

****

Tusha slipped silently into More's establishment. He had his back to her, as he rearranged his produce. She moved to stand just beside him, waiting until he noticed her.

"Ha!" he said, shocked, when he turned. Stepping back to peer at her, like a farsighted individual, he added, "Loki's little she not dead, after all."

She quickly switched to his tongue, answering at a mere whisper.

"Does More still wish to leave this place?"

He frowned, if you could consider that a tree creature could pucker its brow. "More go, if he could. Yes. Why?"

"We have found a way to the world above. Come with us, we leave night after this."

"Ha!" he said again, then thought a while. At last, he spoke regretfully. "More cannot live on surface. He have nobody to talk to, and primitives of my kind up there are ...stupid."

"More is afraid," challenged Tusha.

"Yes," he agreed quietly. "Be alone there. Better stay here. Have lived beneath for so long; don't know how to live another place. But, More keep secret. When you leave above place, send space flier back for More. I go then to Loki's land."

"Ah, Moore." Tusha shook her head, saddened.

"Okay then," she agreed. "But don't you betray us. Someday, I'll come back and free you. I promise."

"More know. Sometime, you be Queen again. More say, proud to know you, then."

Tusha laughed.

As she fled back toward the kitchens, she wondered:

Does that old Root have the foretelling eye?

****

271

The urgent hungers for food and fleshly release abated; the brawling and antagonistic challenges lessened; and the frantic gratification of open coupling ended.

The dogs grew still, each participant staggering off drunkenly to its chamber, to sleep off the fatigue from the exertion orgy required, leaving behind their empty dining hall in all its cluttered disarray.

The only activity that remained was in the area of the ever-functioning kitchens.

Tonight was the night!

****

As Tusha made her way along the aisles between the reeking meat cages, the tunnels were deserted. Most cells were empty, save for the last two at the end. Each of these contained ten or fifteen occupants: one cell for women, the other for men.

She knew, the keys to the sliding rail doors were on the belts of the Roog sentries…and all those were gone to their beds. But, that fact did not bother the small human Noor. No one else was with her to see, nor would the beleaguered, despondent prisoners care about how it was done, when the barriers slid away.

Tusha placed her hand against the bars, willed them to glide back into its space. And not only did the gate open, but it did it soundlessly.

In the dimness, all fear filled eyes turned her way.

"We have found a way out," she whispered, but it seemed to ignite no emotion of hope in their breasts. "Go back…to the kitchens…if you wish to be free."

Many slunk deeper into the dark recesses, disbelieving, but one brave woman chose to challenge. "Why should we believe you? It's other humans who help take us off to that place to become…the dogs' next meal."

"Their feasting is over for the night, but the way out we've found is through the kitchen. Come please! When you get there, ask for Darren."

Yet, only two women hesitantly approached the gaping doorway, eager for freedom at any cost. Tusha stepped away as they fled, leaving the barrier ajar, in case the others gained enough courage to follow their comrades.

Turning her back, Tusha slid the second gate open. Five impatient, portly men charged the opening, fighting against each other for the right to be first through. Unlike the women, they obviously had listened in, decided before hand, and would do anything to gain their freedom.

As with the ladies, the rest of the male group held back. Once more, Tusha left the barrier open, in case they changed their minds.

Then she fled down a tunnel off to the side, toward the cages of the pregnant ones.

It is time to rescue Beth!

****

Tusha stepped into the cage that held the young girl. It had only two occupants: one fast asleep, the other sitting despondently, staring into middle distance at nothing.

"Beth," Tusha whispered, gently shaking the apathetic teen. "I've come to save you. We have found a way out."

But Beth gave no evidence she had heard.

The second girl beside them stirred. Tusha gave her no mind; it was the adolescent that had come in with her she felt most concerned about, the shattered sufferer.

"Beth…you want your baby safe, don't you?"

Unexpectedly, the eyes came back in focus, met hers. "No baby...just a dream. Bad nightmare...man...rape," Beth muttered, near incoherent. "Baby evil...kill it..."

"It's not evil. I'll not let them kill it," Tusha soothed. "Come with me. You'll get to raise it."

But, Beth went away again to her escape place, responding no further.

The second girl sat up.

"Take me. Oh, please. Take me!" she pleaded.

As Tusha turned, she recognized the young patient who had come to the med bay in tears. She was the one who had wanted to raise her child, not kill it.

Tusha looked at the teenager's belly; she was very near delivery.

How can I refuse? But, can she make it out through the caverns?

"What is your name?"

"Amara." The child was holding her breath in anticipation.

Tusha knew this was a rash decision, but the recollection of what was to happen to the fetus, should the girl be left behind, conquered and over ruled logic and rationality.

"Okay, Amara. I'll take you both. Will you help me with Beth?"

****

A voice from the cage next door broke the silence.

"You would risk all," it rebuked. "For what?"

Tusha's insides went cold.

Lana! They put her that close.

All the woman need do was reach through the bars to torment these two.

How many times has she badgered them with words? They might escape her probing hands by moving across the cage, but her hateful words could always follow wherever they went.

Tusha, the free one, moved out to the other cage door; faced her nemesis through the bars.

"Why do you risk all for the empty minded one?" Lana challenged.

"To preserve the life that dwells inside her!"

"For one baby, you would risk your life?"

"Yes! They have intelligent human beings inside. Most forget that! Not just down here, but above on the surface, as well. To even save one, would never pay the debt of the countless ones destroyed!"

"Then how about saving the creature inside me?"

Tusha pulled in a breath, as if she'd been punched in the gut.

It's true; the baby Lana carries cannot be blamed that her mother is like a vicious animal, nor is it responsible for the way it was conceived.

"If it had been within my power," Tusha fired back. "I would have saved the other child."

Both knew to what she referred.

"Then take me along this time. I'll help you with Beth, and the other one."

Tusha knew this woman could not be trusted, but whether from self-preservation or sudden benevolent empathy, the logic was indisputable.

Tusha touched the bars of the cage containing Lana; they opened silently setting her enemy free.

"You'd better keep up, old woman," Tusha sarcastically threw back over her shoulder, as she guided the other two girls.

And Lana hurried after, silently, amazingly submissive.

CHAPTER 40

When Tusha returned to the kitchens, Loki and Darren were already directing the would-be escapees up the wall. Near the top, Norris could be seen leading the group, and just disappearing through the hole at the top.

"How many do we have?" she wanted to know.

"With the three you just brought," Darren admitted. "There are only twenty."

"That's all?"

It distressed Tusha that only thirteen from the meat stalls had taken advantage of freedom.

Don't they realize, to remain, are sentenced to a horrible excruciating death?

The Roog like their food live; they prefer the fresh kill!

Loki turned from gazing upward, and catching sight of Lana, hissed his disapproval. He knew who she was instantly, for he'd not only seen to her in the med bay, but had viewed visions of this female's vicious behavior toward her, from Tusha's mind.

"Why this one?" he demanded. "Are there not others more worthy?"

Tusha knew appeasement was needed; yet Loki was being judgmental, and as that was not his usual attitude, she felt justified in giving rebuke.

"Love your enemy," she bluntly fired back, as if she were his mate and had the right to rebuff him.

And Loki took it, as the gentle beast he was.

For a second his image faded. When he reappeared, he nodded sheepishly.

"I've been in here too long," he excused. "My right and wrong has become switched. Anytime you see that in me, feel free to bring me back to Noor morality. Thank you."

At his praise, Tusha, felt a sudden warmth. She realized, her image had brightened and quickly returned to normal, apprehensively looking about to see if others had noticed. All eyes were on the ones above. Even those of Lana, who had chosen to ignore Loki's displeasure.

****

They had just gotten in through the hole with the three pregnant women, when Bom thundered into the kitchen with two of his sentries. Loki shooed the women on around the bend, and turned back to join Tusha, just out of sight at the opening. From above, holding their breath to keep from coughing in the acrid smoke, they watched what transpired below.

"Darren!" shouted Bom irately. "Human beast! Where are you? Are you sleeping on the job?"

Darren unhurriedly moved out from behind the dough mixer.

"Here, master. What is your wish?"

Appeased somewhat by the human's submissive attitude, but nevertheless wishing not to appear to show weakness, the Roog/Feline warden bristled visibly.

As if the human were to blame, Bom growled, "Some of the pens housing pregnant cows were left open. We are missing three heifers, one heavy with calf. They cannot have gone far in that condition; are they hiding in here? It will go hard on you, if you keep them from me."

Darren didn't even contemplate his own danger. Truth be told, in his eyes, he'd never viewed humans as cows. Therefore, without a moment's hesitation, he blatantly lied.

"Haven't seen any cows come through here, of any kind."

Bom growled, eying him suspiciously. After a brief interval, when Darren didn't seem to waver, the giant overseer decided, this skinny human would not dare defy him. Not content with what he'd been told, he panned the kitchen with hooded sleep-deprived eyes, and spied the empty central area.

"Where's the Noor's carcass?"

As if surprised, and only just noticing, Darren replied, "Huh! The she must have dragged it from sight. Maybe she hid it in the storage rooms."

Again Bom growled, once more mistrustful of the human's statement, his eyes boring Darren angrily, but the man held his ground bravely. Finally, the warden turned to his Roog companions.

"Find the body! And bring to me the one marked with butterfly. She will not keep hidden from me!"

Sighing with relief, as Bom left the kitchens below, the two above crawled away after the other runaways.

****

Just as Tusha and Loki reached the other side of the ledge, leading passed the shadowy drop away abyss, one of the men from the meat cage came back to them. Before he ever reached them, the reek of him preceded, filling the confining tunnel with the fowl stench that clung to his body. The man's mood, as he approached, was as lethal as his body odour, his stance accusatory.

"There is no way out! It's a dead end!" he shouted. "Norris sent me back to tell you."

The two Noor looked at one another, knowing what needed to be done, each aware also, Loki would never be able to do it, at anytime. Not yet healed properly, nor at full energy, and being only a physical, the deed needed the mind of a mental, which Loki had not.

"I'll stay here with the pregnant ones. You go," Loki offered, for the benefit of those about them.

Tusha slipped away silently, and as she left them, the human messenger made to follow after, back the way he had come, but Loki grabbed his arm, pulling him back.

"No!" he hissed. "You stay with us! I don't want you discouraging the others."

"We are trapped in here!" growled the man angrily. "Why did I think any of you could be trusted? I should have remained where I was."

"You think you were better off in the meat cells?" Loki exploded. "Then go on back!" Pointing behind, the Noor male felt a need to drive home the hopelessness of the past. "Be sure, when you pass through the kitchens, that you tell them how you want to die, as live meat or stew!"

The man sank dejectedly to his knees, and Loki immediately regretted his harsh words. The confining space, the darkness; his still festering injuries, were all taking a toll on his sensibilities.

"Forgive me," he apologized. "I should not have been so cruel. I am not myself..."

The man remained silent, and Loki again felt the desire to boost morale. "We are not trapped! You are better off than you were; no longer dog meat. She will discover a way out; she found the way up from the kitchens..."

The other looked up at Loki almost hopefully, willing at last to give the benefit of the doubt. And Loki read the man's thought:

The little woman did free us from the cages.

****

Loki felt extremely annoyed with himself; he hadn't meant to lose it. Usually, he was more self-controlled, but it seemed, as Tusha left, his surroundings rushed in on him. It was like she'd been shielding him, and now, with the barrier she had provided gone, all negativity descended in a blast.

From the moment the belt had been removed, his empathic sense had exploded, and now, he realized Tusha's mental side had indeed protected. At present, she was out of range, and would be otherwise occupied, and as Loki had not built up resistance, all hell was upon him.

He couldn't cope. Darkness engulfed him, oppressed his spirit. For a Noor, a light needful being, it was like starvation. He had no source of energy. Yes, he'd stored limitedly from the meager lights in the kitchen, but it had not been adequate even there, to heal his body, let alone protect his mind.

And it was not simply the lack of light that chaffed and bombarded him here in the enclosed tunnel, nor the narrow space his larger frame was forced to endure, but being an empath, the feelings of others were his to experience, tenfold: fear from the man beside him; suppressed anger and hatred in Lana; emptiness and brokenness from withdrawn Beth, and worst of all, Amara.

That young teen was not only terrified, but in agony. Each time, he felt the excruciating hot pulse run along her sides, the intolerable cramping spread over the belly, the deep ache of the lower back, as if the very spine was about to crack, he could only be included, not give aid.

This little female is just beginning the early stages of labor.

Normally back home, he would cushion such a one, absorbing the majority of her pain, but here, without sufficient energy at his disposal, he could only share…and wait with her.

To him this was more physically and emotionally draining than to actually give birth, and it left Loki near madness. It was all he could do not to lash out at those around him. With his size and untold strength, had he not been depleted, Loki had the potential for uncontrolled violence.

To top that threat, he also suspected, the baby Amara was delivering, was caught up in the cord, and turned with feet against the back of its mother. Without proper assistance, the birthing would not only take days, but might well cost the life of the mother.

Loki had never felt so helpless in his life. Depression bordered on madness, and all hinged on Tusha: his shield, his would be life companion, his soul mate…the forbidden lover he could not claim.

If Tusha can't make a way out, all will be doomed to die in these dank, confining, black tunnels. And most likely, I will be the first to go, because I lack a light source.

Where will that leave my treasure? I refused to violate her further believing she needed the freedom of choice.

Was it all for nothing? Should I have simply accepted, and given in? If there is no future, why did it matter?

In the darkness, tears formed, slipped down the half Noor's cheeks. He deeply regretted his lack of action, wished he'd done differently.

But, he wasn't one to give up easily.

The Almighty governs our paths; each event has a purpose!

But does that plan include my early demise?

CHAPTER 41

When Tusha arrived at the end of the line, the bulk of the runaways were gathered together, while ten feet away, Norris stood by himself, enclosed on three sides by a closet-like dead end. In rejection of what his eyes told him, the man was still seeking the way through.

Norris turned, when she approached.

"I moved them back," he explained. "Didn't want a panic."

Tusha nodded, stepping around him to consider the condition of the barrier blocking their progress.

"Go back, Norris. Sit and wait with them. Let me look on my own."

"I've examined every inch I can reach…"

"A fresh eye, or…perhaps, I can feel something you've missed…"

He hesitated, reluctant to leave his quest, or maybe to admit, she might find something another could not detect.

"Please? Go back."

He looked at her searchingly, his face lit by the small lantern he held in his hand. It was as if he suspected she was something more than human. At last, seeming to think better of challenging, he set the light at her feet, and turned to join the others.

"Take the lamp, Norris. I prefer to use feel."

Obediently, he picked up the small camp item, and moved away.

****

With Norris out of sight and hearing, Tusha began to feel along the sheer surface. Over in one corner, she did find a small indiscernible crack, but no way was it big enough to pass through. Touching the fracture, she widened it, forcing a bend just big enough for someone such as Loki to pass into. Always, she had in mind; he needed more space than others.

But though she had made a small escape hatch forward, the wall was too thick to continue in such a fashion.

Her eyes turned upward.

That smoke has to be going someplace; it does not sit in this space, and the air is not stale. There is a breeze coming in somehow.

The shadows above hid what was up there from her sight.

Might be to my advantage to climb this wall.

And so she did. As she had in the kitchen, Tusha made her own hand holds; around the corner, out of sight of the humans behind, she ascended.

Once again, as on the ceiling of the kitchen cavern, a small hole went through at the very top. She knew, if she were to find a way beyond, it would take time, and she did not need others watching.

Tusha descended; went to Norris, drawing him aside.

"There is a small hole at the very top."

Norris let out a sigh of relief.

"I'll need time to explore," she cautioned. "I may be gone a while. Tell Loki."

He nodded, and turned to seek someone to send to those left behind.

****

At the top again, Tusha realized the hole was too small even for her to pass through. A cool breeze entered this part of the tunnel, but she could also feel an extreme heat beneath that draft.

That doesn't bode well.

With her hand, Tusha touched the wall surrounding the escape hole. It shimmered, and widened, until it was large enough for Loki to fit through.

But now, heat rushed it with vengeance, stiflingly so, like a vent from hell. Yet above it was the scent of fresh air.

Two currents? One stream of intense heat, another of cooling vapors, one atop the other? The upper shaft beyond must have fresh air, while something hot ran beneath; a lava vent?

Is what lies beyond more deadly to us, than what we left below?

Tusha peered inside:

A sheer drop...but light. Dimly lighted, and a glow far below.

Also beneath, measuring at about a depth of some fourteen feet below, a ledge.

The others will never get down there, especially the pregnant girls. How can I make an easy path to it?

It won't work to just use hand holds...especially for Amara, with her extended belly. She will lose her balance leaning out...she'd fall to her death.

Then an idea struck her:

A rope ladder! With that, one could swing out; it would give the needed equilibrium, and still leave enough space against the wall to accommodate.

And with that thought, a rope ladder formed, complete with iron hooks, clamped to the lip of the entrance hole.

Tusha made her way down easily, until at last she stood on the ledge beneath. It was larger than she'd anticipated, wide enough for three people to walk abreast.

Dropping to her knees, and then to her belly, she peered over the edge. Thousands of feet below ran a river of red-hot steaming lava.

She shivered; then stood up. The shelf extended out of sight to either side.

Back to the left, the way we came seems unnecessarily back tracking. Surely to the right is the way out. But to check both will take far too long.

Standing in indecision, her back to the ladder, she did not see the movement until Norris appeared at her side, materializing like a black shadow into light.

Tusha spun on him, for an instant angry, not at Norris, but at herself, for not having sensed his nearness sooner.

"What are you doing here? I told you to stay back!"

"You are like Loki, aren't you?" Norris stated quietly. "Your secret is safe with me."

Tusha chose to ignore his observation.

Well, that knowledge is out, so what can I do? Erase his memory? Not a good idea!

"Two ways to go," Norris observed, after a moment, taking her silence in stride. "Will take a lot of time to explore…time we don't have."

Tusha nodded, deciding to trust him.

"Be silent, while I try something."

Stepping back to the wall, dropping to her knees, she leaned against it, and closed her eyes. Sending her mind down the shelf to the left, she ran in bodiless rapidity to its end.

With a distant voice, she told Norris, "Dead end, about a mile away on the left. I'll check the right."

He did not question, simply accepted what she'd said, choosing not to doubt. He waited.

Once again, she travelled by mind to the end of the right fork. There, a dead end, as well.

Tusha sighed, and rose to her feet.

"Go back, Norris. I'll go alone now."

"Someone needs to watch over you. I'll send Loki."

"No! Loki is not well enough yet. Leave him rest with the others. I'll come back soon. Go!"

And so he went back, up the ladder, disappearing through the hole, trusting she would find the way out.

****

The purpose for sending Norris back was just to have privacy to make the next section without prying eyes watching.

Somewhere, there has to be a place to get through, and I'm going to find it, or carve all the way to the surface myself!

CHAPTER 42

At the far end of the ledge to the right, Tusha again went to mind search. Across the vast empty void, the deadly drop to death, the wall on the opposite side held some promise; no escape hole, but a thinner partition.

In a bodiless state, she passed through the granite barrier, and came out in a cavern as cool as any dark night on the surface. At a farther distance she saw a sloping sand slide, and beyond that the roots of trees travelling up through the soil above.

And there, between the roots, a yawning mouth swallowed the starlit sky!

The way out! Maybe a mile's distance, but...so out of our reach; to us, as far away as outer space.

Or is it?

In her body once again, pondering, Tusha searched for a means to cross the yawning chasm.

She turned and gazed back the way she had come; two miles of treacherous ledge along the lava valley, with a drop off of immeasurable yards below, then the escape hole leading back to the others.

I can't ask them to return to their death sentence. Not when the way to freedom is so close. I'll have to make a way over the abyss.

Returning her attention to the far wall, Tusha considered the length of the space; by her judgment, at least thirty feet.

It needs a bridge, but can I make something that large?

Crawling to the very brink of the cliff, she looked down. Far below, a ribbon of luminous molten material travelled across the valley floor, eating up rock as it made its way along, and finally disappearing through the wall just under her.

Tusha shivered with dread, as she gazed over the precipitous drop, envisioning falling to her death. Then resolutely, she turned her mind to the matter at hand.

Closing her eyes, so the view below would not distract, she spread her arms to either side, touching the ledge beside her. Abruptly will took over, materializing her ideas, as she formed them in her head.

Just beyond her fingertips, a base of rock took form, like the flat surface of a rail type bridge, only of transparent, clear stalagmite, yet solid enough to support multiple persons as they crossed. First one foot, then two; a filigreed structure inched across until it measured two yards across and five feet forward, where it again dropped off into space. By the time this was accomplished, Tusha was panting with the effort, and perspiration dotted her brow.

She longed for just one swallow of water, but she had taken none with her.

Tusha knew she must take a break; besides she realized she could not mind reach to build further without moving forward; this exercise just took too much effort. As a bonus, however, she was also aware, she could draw extra energy from the light source deep beneath her.

After a short rest, the human Noor crept forward, until she was once more at the edge of her artificially formed pathway. Shutting her eyes once again, Tusha continued building the next five feet.

A break, another span, and so on, until her body was not only covered in reeking sweat, but leaking cuts, as if she had deliberately sliced herself with a knife; also present were unexplained bruising, and small festering sores. It appeared extreme mental work took a visible, physical toll, as well.

Half way across, oblivion took her.

****

Her first awareness, when she came to, was that she was perilously suspended, her left foot and hip hanging out into space, over the edge. Lying on her belly had saved her, but the energy to roll over, and across to safety, was still not there.

Tusha lay immobile; added to the discomfort of dry damaged skin, was the stinging, burning pain from multiple oozing cracks along her arms. A tender tongue, and the metallic taste of blood in her mouth, also assaulted her fragile consciousness.

Was I convulsing while unconscious? Did I bite my tongue, or merely clamp my teeth with the effort to remain in this reality?

She would never know, as there was no one there to look out for her.

It was then she became aware of the intense heat rising up from the valley below. She took a labored breath. As time passed, her difficulty breathing eased; energy gradually returned, enough so she could roll to her other side, and then to her belly again, out of harm's way.

Oh, how I long for a bath...or just a cup of water...

But, she must return to work; she was only half way across.

The others are waiting!

Moaning like a grieving beast, she carried on, each five-foot span causing internal pain, as well as external. Tusha knew, organs were being damaged; aging was progressing.

How much more do I have left to give?

She never knew if she reached the other side. Once again, the world fled away.

****

Tusha thought somehow, someone had come and carried her back across to where she had started. When she awoke, she was seated against the cool granite wall; arms at her sides, her hands open, resting on the ground. In front of her lay the finished pathway, a marvelous display of incredible power.

As she gazed out over the expanse, she realized, on the far side was the ledge leading back to the others. She had made it to this side, before passing out.

But, she was still alone.

Desperately weary from her labor, she rose to her feet, and turned to face the blank barrier behind her. Tusha never considered not performing the next step.

It has to be done!

She touched the granite wall. It shimmered; a tiny hole appeared, widened, growing ever larger, until the gateway to freedom was large enough to pass through in a crouch.

Then, once again, the battered being sank to a semi-conscious state, sprawling half in and half out, across the lip of the portal, as cool air flooded over her.

****

At last, hours later, life began again. And still later, Tusha stood beneath the slope of gravel leading upward to the yawning aperture above.

Freedom was there; a beautiful moonscape, framed by the roots of a dead tree, surrounded by large boulders.

The thought ran through her head:

I could escape on my own, leave the others to chance finding the way out on their own. It would be so easy. But no...it isn't right; it isn't fair to them.

It is time to go back!

With heavy feet, and aching frame, a body that now looked eighty, Tusha returned the way she had come. It was easier now that the way was formed, but still extremely taxing. Half way down the ledge that skirted the lava river, at a spot where the outcropping spread inward in a circular space, causing a platform like a roadway rest stop, Tusha sank to her knees.

Too weary to go on, she lay down, and abruptly fell asleep.

****

Tusha woke to someone shaking her, and wondered for a second, whether she had dreamed it all. It was Norris. Once again, he had disobeyed her instruction...and it made her glad, that he had.

Tusha sat up, stretched, and yawned hugely. In her sleep, much of her fatigue, along with the worst of her injuries, had disappeared. Her appearance had also returned to that of someone of sixty plus years.

"You couldn't wait for me to return?" she rebuked in an annoyed tone.

"You've been gone for days!" he answered in surprise. "Most think you have abandoned us; others that you must be dead. They are despairing back there. The food we took has near run out. And here I find you sleeping." The last was given with such disappointment in his voice Tusha felt shame.

Then the words he'd spoke sunk in, that is at least one.

Food! Golly, am I ever hungry! I think I could even eat that Roog stew...maybe.

And then she came back to reality.

"Sorry. I only meant to rest a while. I did find the way out."

His jaw dropped in astonishment, as if he had given in to doubts himself. "You did?"

"Yes. But, it's a long way off."

He sighed. "No matter. You have seen the sky?" She nodded. "I haven't seen daylight for twenty years," he marveled longingly.

"Norris?"

"Yes?"

"I'm so tired. Would you go back to get the others? I'll meet them beneath the drop down hole where the ladder is."

"Yes!" he exclaimed jubilantly, and turned to go.

"Norris? You don't have any water with you, do you? And food?"

"I'll bring you some. I think Loki has a bit of water left." And then, like an apparition that had never been there, he was gone. Tusha turned over, and went back to sleep.

CHAPTER 43

Almost everyone was through, and down the ladder, before Loki put in an appearance. He came first, staying beneath Amara, guiding her as she moved down. Their descent seemed to take forever.

"She's in labor," Loki explained, when their feet were on the ground. "She's weak. It's been going on for days, but I don't think it'll be more than another half hour. Is there somewhere I can lie her down?"

Feeling guilty, because she'd delayed in coming back immediately, Tusha was quick to give directions. "There is a jut-in about the middle of the pathway to your right. It's a good mile away."

"I'll carry her."

Loki scooped up the young mother-to-be, swaying with weakness, before he turned, gained his equilibrium, and took off at a run.

For a moment, Tusha stood there stunned, feeling abandoned, overlooked, slighted.

He didn't even ask about my welfare.

Nor had he noticed her bedraggled state.

Rebellion welled inside her, coupled with jealousy and anger.

After all I went through to make the way, he could at least say thank you.

Then she realized that Loki too was suffering.

An empath feels more deeply from those around him, and being physician he is concentrating on his patient, whom he's been tending for days. He may be out of the belt, but the tunnel back there was dark with no source of energy. He's been handicapped, as far as helping is concerned.

And another fact was brought to her mind:

He knows nothing of what it took to make the way out. He cannot be blamed; he did not deliberately slight me.

****

As Loki ran, he realized the available energy resource below. He had no time to seek the source, but he guessed it was lava based, and knew the danger it presented. Miles below, a river of molten power gave dim light to the shelf above.

This meant he could absorb, gaining strength.

I still won't have the power to actually heal, but I'll have the ability now to assist, and ease this girl.

His speed increased, until he was a mere blur, passing on the inner side of the stumbling but eager escapees, walking single file.

Panting with the effort, Loki arrived at the platform Tusha had directed him to. Amara was just moving into a very powerful contraction. Weary with the long ordeal, she had little left to give.

He placed her gently on the powdered soil, willed a blanket beneath her, and absorbed much of her pain. As he doubled over with the force of the contraction, she sighed with the ease he'd given her.

Loki knelt beside her, his mind going inside, and once again using mind will, moved the cord from the baby's foot, so it could deliver freely, and carefully prodded until it turned face down.

And none too soon, the time was at hand.

Tusha found Beth, walking with Lana. As she joined them, she noticed no change in Beth. She was still walking in a daze, oblivious to her surroundings. Lana, on the other hand, appeared to have become a gentler person, guiding the other girl carefully by the hand, watching to make certain she did not step away, and over the precipice.

Has Lana been her caregiver all this time? The experience seems to have mellowed her.

If that were the case, Tusha had missed much during her time away.

What really went on back there?

The temptation to mind read was near overwhelming, but the human Noor found her conscience telling her, to invade privacy would be wrong. Loki had taught her that, by blocking her probe.

Arriving a short time later at the mid-point platform, the women heard the strident scream of a newborn infant. Tusha enthralled, moved up beside Loki.

He laughed triumphantly, when he caught sight of her. Cradling the small bundle in the crook of his arm, he seemed on the verge of collapse himself. He was trembling visibly, as if he'd been the one doing all the hard work of delivery, and not poor Amara.

Tusha suddenly realized what he'd done.

He has indeed borne the brunt of the pain! And is suffering the resultant fatigue.

"The first born of our freedom fighters!" he proclaimed with fervor. "Want to hold her?"

Tusha grinned broadly, and held out her arms.

****

Lana had made a show of changing, and so far Loki had bought it without questioning. Until now, there had been no opportunity to dispense with the encumbrance of Beth. It would be both obvious, she had done it, and ineffectual, if Loki was there to intervene.

They stood cooing over the baby, encouraging the mother, congratulating each other at getting this far.

With their backs turned, intent on the tiny infant and Amara, no one will be able to move quickly enough to prevent.

Lana scowled, let go of Beth's hand. The blank-minded girl suddenly came alert, moved to the brink of the precipice, stood there looking down.

All I'd need to do is give her a slight push.

Lana waited, somehow growing a conscience in the last moment, hesitant to do the dastardly deed.

She turned away, moved toward the other three.

Just a tiny peek at that thing they think so precious, and then...

****

Beth studied the luminous river far below, her mind finding sudden amazing clarity. Life these last months had become unbearable: the beastly frightening dog people, malicious Lana's taunts, and the vision of her eating what she'd brought forth from inside her, had sickened the girl's reality, soured her soul. Then the lustful man she'd been corralled with, so he could rape and brutalize her, over and over again, the shame of her own immoral need, had made further existence meaningless.

Beth had wanted to end it long before this, to kill what had infected her from the inside. She knew fully what she was doing.

Oblivion will come; the end of pain and suffering. That's all I want. Don't believe there is punishment in the hereafter. If there is a God, he would not allow this to happen to me.

My father, my mother, my boyfriend; they are all gone. Why not go, too?

This is what I want!

****

When Lana turned back, it was already too late. There was no unsteady tottering, no scream of fright, as the decision was regretted. The girl simply stepped out into empty space. There was a quiet whoosh…and Beth disappeared.

The thought went through Lana's mind:

I could yell, give a warning.

But she rejected it, only sucked in her breath, at the sudden joy of the release of her burden.

****

Tusha turned, the baby still in her arms, sensing more than hearing something behind her. Seeing Lana standing alone, with what appeared to be a shocked look of denial on her face, the elder woman assumed correctly what had happened. She thrust the baby at Loki, moved like a rapid blur to the edge, and was down on her knees in a second.

It took until then for Loki to realize Beth was missing. By then Tusha was down on her belly, her hands extended over the edge. Loki carefully placed the baby on Amara's tummy, then moved to the edge himself.

Far below, he saw Beth suspended, turning in slow-motion circles, a pantomime frozen half between their upper ledge and the lava river below. The girl had her arms extended to her sides, as if she meant to fly.

Did Lana push her?

And then he realized, all action below had stopped. Beth wasn't moving, nor was she falling.

Only once had Loki seen this done. Liam had rescued a falling comrade, by freezing time, and gradually raising the male to safety.

Loki got down on hands and knees, watching Tusha intently. Her pupils were dilated, staring fixed, colored a rainbow hue.

Yes! She is doing what Liam did. But I can't give her of my strength, as I've done for my mental. I don't have the energy reserve.

It was then he noticed how scarred and aged her body had become, the many cuts appearing by the minute, the oozing bloody sores gaping.

Oh, Almighty! She'll kill herself trying!

And just at that point, Tusha crumbled. If he had not reached out and caught her, she would have slid over, as well.

CHAPTER 44

He tried to bathe her sores with the little water he had, a half filled bottle supposed to be for drinking. As she had done for him, he gave what ministrations he could. She was dreadfully damaged, both physically and emotionally.

Tusha moaned, and opened her eyes.

He saw when memory surfaced; it was mirrored in the deep blue eyes.

"Beth?"

"She's gone," he returned, sadly. "You tried. No blame…"

But she growled at him, like an angry mistrusting animal. "Go away! Leave me alone!"

Loki backed away, feeling the rejection, turned, and decided to check on his other two patients.

He knew Tusha didn't mean it the way it seemed.

She needs to cry it out, to grieve, but…there is no time. There are people counting on us, strewn out across the pathway leading out, all in various stages of fatigue, some near starvation. Their safety must be my priority.

Loki caught up mother and baby, preparing to carry them on. He stood to his feet, looked back at Tusha, deciding to chance it.

She will not do the same as Beth. Tusha has fought too hard, for too long, to give up now. She just needs some time alone.

"I'll stay with her," Lana offered.

"No, you won't!" Loki hissed, his temper thundering to the surface. "You come with me! I don't trust you!"

****

The minute the others were out of sight, the tears came in a hot flood. It was as if the death of Beth had magnified all losses that had come before: first her children, then her freedom, and nearly her life.

How many times now have I been courting death? But I still go on with life...at any cost.

Something in her prevented her ending it all.

I just have to get passed this hurdle!

Her heart longed to be taken care of, to belong somewhere, to someone.

I just want to go home, to that place that no longer is mine, but it's ceased to exist. My treasured family memorabilia has all been snatched away! Even now this second time, that last picture was lost, when Loki and I were forced into the kitchen.

The tears came fast and heavy; her depression took the upper hand.

And the loss of material things was not the worst of it; the tearing away of those she'd loved smoldered the most; the life that had once been could never be retrieved.

In retrospect, I was lonely and felt neglected, but at least then, I had my freedom, and once in a while contact with those I cared about. I could worry about my children, encourage as they solved their problems, watch as the granddaughters matured, and pray for them. In my mind, I could view their faults, silently rebuke, and offer advice. I could watch quietly, hoping for change. The loss of that leaves a huge gaping hole.

Until now, she'd kept that painful fact at bay. Existence, survival down here, had taken all her thought and energy.

She had assumed she would never get to go back.

By now, my children had grieved and moved on, forgotten me.

Having changed so much in mind and body, it seemed unwise to inflict her condition on the younger generation.

It's best I remain dead to them. I'm not sure I'll ever search them out.

After all, why should I?

Grief turned to unwarranted anger focused on her children.

The loss of Beth had opened a grievous canker that had been there for years.

That young girl had always reminded Althea of her granddaughter, Iora, with her protected lifestyle, and shy withdrawn nature, her tendency to give up in the face of adversity. Iora's mother had always kept her close, first in the early years treating her like an adult pal, then becoming so protective, the girl was defended to others whether she was right or wrong.

In personality, Moriah resembled Lana. No advice was acceptable, especially coming from her mother; she wanted only a listening ear, and grandma better not dare criticize. In her daughter's opinion, Althea had always had it wrong, was to blame for the conditions in their past, and her decisions had been stupid from beginning to end.

For a long time, Althea had felt rejected, used, there only to fill her daughter's needs, either for physical help, emotional comfort, or to take up the financial shortfall.

When that was not required, she'd been expected to vanish into the background until further notice.

There had been a deep, insurmountable rift between them.

Tusha tried to stop her mental tirade, brushed at the tears, and made an attempt to remember something positive...and failed, as her thoughts went to her son.

Nyle, when at his worst, could be likened to Bom. He had a certain lack of concern for his family, and a likelihood of exploding into anger, rather than showing affection or concern toward his parent. She remembered vividly once when her behavior hadn't pleased him; she had feared for her life. Nyle tended to hold a grudge. He hadn't spoken to her for six month after, and that had been getting off easy.

In his eyes, someone else was always to blame, never he. Like his sister, he tended to be so involved in his own ideas and affairs; he simply forgot his mother existed.

But, at least, Tusha reminded herself:

He has his good side; his love for his own daughter is unmatched.

Althea had never gotten to know Kaudy. Only once had she seen her, at six weeks old. Nyle's wife had always prevented any further association.

No, I have no reason to go back. I was always such a thorn in their side. By now, they have gone on with their lives, and I have no value to them.

I have Loki now. He will cushion my transition.

He is unlike any man I've ever known. He is gentle, humble, and keeps wisely private, until action is needed. But sometimes, he's too trusting and confident. He errs on the side of rashness, not backing down when he feels the need is justified. That's how he came to be here, both at the beginning, and in that most recent encounter with Bom.

But then, even Loki tends to ignore my accomplishments. If he approved, at least he didn't say so.

At this moment, Tusha could see only the dark side. She could not bring herself to stay positive. In her present state of mind, she was incapable of clear thinking; her memory was selective. She knew she was wallowing in self-pity, but she thought that it was warranted.

Do I not deserve even an iota of respect and recognition? It seems, it doesn't matter what I do, it is of no benefit in the long run.

Her body shook with anguished sobs; disappointment made her breath come in ragged gasps. With little energy left to fall back on, the tears soon were spent. Then Tusha simply sat there, vacant-minded, numb, waiting for peace.

At long last, with a resigned sigh, she let the past go, prepared to face the immediate future, and rose to her feet. With steps dragging, she took the path, to follow after Loki and Lana.

CHAPTER 45

Loki kept his pace gentle, striding resolutely toward the freedom door. Still Lana had to nearly run to keep up to him.

As he reached the bridge across the gorge, he stopped abruptly. Lana nearly ran into him. He shifted his load, reached back to stop her forward motion, not because he particularly valued her as a person, but because he wanted no more deaths on his watch.

Loki had reached the point where his own feelings had gone numb. Empathy had its faults; after a time overload ensued. And in his own beleaguered condition, he could tolerate no more.

Loki stood examining the intricate platform that spanned the yawning chasm.

There is no way this is natural! Stalagmites don't grow together to make such a perfect filigree network, let alone on a horizontal plane, across a steaming hot open space of this length.

This is mind work!

Most beings viewing this would not realize it was mind-formed, but Loki knew the potential of a Noor mental.

But even Liam can't do this!

And there was no one else…except Tusha!

Uel had told him, Tilk, the mental Noor queen, had once had unmeasured mind-strength, but until this moment, he hadn't believed such a thing possible.

If Tusha has done this, what have I created? I only meant to save her life; one tiny human coupled with the essence had become...what? A monster?

I can't be the judge of that; it's for those of mental aptitude to decide.

Again, he surveyed the thirty-foot length; it had a width of two yards, and was the thickness of at least half that.

How did she find the power to form this? And with limited light available to her.

He shook his head in disbelief. But, then he was reminded of the petite woman's physical state, the aged countenance, the oozing cuts and open sores.

Loki shivered, as he realized the agony Tusha must have endured.

How many times did she pass out while doing this? No wonder she was gone so long!

And still, as low on energy as she must have been at the end, and suffering from unbearable exhaustion, she had tried to save Beth.

Such power!

If she had a predilection for revenge, or even mild self-indulgence, imagine what she could do.

But as selfless as Tusha appears to be...

She is mostly a follower; her leader skills seem nil, and she is unschooled in the methodology of mind-practice; maybe...as other Noor have, she will travel the path to integrity when she gains her peak.

Yet, one wrong experience could turn her the opposite way, and that worried Loki.

No! I'm certain Tusha will never be a dominating, self-centered, lethal dictator. It just isn't in her basic nature to hurt others. I have never known a female with this level of self-sacrificing disregard for her own welfare.

At home males lived in the shadow of the females; their duty was to serve and protect, and some of their partners took mild advantage, but most were benevolent. Still, he knew none, save Dia, who would give their lives for others.

Tusha is a rare find; my female needs to be protected from herself!

And then, reality struck him:

I can never claim her!

I can never tell her how proud I am of her, how much I love her. It is not my place.

My duty is to take care of her, help her reach her potential, to feel good about herself, show my love…and I have failed miserably on all counts. She has every right to be mad at me!

And to make matters worse, he was about to disappoint her once again.

Exceedingly grieved at heart, Loki started down the bridge with Amara and the baby in his arms, Lana travelling after.

CHAPTER 46

When they finally rounded the bend, leaving the dark tunnel of the last leg, and stepped into the open space, with the sand slope that led upward, they found all the refugees huddled together, just short of the exit. As if they feared to go on without proper guidance, or realizing freedom was so close at hand had panicked, they seemed afraid to actually take the step of leaving captivity, doubting they could survive, not knowing what to do on the outside.

Norris and Downy came to Loki, the woman exclaiming profusely at the sight of a living newborn; Norris seemed simply relieved to see them.

The black man immediately realized two were missing.

"Where are Tusha...and Beth?" His tone told he feared the worst.

Loki lowered Amara to the gravel, while Downey took over immediately, hovering protectively at the side of mother and child.

His back still turned away, Loki answered. "Beth went over the cliff." He did not elaborate beyond that, laying no blame.

Norris sucked in a breath. "And Tusha?"

"She needs some time...she tried to save her..."

Loki left the thought hanging, deliberately, allowing Norris to imagine all sorts of scenarios.

"Is she hurt bad? Will our liberator survive?"

The Noor refused to speculate. "I'm going back to get her now," Loki stated.

Norris abandoned his questions. Perhaps, he didn't want to know, or dreaded to be told the whole story. Acceptingly he let it pass, certain that in time, he would gain the details. He was much like Loki, a watcher, a listener, but considerable wisdom was under his mantle.

Loki turned to glare warningly at Lana, who had backed into a corner by herself. "Don't let that one near the baby," he ordered.

Curiosity got the better of Norris; he voiced the question uppermost in his mind. "Was Lana responsible for Beth's death?"

But Loki made no answer, left the idea hanging in the air.

****

Loki found Tusha halfway across the bridge. She didn't meet his eyes, still seemed to be nursing a grudge against him, or so he assumed.

Taking in her obvious lethargy, he realized it was more resignation and despondency than actual displeasure with him. Her eyes were half swollen shut, her cheeks sallow and sunken; she looked a wizen ninety, stooped, broken, despairing. She had cried herself into a state of stupor.

His heart went out to her. Desire to heal away the hurts, both physical and emotional, thundered to the surface, but his own previous injuries, never completely dealt with, were burning and festering for lack of water, and having gone so long without adequate light, the energy behind his ability was nil.

It struck him then.

Since Tusha has developed her Noor nature, she has never known a true light source; she has never been in the sun!

In awe, he marveled.

Considering the power she has already displayed, what magnitude might she be capable of when she finally steps outside?

But now, at the very least, I can ease her aches.

Loki reached out, and touched her hand.

Sensing the desire, and the motivation behind his action, she pulled back, extracting that small member.

"Don't!" Her voice came out a hoarse whisper, but the force was there, and the annoyance. As always, true to her inherent considerate nature, she wanted no part in using another selfishly.

So he conceded, yet quickly sought for another means to help.

"I'll carry you," he offered.

"No! Leave me be!"

Admitting defeat, he turned, and walked next to her, gauging his steps to match hers. Stubbornly, she moved ahead of him instead.

He knew she meant for him to follow; obediently, he did so.

****

Travelling that last mile through the darkness, Loki watched Tusha. The glow around her body was so faint, visible only here in the utter blackness.

She has used her powers constantly for days, without having adequate means to replenish the energy used. Eventually, she is bound to go down completely.

He waited, patiently, watching as she faded slowly. Expecting it. A half hour's walk from the exit opening, like a rag doll, she folded toward the floor of the tunnel. Quickly moving forward, he reached her side, and scooped her into his arms, before she fell.

Her head sagged against his shoulder, flopping like an inanimate toy doll. He cuddled her close, relishing this last close contact.

If only Liam can love her as I do, all will be well, but I must step aside, wait for my mental to notice her. Until then, I must forfeit my claim, and give no inkling I've found our future partner.

Everything in him rebelled. Loki didn't want to do what he had to do.

The rest of the way, he carried her, moving at as leisurely a pace as he dared…to delay the inevitable.

CHAPTER 47

As he rounded the bend, into the semi darkness of the moonlighted space, Loki found all humans just as he'd left them...save for one.

He frowned. "Where's Lana?" he demanded, looking about apprehensively.

Norris rose to meet him, answering with an offhand attitude. "She preferred to take immediate advantage of the prospect of freedom. About an hour ago, she just walked through the opening into the night. Guess she didn't want to be here when you got back."

Loki grunted disparagingly, shifting his burden. "And...were the Roog out there to welcome her?" he asked hopefully.

Norris laughed, identifying with the frustration of the Noor male, excusing the uncharacteristic lapse of compassion.

"None that we heard from in here."

Sighing with relief that that woman had not brought about their recapture, Loki eased down to a sitting position against the wall, yet not relinquishing the treasure in his arms. He leaned back, with the still unconscious Tusha on his lap, her head against his chest, holding her close, as if he planned to keep her there for eternity.

"We'll just wait here for the sunrise," Loki suggested. "Give Tusha some time to recover. By then the dogs should all be asleep."

Norris studied the elderly woman in his arms, shaking his head. "What's happened to her?" He slipped down to sit beside Loki. "Does every Noor suffer like this when they use their abilities?"

Loki furrowed his brow.

What is this? The man knows Tusha is no longer fully human? When did that happen?

Did she tell him?

Norris anticipated the unspoken queries.

"I watched her go mind-travel, and...I know, she made the first hole...and the down ladder. I will not tell," he added in a whisper.

Loki made a quick decision.

If Tusha chose to trust this male, so will I. She is a good judge of character.

He explained. "Since I infected her," he confessed. "She has had no contact with a real energy source. For us all, the sun is best. Because of this lack, her mind takes substance from her own body, like a starving marauder might blindly mistake its own extremities as food."

Norris shivered in revulsion. "You are self-mutilating? Cannibalistic?"

"Not usually. It is a deficiency found only in an instant healer, and some of our stronger mentals, more so, ones that are female. Tusha, being inexperienced, and self-taught, was unaware, and unprepared to handle the handicap. She does not know how to alleviate or correct it. She is like a child, still learning. And I cannot instruct her, as I am merely a physical."

"Can she teach herself?"

"Hopefully...when she has a taste of sunlight. She also learns from watching it done."

"Why don't you just heal her yourself?"

"Not enough of a light source. And we both also need water…"

"So, that's really why you want to wait for morning?"

Loki nodded quietly.

Tusha stirred, slowly opening her eyes, ending any further discussion.

****

They stood in a boulder-strewn field, in the bright sun, watching the humans cross the sparse grass, and disappear into a band of trees beyond.

Tusha was awed.

It is summer up here on the surface. I have been underground for near nine months.

She turned to watch Loki, his eyes closed, as he raised his arms to the hot sun, soaking up its light, as if he were a winter-starved tree. His dirty and battered stark naked body seemed to shimmer, like a desert mirage.

She slipped into his mind to watch what he was doing, curious at the phenomena.

His still festering wounds vanished, as did his tail. He had willed it to be non-visible. The filth from the prison disappeared, and clothing: leggings, a long sleeved collarless shirt, took its place. He stood there, looking more humanoid than feline now.

He's handsome, when he's fully healed. That mop of ginger curls. And the muscular chest, powerful legs, not half bad either.

Tusha shivered with want, then shaking it off, turned her thoughts to other things.

Loki lowered his arms, but remained gazing into the sun, as if he were absorbing its rays like a shower of water, washing away the ugliness, relieving himself of all the horror, pain and tragedy he'd experienced in the bowels of the earth below.

Shocked by his transformation, and what she'd seen him do with his mind, Tusha marveled.

What a handicap! He is unable to instruct me, as any normal person might. Yet he can do this, and by accomplishing it, show me the method. It's a puzzle. So this must be the difference between a mental and a physical: one tells, the other shows? Incredible!

She turned her eyes toward heaven, staring up at the sun. Now, she could feel it too, an energy gained from that great glowing orb; it tingled on her skin, invigorated the mind, so sharpened your powers, they leapt to the forefront, waiting to be used.

Is this what it means to be Noor? Dare I try what he has done?

****

He turned, and was astounded, as he watched her close her eyes, raise her arms, and like a learning toddler, imitate his actions.

How fast she absorbs knowledge; things that have taken me years of practice to perfect, she instantly comprehends and is skilled at, simply by watching the process of my mind. It's not even necessary to teach her; her ability to fathom is phenomenal!

Loki observed, as her body changed. The bruising, the angry wounds, the festering sores, all disappeared in mere seconds. The elder wizen creature became a beautiful younger maiden, with a short crop of silver white waves crowning her head. Even from where he stood, the hair looked soft as infant silk; the ends curling up around her ears and across the back of her neck. The skin of her face was pale cream-pink, smooth and unblemished; even her exposed arms were free of the former ancient age.

The lashes that swept her dusty-rose cheeks were long and white-blond; the lips beneath, soft and sensuous.

Loki's eyes dropped, caressing over the grubby shirt and jeans, as they changed to a clean frilled blouse and dark slacks. She now stood, approximately five foot three, still lean, small breasts, full and firm; tiny waist; hips curvaceous, slim long legs, and tiny naked toes.

He caught his breath at the sight of her.

This stunning creature could be mine...if I choose. But...I must wait.

It was then he realized, in this unguarded moment, her mind was open. He saw what troubled her; all that had gone before, prior to her capture, the hurtful things said to her by both daughter and granddaughter; the anger and neglect forced upon her by her son.

So this is why she fears to go back into this upper world!

Suddenly aware he'd caught this glimpse, she quickly blocked him from seeing more, but he'd garnered enough to know, he must give rebuke; direct her to a more pleasant mindset.

CHAPTER 48

"Don't hold a grudge, Tusha. Don't let the past spoil the future," he cautioned.

Knowing exactly to what he referred, and realizing he was right, she was silent.

Sympathy was in his very words, as Loki continued. "I know that children can be very unwise and selfish creatures, even after they have reached maturity. Many have the idea they are the only ones hurt in life; and they blame all unsatisfactory situations in their world on the elder generation. But we know, even if it may hold true in some cases, it is rare that any parent has total responsibility.

"Sometimes, the cruelty of the young ones scar deeply, hurting those who sacrificed everything to bring them to the place they are. They repay with disrespect, take advantage excessively of a generous spirit, and when refused what they want, they strike back, by abandoning those who love them unreservedly."

Tusha suddenly got the impression Loki was not just speaking of her relationship with her children, but as if he was the father. Her conscience had her feeling guilty of the crimes he listed.

It's true; perhaps I am like his child, though it has come about unnaturally.

"Always be my gentle butterfly," he encouraged. "Not a venomous snake."

Tusha recoiled at his words.

Am I a vicious creature? Perhaps...deep inside.

He continued. "Our agape love is always waiting, hovering beneath our silent observation. It's not rebuke; sometimes it's regret…"

Puzzled, Tusha wondered.

Is he identifying with me, or is he speaking of himself?

She well understood the feeling he described.

If I were able to rewrite the past, I'd do many things quite differently. Yet, I will always love my children, no matter what, even if that love is not reciprocated. They will be a part of me until the day I die.

"We have no guide book to go by," Loki went on. "We stumble through and make mistakes…that may or may not need forgiveness. But once the young ones are parents themselves, and are in a similar situation, they will at last understand the heart behind the love of the elder…" He paused. "Sometimes, however, that knowledge comes too late, and they can never make up for it; they can no longer tell them they are sorry…"

Loki went very quiet for a moment, pondering something in retrospect, as if he had suddenly been hit by an ugly comparison to his own past.

After a time, he continued, as if encouraging himself. "No matter what they do. Or what they may become, we must always love them…"

Once again, his words seemed to have that double meaning.

Tusha felt near to tears, sensing something very heavy under his soliloquy. She wasn't sure if she had done something to offend him, or the reprimand applied to her relationship with her children.

Maybe it is both?

It even seemed Loki had an ulterior motive behind his words, a warning of some impending wound about to be inflicted, almost as if he were apologizing before the act...

****

"When did you get so wise," she asked softly. "For a physical, you have wisdom beyond your function."

He grinned sheepishly at the unexpected praise, recognizing in his apprehension, he'd begun to ramble. "Sometimes," he excused, tongue in cheek. "When a physical falls in love, he becomes like a mental..."

Tusha's eyes went huge, and she sucked in a surprised breath. It was the first time he'd spoken aloud of his sentiment.

Loki looked away.

I will have to be careful how I do this. I know what I am about to do will hurt...maybe, if I strike quickly?

He sighed heavily. "You will not understand the why," he stated bluntly. "And no doubt, without that full knowledge, you will be angered by what I am about to do..."

He felt sudden dread from her, and it initiated a protective response in return. All he wanted to do was kiss away her fright, tell her that he would never physically hurt her, but he kept his head turned away, so he would not respond.

He then delivered the hurtful blow.

"I must go back inside..." he declared quietly.

Once again, she sharply inhaled from the shock.

"But, you're coming back? I'll wait here for you."

Loki ignored her. "You are safe for now. Stay safe."

"What do you mean? Aren't you coming with us?"

It was as if she was deliberately playing dense, couldn't grasp the concept of him leaving her. So he dug the pit deeper.

"I must go back down. If I don't, I'll be a fugitive with not only Bom hunting me, but the entire universe. I'd never again see my family; my mental would be lost…"

Even in his ears, the excuse sounded selfish.

"What about me?"

He sighed.

Yes, what will become of her? She'll be free…

"Keep safe. Please…"

It is best not to prolong the parting.

So, he simply vanished, teleporting to the portal leading down into the kitchen. He hoped she would not follow, that in time she would forgive him.

Let me go Tusha. I have to do this; it is the only way.

CHAPTER 49

Tusha gazed absently at the world about her, and for long moments, she merely watched as those they had set free tramped away, disappearing into the distant trees. When they could no longer be seen, she just stood there.

Silently, she waited, hoping Loki would have a change of heart and return. With a mind probe, she reached out to find him, but he had his thought barrier up. He had shut her out.

He means for me to forget him…

But I will always remember you Loki; You gave me life. And even though you might not want me, I will someday search you out; I will not let you die in that demon place!

I will go back in…when I am more experienced. I will rescue you, and if you've been sent somewhere else, I will find you…even if you don't want to be found!

But that resolve evaporated, as the full impact of separation hit.

Suddenly she dropped to her knees, screaming in violent rejection of her circumstance. She raised her fists to the sky, then doubled over, as if the agony was in her belly, and not her heart.

Her cry became a wail, like that of a Siamese cat, wandering, seeking the soul of the kitten she'd just found dead. Tusha gave way with abandonment and disregard; her mourning keen fled across the fields for all to hear.

And the Noor female grieved: what might have been, the travesty that had been played out at her expense, the loss of a supposed mate. Her body shook, and the tears flooded; for long moments she cried. Then, as defeat turned to anger, she stopped abruptly, turning to thoughts of revenge.

In that moment, when wrath took over, Tusha forgot all of Loki's words. She gave one last exasperated scream at the sky, the hot tears fled, and with a cold calm, she took a deep breath of resolve.

Bitterly, she vowed she would never trust him again.

If he can so easily forget me, why should I remember him?

She resolved three things at that moment: first, she would make it her life's work to set free the humans in the pens beneath her feet; second, someday she would mete out appropriate justice to that malicious overseer, Bom; and thirdly...

I will never forgive that Noor male for leaving me behind!

You have just become my enemy!

One more thing she decided:

I will never again be your Tusha. No! I will change my name, hide from you Loki. You will never find me!

And then she cried again. Utterly confused, she retracted all decisions made previously.

Almost as if the Almighty wanted to weep along with her, the clouds pulled up over the sun, and it began to rain.

****

Loki stood in the kitchens, refastening the dreaded belt. He drew in a sharp breath as the painful probes pierced his tender flesh. He'd forgotten about the agony of the drain-away energy reversal.

Darren watched him with accusation and puzzlement in his eyes.

The Noor couldn't explain why, but he felt guilty, a need to defend his actions.

"I have to," Loki excused. "Or Bom will find the escape route…he will follow, and hunt her, and…you know how that will end. I needed to buy them time…"

Darren nodded silently, but still seemed unconvinced this was the best way to go.

EPILOGUE:

More was standing in the doorway of his shop; he saw Loki as he passed through the tunnel beyond.

So, the Noor male has survived. Good! Now maybe, Bom will be dealt with.

It was just a matter of waiting.

Absently, More wondered where Loki had hidden the little queen.

****

Like an errant kitten being berated in disgust by its owner, Bom's large hand suspended Uel by the back-skin behind his neck. When Loki stumbled into the med bay area, the warden was shaking the Feline violently.

Turning, dropping his prey, the huge Roog Feline growled deep in his chest at the intrusion. Uel, forgotten for the moment, crawled beneath an exam table to watch.

I thought I'd done away with this blight! How is it that Noor survived?

"So, you still live, do you?" Bom barked. "And now I suppose you think I must release you?"

Loki stood his ground. "My term is up! Even the extra time you added on."

Bom snorted. "You have no rights here!"

"I have the right to demand freedom, and you know it! And...I want Uel released, as well. He too has served his time...long ago. His release time is long past. If he is not let go, once I am out, I will plague the council, until he is released. For your own good, you'd be wise to do as I ask."

The administrator shifted his weight, thinking. He knew both of these males could be more trouble than he needed. Uel alone, he could handle, but together, they could secretly undermine him. They had obviously done so before.

"Very well," Bom agreed. "I've had enough of you anyway. But…we'll discuss my terms when you leave."

"No conditions, Bom! We're done!" Turning to Uel, peeking out from beneath the exam bed, Loki added, "You will join me on my momma Dia's med ship, Uel."

Bom growled, ready to dispute. Loki met his eyes with fierce warning in his own, and the half Roog knew it was time to cut his losses.

He turned, and strode from the room, purposely ignoring the two behind.

They are my prisoners! How dare they tell me how to run my kingdom!

****

Needing to impose his authority, and to have the last word, as Loki and Uel were loaded onto the transport, Bom bent down to whisper a warning to the Noor. He switched to the Roog tongue, so that Uel would not fully understand. He knew the Noor was a linguist; Loki would not need a translator to comprehend.

"Listen, you Noor half-breed," he hissed. "I will tell you this just once. If you speak of what went on here, I will have you back so fast…not only you; I will have your entire family, including all of your matriarch Dia's ship staff, imprisoned. And you know I have such power…I will take their lives, and yours, before I am done. Do you understand? Your silence buys their freedom, as long as you keep it!"

Loki nodded, ever so imperceptibly, then stepped into the shuttle. The door slid shut, and Bom grunted in triumph.

I have won!

****

As the door shut, Loki had the nagging feeling; his release had gone too smoothly.

Bom is up to something!

He wondered where Tusha was at this moment, and if after all, she was really safe.

****

Bom chuckled to himself.

Now to find that she of his!

The Noor male had done exactly what he'd expected of him. They had searched the entire facility, from end to end. The little one with the butterfly tattoo was nowhere below ground. That meant, somehow, the Noor had returned her to the surface.

The hunt has just begun! It will be so invigorating!

###

About the Author:

Margaret Afseth, a Canadian novelist, grew up on the prairies. She raised her four children from preschool age to teens on her own. Now, as a widow and grandmother, through the encouragement of her family to follow her dream of writing full time, and publishing her work, she has stepped to the publishing stage in the latter years of her life.

Since her late teens, Margaret was always an avid reader and clandestine writer, but due to discouragement, and the unfortunate hard lesson in which her first novel was destroyed by a misguided counselor, she was too publisher shy to go through the gauntlet of the critics...until, that is, the ease of on line self-publishing became available.

In February 2013 Margaret published her first sci-fi thriller the Aopato Chronicles.

Discover other titles by Margaret Afseth at
Amazon.com

Aopato

Remedy

Turn Back

Hidden From View

If you enjoyed this book, here is a sample of book two of the Noor Chronicles; coming soon:

SOUL SAVER

By

Margaret Afseth

PROLOGUE:

Ice at the water's edge; steam clouds rising in the air; the gurgle of a gently rushing watercourse just out of sight. Trees covered in hoarfrost above; dark obscuring everything.

Liam crouched in the bushes with the young ones, waiting near the river bank, until it should be safe. In this disguise, it felt cold, damp, uncomfortable. Static made the fur of his body tingle.

The water nearby filled him with dread, but this was where he'd found the young kits hiding. It was dangerous here; the youngsters could fall in; the humans had a weapon to drown the pair, and if the Roog came along, they too might use it to their advantage. Thankfully, the dogs preferred to stick to land.

This human world had always seemed hazardous at best, and this time it was more so; they had much too long to wait before he could give the signal for pick up. The shuttle was caught beyond the solar system, concealed, cloaked, avoiding a Roog battleship.

"This spot is not secure; we need to get beyond the buildings," Liam decided. "Darkness might hide the smaller primitive cat, but not those of us who are larger."

"Where should we go, poppa?" asked the five year old male.

Liam gestured toward a path above, and they ascended the bank together quickly. Once up there, the way led along the embankment, through an illuminated park that was adequately treed. But the light made the elder male uneasy, wary, cautious, yet he had little choice but to take this route.

"Poppa..." the female complained. "I am cold."

"I know, little she. When we are at a safer location, I will build you a fire."

In his lifetime, Liam had saved many across the universe. When he found them, they were most often alone, their parents killed by Roog, or captured, which was as good as a death sentence in itself. And though the parents had hidden and sacrificed for them, setting out the beacon for rescue, by the time Liam got to them, the little beings were foraging to survive, in bins of garbage behind the businesses. Upon his arrival in their hostile environment, he became their lone protector, and this fact alone bonded the little ones to him.

Because of his age, many of the children called him Poppa, a nick name implying grandfather in his culture. Liam cherished this designation!

Always, when bringing them in, he made certain they were adopted by a new family, and kept in touch, returning often for visits. Because of this, wherever he went he had a welcome, and was called Poppa by the younger generation. It was the closest he could come to having children of his own.

And this had been how he had staffed his momma Dia's med ship. He had once been a lost kit himself, alone, different. Dia had taken him in, accepted his unusual character and parentage.

****

Liam heard the crashing, blinded, panicked escape of the person fleeing toward them before the creature stumbled into sight. When the human woman broke into the path directly ahead of them, the left side of her face next to her eye, and down the cheek, was covered in dry blood. She was limping, gasping with exhaustion, running erratically, eyes closed, arms outstretched before her, feeling her way along.

Suddenly, she caught her foot on an exposed root; went sprawling, right into Liam's arms. He reached out to catch her just before her knees found the leafy peat beneath their feet.

"Help me," she pleaded, in a voice that was soft and raspy, weak from fatigue. "They found me."

She must think I'm someone she knows.

At their touch, due to his empathic ability, Liam became aware of two things: first, she was trembling with unreasoning terror; and second, she'd been drugged excessively, and the preparation was just beginning to effect her. She went limp against him, going senseless.

Liam sniffed at the air.

Danger is coming! I can smell the obnoxious odor of Roog.

It's time to leave the path!

"Hide, little ones!" he growled urgently in the Feline tongue. "Under the bushes. Quickly! Our enemy approaches!"

Lifting the unconscious female, he rapidly followed his charges, to dive and burrow with them deep beneath the foliage.

Their escape was none too soon.

Liam held his breath as the giant hunters loped by, moving upright; as always, unaware and unperceptive, expecting their quarry to be far ahead, and not beneath their feet. Large, with unconcealed dog-like heads, their bodies were camouflaged in human garments.

Liam was intimately familiar with masquerade practices. It was a strategy used by both Roog and Feline. Whether on the hunt or fleeing, each wore a camouflage belt, which could change the outward perception of their visible image. His father's race used it to protect themselves, whereas the Roog employed it mostly to confuse their prey.

The colossal dog creatures hunted humans as food. And just as easily, would kill or torture any of Liam's kind, just for the sport of it. It was their favorite pastime to seek the weaker young, and especially all females. No life was sacred or safe from them.

It is unusual though for them to wear only half disguise. I wonder why they've become so brave?

The young kits beside him flinched, as the pack passed over them. The female gave a hissing moan. Liam stroked her fur, and cautioned.

"Shush, little she. They will hear."

Liam knew their cover was good, the bushes large and full.

The male twin worriedly added his challenge.

"They will scent us, Poppa?" he whispered fearfully. "They can find us?"

His tone said much, revealing just beneath the surface, the memory of the last encounter, in which they'd lost their parents to these beasts of prey. The grief was poignant.

"If I can help it; they'll not have you," Liam disagreed in a low growl.

The woman beneath him stirred. Roughly, to silence any sound, he placed his hand across her mouth, clutching her tightly in his arms. Her reaction was to struggle against his hold.

"Be still!" Liam hissed in human English. "I am not your enemy. They will hear you."

She went quiet in compliance, easing into his shoulder.

On high alert, Liam listened as the diminishing sounds faded. The fog was descending around them, but he knew it would not really hide them. Their dark bodies would soon stand out, visible shadows against the white.

And the Roog would turn around when they realized they had lost the trail.

When Liam was certain the enemy was out of range, he risked speaking again.

"Come children. We must keep moving."

He rose, easily lifting the human with him. Still carrying her, he proceeded along the path away from the threat of danger. For safety, he kept her lips covered with the palm of his hand, just to make certain she did not cry out.

A moment later, the female made a weak attempt to pull away his hand. Liam stopped, knowing she wished to communicate.

"Will you promise not to cry out if I remove my hand?" At her nod, he loosed his hold, and added, "I am Liam. I will see that you are tended to."

Though in an obvious drugged state, she wanted to be let down. Rather than argue, he let her try to stand. Her legs buckled, so he scooped her up again, and took off at a rapid pace, the young ones loping after to keep up with him. He stopped to rest only when the little female began to lag. By then, his burden was once more in oblivion.

He knelt with the human on his knee, giving the young ones the break they so desperately needed. Looking about him, Liam noticed the end of the park was just ahead.

As he rested, he took note of the woman he carried. He reproached himself for taking on this unnecessary challenge.

Why am I taking her with us, anyway? I could just leave her in the entrance of a building, where her own kind would find her, and give her medical treatment. It would certainly be easier on the kits.

Yet he feared, if she wasn't found immediately, the delay might cost her life.

Liam shook his head, frustrated at his dilemma.

He examined the wound next to her eye.

That was inflicted by a taser!

Raw and still bleeding, the damage seemed to be more inside than exterior.

Her eyes must sting and burn when she tries to open them. Her head is throbbing constantly, yet she's not uttered a word of complaint, as if she's used to constant pain.

Odd.

Perhaps, it's a blessing she cannot see; that way she'll not realize we are not of her race.

He passed his hand across her forehead attempting to ease the pain the poor women was experiencing. In shock, Liam unexpectedly connected with her inner mind.

Recent and some past memories flashed by in an instant; among them, a vivid recall of a scarred and ancient appearing female. In that spilt second, Liam became aware the one he was viewing was half Noor as he was. He also watched as the she Noor used her powers in a vain attempt to rescue a third woman, and realized that the one he held in his arms, had somehow been responsible for the situation.

A hatred of such intensity, focused on this elder, emanated menacingly from his charge, at this recollection. Liam pulled away in disgusted outrage. He studied the face before him.

Am I harboring an enemy; someone dangerous to me?

Rebuking himself, he shook away the thought.

No! I cannot be a judge. I am a healer; rescuer. I do not have all the facts.

He put the memory away, and went to other things he had seen.

A more recent experience was the one in which the human had encountered the Roog. Two had surprised her, the first, coming from behind, had tasered her, while the second had shot a drug into her opposite shoulder. She had jerked away involuntarily, before the complete dose had been administered.

Liam sat thinking; he grew hopeful.

She may not have gotten enough to kill her, after all.

He noted a distinct change in her breathing.

She's awake again.

"Do you know where you are female?" Liam asked. "Who am I?"

"Liam," she answered groggily.

"Do you have a name?"

"Lana."

"And...how did you escape from the Roog, Lana?"

"I...I played dead. It always works. When they turned away, I ran."

Liam frowned.

First off, she didn't ask what a Roog was; she already knew. That alone proves she has had experience with them before. For such a one, they won't stop looking. And that is decidedly bad for those with her.

The young male kit tugged at Liam's elbow, mewling in fear.

"Poppa, we are afraid..."

His responsibility thundered to the forefront. He'd completely forgotten his charges.

Ah, yes. Young Felines, when stressed, are especially sensitive to my mood changes. I assumed I wouldn't need to cloak.

And they feel exposed out here.

What's wrong with you, Liam? You addlebrained dimwit.

"Sorry," he murmured contritely. "Forgive Poppa, little ones. I got distracted."

Shifting the woman, Liam stood to his feet, and looked about him. "We need to find a place to shelter." Then he added in human, for the sole benefit of the woman in his arms. "Do you know...is there a building nearby where we can find medical attention?"

She was confused, her head lolling against his chest, too heavy to hold up. "Homeless...shelter," she uttered with difficulty. "Take...the street...going west."

Can I trust her word?

Liam panned the view beyond the park, and saw, just ahead, the street in question.

"They...are having...a holiday..." Lana sighed heavily, fighting the drowsiness. Her words slurred. "Should...be open...though."

Holiday?

It was then Liam noticed, in the distance, small children in costume: ghosts and goblins, witches, and some, only in monster masks. Each one carried a small bucket or cloth sack.

I've read of this practice from their histories. The festival is called Halloween. The children are given treats when they beg at the doors of the houses.

No wonder the Roog dare to walk undisguised on the surface this night!

"Stay close, little ones," Liam ordered, taking off down the fog filled street. "I will keep the pace slow, but we cannot stop to rest again. Keep in the shadows, so we are not noticed."

Lana had once again drifted off into her drugged sleep.

Five blocks later, just when Liam was beginning to wonder just how far away this shelter was, and if maybe he had missed it, the woman rallied again.

"Put me down," Lana pleaded, struggling weakly against him. "I can walk..."

She'll slow us down. Oh how I wish I'd not taken this on. Just being with her is dangerous. If she's tagged, the dogs are following. I just want this over with!

But the weight of her was getting too much to carry, and Liam needed to relax his muscles. Rather than argue, he slowed, shifted Lana to her feet, and supporting still, his arm around her, they gradually proceeded.

Lana made it just one block, when her limbs gave way beneath. It had been just enough reprieve to give Liam new energy. He caught her up again, and she sank against his shoulder gratefully.

"Why can't I see?" she quietly whispered, as they went on.

"They blinded you with a taser blast, hoping you couldn't run."

She laughed, and the sound was filled with spite and premeditated malice.

"Fooled them, didn't I?"

He did not smile at that. He knew for certain then, she would mean him harm, as well, if she discovered what he was.

Oh, yes, little she. You are a smart one. I'd best be careful in my dealings with you.

Thankfully, Lana passed out again.

****

Just ahead Liam caught sight of humans blocking their way. There was nowhere to go but through them, not with Lana in his arms.

How much farther is it?

Liam made a quick decision.

From birth every kit was taught to use a camouflage belt. He'd equipped the young ones immediately upon arrival. Liam dropped into the lower Feline tongue the primitives used.

This was a language used mostly in battle, more sounds, hisses and growls, than actual words.

Liam warned, "We approach man. Go human, and stay that way until I tell you otherwise."

The small pair obeyed him without question. Each depressed the middle buckle on their belt, and shifted shape.

Liam, being Noor, a Mental with powers beyond any known others, able to manipulate material, and a shape-shifter, as well, needed no belt.

From a man-size Feline, Liam became a humanoid; his tail vanished; the tiny cat ears slipped beneath his hair; the eyes changed; the nose elongated. No longer was he covered in soft short fur; jeans, a bulky sweater, and a shiny, brown leather jacket replaced that covering. Pliable matching mukluks covered the once paw-like feet.

Beside him, the kits became identical twins, a boy and a girl, with short wavy black hair and tanned brownish skin. Each was dressed similarly to Liam.

Now, the group appeared to be just a father walking home with his children...carrying momma in his arms.

Liam hoped it would be enough to protect them.

****

Until this moment the darkness had shielded them, but presently they were coming up on a street lamp that would illuminate them fully.

Just ahead, a prostitute leaned into the open window of a car talking with the lone front seat occupant inside. Like a wild primitive in heat, her rear was raised, one high-heeled, booted foot moving back and forth, like a flicking tail. With her short skirt and fishnet stockings, it was clear she wore no undergarment.

Humans are such perverts! They have such a perchance for immorality.

The young ones do not need to see this!

Liam felt the children shudder, as they came abreast of another pair of women, standing in the lamp light, as seductively attired as the first. He realized, their reaction was not fear, but revulsion, as they read body language that was considered depraved in their culture.

To comfort, Liam spoke softly under his breath. "Little ones, pay them no mind."

But what was meant to ease, turned the eyes of another, standing back in the shadows, toward them. Liam had failed to notice until too late, because his mind was focused on the backseat passengers he'd just noticed in the car.

This new human was male, dressed all in black clothing. He had blended way too well with the darkness. Now, as he moved toward them threateningly, Liam almost hissed with the abruptness of the shock, before he caught himself.

"Well now," the human challenged as he came out of hiding. "Just what do we have here?" He laughed contemptuously. "Shouldn't keep your drunken bitch up so late." He grinned lecherously. "If she weren't so ugly, I could put her to work."

His manner changed abruptly. "Maybe, you got some money on you, eh? How about handing it over, bud?"

Liam's timid, non confrontational Feline nature took the upper hand. "We have no currency. Honest." he declared truthfully.

The man eyed him with suspicion for long moments, decided there was truth in the statement, then suddenly, he caught sight of the young children peeking out from behind Liam's back.

Liam slipped into the man's mind, watching the lustful hunger flood over him, as he spied the young girl. He cringed, and shivered visibly.

"Now, your kid," the human observed solicitously. "She's just ripe. She'd be worth a lot to me. I have guys lined up, who'd pay plenty for her."

The man spoke directly to the five year old. "What say, honey? Would you like some candy? Come with me, and I'll always take care of you. Leave your old man, and come live off the rich. I promise it'll be worth your while."

It was a good thing the little she was so very terrified; if she had hissed at him the way she wanted to, their cover would have been blown.

Am I going to have to use my powers to protect, after all? Even here a young female is prey!

But the man was abruptly pushing passed them, seeing danger to the girls he already had. An unmarked police car had slowly approached, and those inside were accessing the situation on the sidewalk.

"Get out of here," tersely growled the pimp, motioning toward a side street escape route. "I'll catch up to you later."

Liam didn't need to be told a second time. He fled into the night, his strides long and rapid; the best he could do without actually running. His little charges did have to scurry to keep up.

Behind them, the policemen were too intent on the women and their handler, to challenge Liam and his entourage.

Minutes later, they came out on another street, and came upon the entrance of an emergency clinic. Liam breathed a sigh of relief, placed his burden just inside the doors, with the hope she'd be found shortly, and tended to, then stepped outside again.

With the two disguised kits in his arms, he teleported to the edge of the city, where he quickly found an old abandoned barn in which to spend the night safely.

TO READ MORE PLEASE GO TO AMAZON.COM TO PURCHASE.

www.ingramcontent.com/pod-product-compliance
Lightning Source LLC
Chambersburg PA
CBHW030920050726
47498CB00003BA/832